THE BUREAU

VOLUME 1

KIM FIELDING

Tin Box
— PRESS —

PART I
BOOK ONE: CORRUPTION

CHAPTER 1

*T*HE CROWD was restless tonight. Men reeked of sweat and liquor as they shifted on the creaking wooden seats. Rough voices whispered, and sometimes one of the men called out. Demanding words, angry words. Tenrael knew that by dawn he'd be bruised and bleeding. His back to the audience, he tried to stand straight despite his fears, tried to keep his breathing steady. But he couldn't stop the slight tremor of his wings. A black feather drifted down and landed near his foot. His owner would collect it later and sell it to someone for a dollar or two.

The air inside the tent was sultry, and sweat trickled down his bare skin, making him want to twitch. He would have liked to wipe the stinging saltiness from his eyes. But Davenport preferred to begin the show with Tenrael bound, his wrists shackled overhead and his ankles tethered to the stage. Even his neck was kept in place, a tight chain fastening his collar to a metal support. The chains weren't necessary—Tenrael couldn't flee—but they gave him a mystique of danger, which excited dark fantasies in the marks' heads.

Davenport began his usual patter, punctuating his words with occasional slaps of his cane against Tenrael's body. The blows were calculated to make impressive noises more than to hurt, although the stings made Tenrael flinch.

Tenrael didn't listen to Davenport's words; he could easily have recited them himself. He stared at the wall of the tent, imagining figures in the stains on the dirty canvas. One splatter of mud resembled a soaring bird, another looked like the moon rising over faraway mountains, and a third was the crest of an enormous wave.

"That ain't no demon!" yelled a familiar voice from the crowd, interrupting Davenport midsentence. "Them wings are fake." As intended, the rest of the audience rumbled agreement.

Davenport whacked Tenrael's ass; then he poked his cane tip into the narrow space on Tenrael's back, between his wings. "I assure you, *this* is the genuine article. But perhaps you'd like to come closer and see for yourself, my good sir."

As the crowd cheered and clapped its encouragement, the caller—in fact, Davenport's employee, Ford—stomped forward. Tenrael fought not to tremble as Ford clomped onto the small stage. The man wouldn't do him much damage now, not while he was playing the part of a mark. His favorite time for torment was very late at night, when Tenrael was already raw from whatever the marks had done to him. Ford was an artist. He knew that in those cold, dark hours it would take only a few well-placed touches with a blade to set Tenrael screaming and begging. Sometimes not even that—sometimes it took only a few well-chosen words.

But now, Ford simply followed Davenport's urgings to test Tenrael's authenticity. He prodded the wings and yanked a feather free, laughing as he held it up for the crowd to see. "Damn! That really was attached!" Then he walked slowly around to face Tenrael's front. The audience hadn't seen that side of him yet, and Ford pretended it was his first glimpse too. His eyes widened, his jaw dropped, and he pretended to stagger back. "Holy shit! Them eyes! Ain't nothin' human about them!"

Of course, the audience clamored loudly, wanting to see for themselves. Davenport worked the creaky pedal to turn the little platform on which Tenrael was bound. The platform moved slowly. Tenrael didn't close his eyes—that would only earn him punishment—but he kept his head bowed as deeply as he dared, his gaze unfocused. He didn't need to see the men who gasped at him, at the small red horns that protruded from his black hair, his orange eyes, his hairless torso devoid of navel. He knew they wore battered brimmed hats, sweat-stained shirts, patched and threadbare jeans and overalls, old boots that needed resoling. He knew their faces had reddened with excitement as they realized the creature they'd paid fifty cents to see truly *was* a demon. He knew some of them eyed his flaccid cock and hairless balls, hanging so vulnerably between his legs, just as they'd no doubt been staring at his ass before Davenport turned him.

Ford hurried off the stage and resumed his spot in the audience, while Davenport stroked his cane and beamed. "So you see?" he crowed. "I present to you tonight the genuine article, plucked from the depths of hell itself!"

That was a lie. Tenrael had lived atop sheer cliffs, not in any depths, and he'd flown night skies, bringing nightmares and troubling thoughts to sleeping humans. So long ago. And it wasn't Davenport who'd captured him; the bastard's grandparents hadn't even been born yet. Another man had laid a clever trap; then he'd ensnared Tenrael with spells and incantations and the mark he'd branded onto the soles of Tenrael's feet. Eventually that man had grown bored and sold him, and later his second master lost him in a card game. And so it went. Tenrael didn't know how many years Davenport had owned him. It didn't matter.

Davenport blathered smoothly onward, spinning tales the marks swallowed eagerly. How the demon had been vicious and terrible, deflowering virgins, ruining men, eating babies for dinner. The more violent Davenport's stories became, the more frenzied the marks grew, roaring their approval every time the cane struck Tenrael.

Finally, Davenport boomed, "Thank you for your attention this evening! For only fifty cents, you now have a story to tell your grandchildren. But perhaps a few of you wish there was some way to exact vengeance on this creature for the great wrongs it has committed." He dropped his voice very low, forcing the marks to grow silent and strain to hear him. "We can make private arrangements for such a thing—at the cost of fifteen dollars."

The marks grumbled loudly at that. Fifteen dollars was a week's wages. On cue, Ford stood, a sheath of grubby bills clutched in one hand. "I've got ten!"

While the marks waited anxiously, Davenport appeared to consider. Finally, he nodded slightly. "Well, since you have been an excellent audience... a discount, just this once. Ten dollars."

It was still a lot of money. Most of the men filed out of the tent, chattering to each other in excitement. They would find cheaper entertainment, which would also profit Davenport and the carnival. Perhaps a sandwich from the booth next door for ten cents, and watery beer or a shot of bad liquor for two bits. Or they could pay another fifty cents for entrance to the largest tent, where more items from Davenport's collection were on display: the tattooed lady, the lobster boy, the two-headed snake. If they had two dollars, they could dance with a painted woman to the sounds of a scratchy phonograph, and for three dollars more she'd take them into a small curtained enclosure, drop to her knees, and suck their dicks.

But six or seven men remained in the tent with Tenrael, their eyes flashing. Ford wasn't with them, but they didn't notice. They eagerly handed their money to Davenport, who took it with a small bow and slid it into his pocket. "Just give me a few moments, gentlemen," he cooed.

They milled around, watching as Davenport released Tenrael's chains. He collapsed to the floor when his arms were freed—he'd been bound in place many hours—and the marks grunted with surprise and scrambled back. But then Davenport attached a leash to Tenrael's collar and tugged hard. "Come!" he commanded.

The brands and spells were stronger than any chains, robbing Tenrael of the ability to refuse his master. He staggered to his feet and followed Davenport through the flap at the back of the tent, into a smaller space that reeked of blood and sweat and semen. Davenport didn't even have to order him then. He just pointed with his cane, and Tenrael meekly bent over the metal framework that awaited him.

Davenport shackled him in place, keeping Tenrael's arms bound downward, his legs stretched wide, his ass raised high. Tenrael hung his head so he wouldn't have to look at the objects on the nearby shelf —objects the marks would soon be using on him and in him.

In a parody of tenderness, Davenport stroked Tenrael's lower back. "Give a good show tonight, boy. Scream nice and loud so I don't have to bring Ford in to liven things up." He laughed and slapped Tenrael's ass.

Tenrael screamed very loud that night. Ford came in anyway.

EARLY THE NEXT MORNING, Tenrael lay curled tightly in his cage, pretending the metal bars gave him refuge. His eyes still closed, he heard the roustabouts chattering lazily as they struck the tents and packed everything away. He grunted in pain when some of the men lifted his cage, carried it across the hard-trodden dirt, and shoved it roughly into the back of a truck. He was glad for the false sense of privacy as they covered the cage, despite the odor of the mildewed canvas.

Soon afterward, the truck motor roared to life, and Tenrael felt the familiar bumps and jostles, each one bringing new agony to his broken body.

It wasn't the pain that bothered him most. It would pass; he would heal. It wasn't the constant humiliation, the total loss of dignity, the unwanted invasions of his body... those tortures were familiar now too. He was as accustomed to shame and degradation as he was to his shackles and cage. What hurt most were the memories of flying, fierce and proud and free. And the knowledge that his future contained only endless towns full of rubes eager to hand over their money to Davenport.

In the musty darkness of his cage, with the sounds of the engine, creaking springs, and rolling tires as camouflage, Tenrael wept.

CHAPTER 2

THE CHAIR squealed a protest when Townsend plopped himself down behind his desk. His fine gray hair was oiled carefully into place, but his face was florid, and he was overflowing his expensive suit. "Got a job for you, my boy," he announced.

Charles Grimes took a seat on the low chair in front of the desk and waited. He knew his boss would take his time spilling the beans. Townsend liked an audience. He'd once had aspirations in politics, until he'd realized nobody was ever going to elect a guy who'd spent his younger years hunting monsters. So now he contented himself with orating at his underlings.

With slow, deliberate movements, Townsend splashed a few healthy inches of scotch into a glass. He didn't pour any for Charles. Then he removed a cigarette from an elaborate silver holder and lit it with a gold lighter. He inhaled deeply, puffed the smoke out, and swallowed almost half the liquor at once. Then he smiled. "This one's right up your alley."

Charles stretched out his long legs and raised his eyebrows questioningly. He didn't say anything, though. Two could play this game. He wasn't in any hurry.

Finally, Townsend huffed. "Got a call from Kansas."

"That's the Chicago office's jurisdiction."

"Yeah. But they ain't got a specialist. We do."

Charles narrowed his eyes and crossed his arms. "What specialist?"

Townsend drew deeply from his cigarette; then he blew a perfect smoke ring before stubbing out the cigarette in a silver ashtray. He drained his glass, seemed to consider refilling it, but shrugged instead. "According to our sources, there's a demon in Kansas."

"A demon." Charles wished he could smoke too, or down a generous slug of booze. But repeated experience told him trying either would only make him ill. He uncrossed his feet. "A demon in Kansas?"

"Yeah. Apparently, someone summoned the fucker and now it's in a carnival freak show."

Charles hoped his wince didn't show. When he was five or six years old, a man with a tall hat had knocked on the door of their modest house and offered to buy Charles for a thousand dollars. "I'll make a star of him!" the man had proclaimed. Ma fetched her shotgun and told the man she'd pull the trigger if she ever saw him again. A few days after that, she and Charles had picked up and moved far away. For a long time afterward, the man haunted Charles's nightmares. Hell, sometimes he still did.

"If it's been summoned, someone's got it under control," Charles said. "It's not dangerous."

Townsend lit another cigarette. "Maybe not now. But what if its master decides to use it for something other than a sideshow? You remember that nasty business in Bakersfield."

"That was before I joined the Bureau."

"Yeah, but you heard about it. Everybody heard about it. There were goddamned newsreels about it. How many dead? Eighteen?"

Charles worked his jaw. "Nineteen. The little girl died a couple months later."

"Right." Townsend pointed his cigarette at Charles. "I ain't gonna have another Bakersfield. Not on my watch."

"But it's Chicago's problem, not ours."

"Normally, yeah. But Chicago hasn't got anyone like you, angel."

"I'm not an angel." He wasn't. His mother was human. And his father... well, maybe not. But there didn't seem to be anything angelic about knocking up a pretty girl then skipping town. Anyway, Charles had given all that up. He couldn't do much about his milk-white skin or strange eyes, but he dyed his colorless hair brown. And he'd had his wings removed when he turned eighteen. The stupid things were too small to lift him and a real nuisance besides.

Faced with Charles' glower, Townsend merely smiled. "Whatever you are, you wasted that fiend in Glendale after it killed three good agents, and you took care of a pair of 'em up near Medford. So now you're gonna get yourself to Kansas and destroy this one too. Should be easy if it's under someone's control. You can consider this a nice little vacation if you want."

"Nobody vacations in Kansas."

"You can start a trend. Maybe find yourself a sweet little farm girl and get yourself laid. You could use it, kid." Townsend ground out his cigarette. "Now, go see Stella and she'll get you all set up with the travel particulars. I'm expecting a nice thick report from you within two weeks."

Charles sighed. "It won't take me two weeks to get to Kansas."

"Then get a *couple* of farm girls. Hell, get yourself a baker's dozen. You gotta work that stick outta your ass, kid, or one of these days you're gonna break. We're in a tough business. Can't take ourselves seriously all the time." He winked and uncapped his bottle.

They could have sat and argued longer, but Charles would eventually lose. He stood, collected his suit coat and fedora from the rack, and exited Townsend's office.

CHARLES KNEW that Stella kind of had a thing for him. She knew it was impossible because she was twenty years his senior, and he knew it was impossible because she was a dame. But neither of them minded a little harmless flirting now and then. Sometimes he even brought her flowers. When he had to go out on assignment, she always made sure he was well taken care of.

This time she booked him a train compartment—a big one, with a private toilet and a drawing room with a couch—on the *Super Chief*. He spent most of the ride tucked away from the curious stares of the other passengers, reading or watching the barren landscape roll by. He slept well too; he liked the rocking motion of the train beneath him. So even though it was early in the morning when he arrived in Kansas City, Missouri, he felt refreshed.

Normally he'd have rented a nice sedan. Back in Los Angeles he owned a plain old Chevrolet, but sometimes the Bureau gave him something flashier, like when he investigated that necromancer in Hollywood and got to spend a few weeks tooling around in a beautiful MG. But the current assignment called for something plainer, so he took a taxi over the state line into Kansas, where he found a dealer selling an ugly but serviceable Dodge pickup truck. Charles bought the truck outright; then he drove down bumpy dirt roads into the countryside until he found a small-town mercantile store. Ignoring the gaping locals, he bought jeans, three cheap cotton shirts, and a pair of dun-colored boots. He'd almost left the place before he remembered a hat, ending up with a plain straw number.

In the middle of nowhere, between fields of half-grown sorghum, he changed out of his suit and into his new, more rustic clothing. He packed his California clothes away in his suitcase; then he spent a half-hour trudging through the dirt, trying to make his new outfit look old. Sometimes he even dropped to the ground and rolled a bit. He stomped on his new hat a couple of times. Satisfied, he got back into the truck and drove away in search of a carnival.

News of the demon was already old when it reached Townsend's desk. And because it had taken a few days for Charles to reach Kansas and start looking, he had no idea where to start. He drove around for over a week, eating pie in diners and sleeping wherever he could rent a room. He had very good hearing, and he eavesdropped shamelessly.

He heard rumors of a banshee near Dodge City and stories of ghosts in Beloit, but those were Chicago's problems, not his. He made notes of them for his eventual report.

It was in the aptly named town of Plainville that he finally found a lead. He'd rolled in at midday, parked his truck downtown, and strolled around for a while, taking the measure of the grain elevator and passing a few tired-looking women in faded print dresses. Half of the shops were boarded up. He wondered if the owners had gone west in search of jobs or had just grown old and died. But there was some life yet in the diner, and that's where he ended up. Everyone else was eating big slabs of ham and steak, but he had to be content with pie and coffee. Meat didn't agree with him any better than alcohol or cigarettes. At least the pie—strawberry rhubarb—was good.

Three young men in overalls sat at the nearby table. They were tow-haired, with faces and arms deeply tanned, alike enough in looks that they had to be brothers. The oldest was very handsome, but Charles knew better than to be caught staring. Even in LA, there were only a few places where a man could show interest in another. Out here, he was betting the wrong look could get a man killed. Not that he couldn't hold his own in a fight—he was better trained and better armed than any farm boys—but he wasn't here to cause a commotion. He stared at his coffee instead.

"Loan me ten dollars," one of the youths demanded of his brothers.

"What for?"

"None of your business."

"It surely *is* my business if it's my ten bucks."

The good-natured argument continued for a time, like a cart down a well-worn track. Charles daydreamed a bit, only half-listening. It had been so long since he'd felt a man's hard body against his. Several months ago, he spent a little time with a fellow named Walter, who'd been willing enough—but almost too willing. He was a doctoral student at a university, with soft hands and a slight frame, and he probably would have fainted if he knew how Charles made his living. He was dainty and sweet, and not at all what Charles truly craved.

"I bet you're going back to that carnival," one of the brothers said accusingly, throwing Charles from his slight reverie.

"So what if I am?"

"You seen all the freaks already. Why do you wanna go back?"

"Just do."

"Well, they ain't here no more."

"No kidding. But I heard some of 'em talkin' last night, saying they're going to Hullville next." His voice turned slightly wheedling. "Loan me ten dollars and I'll talk Ruby Lancaster into going to the pictures with you."

Further negotiations ensued, but Charles didn't pay them any mind. It was time to settle his bill and drive to Hullville.

HULLVILLE WASN'T much different from Plainville—or dozens of other nowhere little towns—although maybe this place had fewer boarded-up shops than the last. It also boasted a courthouse, an enormous heap of red bricks that had pretensions far beyond a dusty little farming burg, and which loomed over a grassy town square surrounded by low buildings, including two diners and a bar. Charles would have preferred to go to the bar, because it was easier to pick up information in a place like that. But his teetotaling habits would be too obvious there, so he went to Aunt Edna's Home-style Diner instead. Cheery red-checked cloths covered the tables, each with a little glass vase of daisies, but the pie wasn't as good as in Plainville, and none of the customers were as handsome or helpful as the brothers who'd inadvertently directed him here.

Passing down a narrow hallway to find the john, he came to a message board hung just outside the toilet door. Affixed to the board, a gaudy sign advertised Cheney's World of Wonders. THRILLS, CHILLS, AND DELIGHTS FROM THE FOUR CORNERS OF THE EARTH—AND BEYOND! the red lettering promised. RIDES AND ENTERTAINMENT FOR THE KIDDIES AND DIVERSIONS FOR ADULTS. ONE NIGHT ONLY!

Two days away.

Irked that he'd have to wait, but satisfied his quarry would come to

13

him, Charles rented a room in the town's only hotel, a dump that made its living off suckers who had business at the courthouse but lived too far away to spend the night in their own beds. The clerk was a ferret-faced man who wanted to know why Charles was in Hullville.

"Business," Charles grunted.

The man squinted at Charles' cheap, dirty clothes. "What kinda business?"

"Mine, not yours." He could have made something up, but he was a crappy liar. He glared at the clerk instead.

In the end, cold hard cash beat curiosity. The man gave him a key.

The room was small and not especially clean, with a sink near the door and a shared toilet and shower down the hallway. The narrow window offered a view of the square and courthouse, and Charles spent the better part of the following days sitting in front of the window on a hard wooden chair, watching the people below. He longed for the softer air of Los Angeles and for his little bungalow, so close to the ocean he could walk to the beach. He liked the water all right, but his favorite part was the wet sand—neither sea nor land, but something in between.

For two nights he tossed on the hard mattress, sleeping only fitfully. His shoulders itched, and his skin felt like an outgrown suit. He jerked off angrily, shadowy figures dancing behind his squeezed-shut eyes.

Late in the afternoon on his third day in Hullville, he packed his suitcase. Before he left the room, he checked his pockets for his arsenal. Demons didn't require much in the way of fancy equipment, which he appreciated. He'd spent too many years lugging crossbows with silver-tipped arrows, giant jars of sanctified salt, heavy ropes woven of hemp and virgins' hair. Now he needed only a cigarette lighter and the small iron brand created especially for the Bureau. And his revolver and switchblade, which had little utility for demons but which he never went without.

Ferret-Face eyed him suspiciously when Charles checked out.

Cheney's had set up in an empty field about a half mile outside town. Good location—close enough for people to walk, far enough for the noise and other potential disturbances to remain uninterrupted. Several tents of various sizes dominated the field, but there were also smaller trailers and carts, and behind them all, a collection of battered trucks. A few booths offered games of chance. Odors of sugar, fried foods, and sweat hung heavy in the air, and children shrieked as they spun around on the rickety rides.

Charles wanted to hate Cheney and his colleagues, who used trickery to con farmers out of their hard-earned pennies. But the people around him smiled, despite their patched clothing, and Charles conceded that maybe the rare splash of excitement and the taste of the exotic in otherwise drab lives was worth missing a few meals.

He spent some time strolling around, getting a feel for the place. He watched boys try to impress girls with the carnival games, watched parents laugh at their children's joy. Although people glanced at him and a few barkers called his way, he felt almost invisible. Distant and disconnected. Well, he felt that way a lot of the time, even back in LA. As if the world was a party and he hadn't been invited; he was just looking in through the windows.

He paid a few coins for the big tent. It was stuffed with exhibits and gawking locals, and the air was stifling, but there were no demons. A dance floor at one end stood empty and waiting.

The demon's tent was nearby, though. It wasn't open, and the huge man sitting near the flap was clearly there to keep people out, not to take money. But a garish sign hung on the canvas, depicting a hideous creature with red skin, sharp horns, and glowing eyes. STRAIGHT FROM THE PITS OF HELL! A smaller, plainer sign announced DUE TO THE SENSITIVE CONSTITUTIONS OF WOMEN AND CHILDREN, ONLY ADULT MEN ARE ALLOWED ENTRANCE. Charles snorted. The Bureau employed a few women who were about as sensitive as a cannonball.

The show wouldn't begin until well after dark. To kill time, he walked, leaned against a fence and observed, and munched on a sticky candy apple and a buttery ear of corn. Eventually the rides stopped and the children went home. The booths with the games shut down. A few women remained, mostly wandering arm-in-arm and murmuring with their menfolk. Several noisy groups of men clustered near the booth selling beer and shots of rotgut.

A man in an expensive but flashy suit appeared from nowhere to stand at the entrance to the demon's tent. He carried a heavy walking stick. "Gents!" he called. "Come see, unless you're too scared. Hell's own fury captured and chained for your amusement. Only fifty cents, tonight only! You'll be talking about this for years."

His patter continued, and men responded as though bespelled. If the kid from Plainville was there, Charles didn't see him. But plenty of others came, their breaths sour, their shirts sticking with sweat, their faces flushed with drink and excitement. Charles joined them. He handed two quarters to the barker before entering the tent.

Something was on the small stage, Charles could sense it, but a ratty curtain blocked the view. He sat in one of the rickety folding chairs—not too near the front, but not in the back, and on the aisle, where he could move quickly. Soon the other chairs filled and the tent was at capacity. The close air was rank, and the members of the audience shifted restlessly. Charles struggled to stay still; his skin tingled and his lungs refused to fully inflate. And his back *itched*. He would have liked to strip naked and immerse himself in cold, clean water. Instead, he clenched his fists and waited.

The man with the cane took the stage. Davenport, he said his name was. His patter was smooth, well-practiced. He spun ridiculous tales of the demon's evil deeds. No single fiend had ever accomplished a fraction of what Davenport claimed for this one—pestilence, mass hysteria, debauchery of the innocent, political disasters, the deaths of thousands. But the audience didn't know that and didn't care, and Davenport led them into a rising frenzy. Charles shuddered at their fast, harsh breathing and the rotting-flesh stink of them.

When Davenport was satisfied they were ready, he nodded, and an unseen person quickly drew back the curtain. The audience gasped. Charles's heart stuttered before resuming a rapid beat.

The demon was bound with his back to the crowd. He was naked, his arms stretched tautly overhead, chained to a heavy metal structure, and his widely spread ankles tethered to the stage. A thick metal collar circled his neck, with a chain running to the overhead bar. His black hair should have been glossy but instead hung in dull clumps, hacked unevenly short. His lackluster bronze skin was a backdrop to his enormous folded wings, covered in black feathers and drooping slightly as his head hung forward.

Davenport was good. He paused long enough for the crowd to gaze their fill, and then he resumed his spiel. He emphasized his words with occasional whacks of his cane against the demon's flesh. The sound was very loud within the canvas walls, and the demon flinched at each blow, once uttering a choked groan when Davenport hit the tender skin just at the top of his thighs.

When Davenport poked the end of his walking stick against the demon's muscular ass, Charles felt the temperature rise within the tent. He smelled the audience's lust—for sex, for violence—and had to tightly clamp his jaw to keep from retching.

Just when everyone was wound perfectly tight, a man two rows over stood up. "That ain't real!" he shouted. "You're tryin' ta hoodwink us!"

The man was a good shill, Charles thought. Appropriately belligerent and skeptical, and when Davenport invited him onstage, the guy nodded at the audience conspiratorially, inviting them to feel as if he represented them all. He did a good job of prodding at the demon, plucking a feather, and carelessly unfolding one wing to see where it attached to the demon's body. His truly award-winning performance, however, came when he walked around to view the demon's front. "Them eyes! Those ain't the eyes of anything human!"

Everyone in the audience held their breath as Davenport slowly wheeled the demon's platform around.

Oh, merciful gods.

The creature was magnificent. He wasn't pretty, not by a long shot, although he certainly wasn't as ugly as the demons Charles had destroyed. They had been twisted, sharp and gnarled. But *this* one was only beautifully broken, his head bowed, his horns grimy, his eyes clouded, his body heavy, his cock and balls hanging like ripe fruit waiting to be plucked. There was nothing angry about him, none of the fury Charles had seen in other demons. Just... surrender and despair, as sweet as a candy apple.

Whatever else Davenport had to say, Charles barely heard it over the rush of his own blood.

Eventually, Davenport offered the audience a closer experience with the demon—for ten dollars. Most of the men left, but they weren't complaining. They looked stunned, on edge. Charles figured they would work it out by drinking themselves into a stupor, by finding someone to screw roughly, brutally. But a handful of men remained, and they ponied up their money and waited for Davenport and his demon.

Charles didn't pay—not because he couldn't afford it, but because he didn't trust himself. His jaw was tight with jealousy, and the gun weighed heavily in his pocket.

But before he left the tent, he looked at the demon once more—and the demon lifted his head and looked back. Orange eyes widened and nostrils flared; the creature opened his mouth but then bit his lower lip before saying anything. Charles had a good idea of what the demon had bitten back: a plea.

Charles shook his head.

The demon did make a noise then. He threw back his head and keened so loudly the tent seemed to shake. The sound inflamed the men, making them pant eagerly, and Davenport laughed. Charles slipped away.

Music blared from the biggest tent, and raucous laughter rang into the night. Glancing around quickly to make sure nobody was watching, Charles stole around to the back of the demon's tent. More laughter, cruel and guttural, and the unmistakable sounds of a body being hit. Choked screams, strangled cries. Charles' palms bled from the pressure of his fingernails.

Only after the sounds in the back of the tent had ended did Charles return to the front. Nobody guarded the entrance, so after waiting a few more minutes, he stepped inside. The air still reeked, but he ignored the smell and the discarded chains onstage. He walked to the narrow flap behind the platform and cleared his throat. "Hoy there," he called, just loudly enough.

A moment later, the flap opened slightly. "We're done for the night," Davenport snapped irritably. His face was flushed. He wasn't in it just for the profits—he got off on what the marks did to his demon.

Charles could have flashed his badge; keeping a demon was illegal under federal law and in all forty-eight states. But he had no backup, he wasn't in friendly territory, and he didn't especially want to drag Davenport to jail. So he simply smiled. "I want to buy some time with the demon. Private time."

"I said we're *done*. Come see us next week in Arapahoe. Don't forget your ten bucks." He started to walk away, but Charles grabbed the canvas flap, holding it open.

"I want it tonight. I have two hundred dollars."

Well, that made Davenport freeze. "Where would someone like you get that kind of dough?"

"Tooth fairy."

Davenport gave him a long look. "Let me see it," he said at last.

Charles was ready for this. He pulled the folded bills from his pocket, fanned them out so the numbers were visible, and held them up for inspection.

Davenport looked at the money the same way the marks had looked at his demon. He licked his lips. "I'll give you one hour. And you don't do any damage that won't heal within a week."

"Fine. But I don't want him here." Not where the smell of other men's spunk and sweat would fill his nose, and not where anyone could lift a bit of canvas and watch. "Somewhere with no audience. A trailer."

After a brief pause—his gaze still firmly on the money—Davenport grunted. "Give me fifteen minutes to get ready. And don't expect the fucker to be in very good shape when you get him. The crowd was rough tonight."

"Fifteen," Charles growled in acknowledgment. He wanted to shoot Davenport in the crotch.

Twelve minutes later, as Charles waited outside the tent, the shill came to fetch him. "This way." They walked into the dark center of the field, to a sort of clearing surrounded by a forest of tents, booths, and trucks. The trailer might once have been bright, but the paint had faded and peeled, and the moonlight stole the last of the color.

Charles started to step up to the entrance, but the shill caught his arm. "It's used to pain. You can make it bleed, make it shriek, but that ain't what'll hurt it the worst."

Sour bile rose in Charles' throat and he squeezed the gun's wooden grip. "Yeah?"

The man leaned closer, blowing fetid breath. "What you wanna do is *almost* show the bastard a little tenderness, yeah? Just a little stroke here, a soft touch there. *Then* you stab or twist or bash. It's the combination, yeah? Rips the bastard apart."

"I'll keep that in mind," Charles replied coolly. He tugged his arm free and strode up the two steps and into the trailer.

Davenport stood just inside, blocking him. "Two hundred dollars," he said, holding out his hand. Charles handed over the bills, and Davenport counted them before tucking them inside his suit jacket. Then he rapped his walking stick once on the floor. "One hour. No major damage."

"I've already agreed to that."

"And I've already ordered him to obey you as if you were me. You know how it works?"

Charles did. Once a demon was properly summoned, its will was bound to its owner. Unless the incantations were nullified, the demon was incapable of disobedience—although a clever few managed to trick their way free eventually.

"No interruptions," Charles said.

Davenport gave a shallow, mocking bow. "Not for sixty minutes." He stepped around Charles and out the door.

Charles bolted the door behind him. It was a flimsy lock that wouldn't hold if someone made a real effort to get in, but it was good enough. He'd already seen that the shutters were closed over the trailer's tiny windows. He took a deep breath before turning to face the demon.

The demon knelt on the dingy floor, legs spread, head drooping forward. His wings were pressed tightly against his back, and his hands rested palms-up on his knees. Angry welts striped him, and blood and other fluids streaked his skin and matted his hair. He trembled slightly, but whether from fear, weakness, or pain, it was impossible to tell.

After Charles stood quietly for several moments, the demon finally lifted his eyes—and gasped.

CHAPTER 3

HE MEN had been especially brutal tonight. Tenrael hurt inside and out, and he yearned for the false sanctuary of his cage. What troubled him most, however, was the man he'd seen while still in chains. Actually, Tenrael wasn't at all sure it *was* a man. His scent was odd, for one thing, sharp and sweet above the stink of the crowd. And his eyes—they were the strangest shade of green, pale and transparent as bottle glass. But mostly he *felt* different. He made Tenrael's nerves buzz in a way that terrified him.

Tenrael had been sure the strange man was there to destroy him, and he'd almost begged for it. But the man had shaken his head, denying Tenrael even that mercy. No surprise, perhaps. The world held no mercy for Tenrael's kind.

So tonight, more than ever, he longed to curl up in his cage and shut out the world, at least for a little while.

But Davenport and Ford had confused him, dragging him across the lot to a trailer instead. When Davenport made him kneel on the floor, Tenrael understood. Over the years, a few people had paid to spend time alone with him. The experience was never pleasant. The weariness itself was nearly enough to make him weep.

Until he caught an odor like ripe oranges and looked up to find the strange, pale man staring down at him.

Tenrael did the only thing he could do. He allowed his upper body to collapse until he was fully prostrate, his arms spread beseechingly. "Please," he whispered.

The answering voice was rough. "What's your name?"

"Tenrael."

Tenrael couldn't see with his face pressed to the dirty floor, but he heard the slight tap of a foot. "Tenrael," the man said thoughtfully, drawing out the vowels. "Yes. A bringer of nightmares."

Shocked into lifting his head, Tenrael gaped. "You... you *know*?"

"I know the names of five thousand demons. The Bureau drilled me until I had them memorized." He sighed slightly. "I'm Charles Grimes."

"What... what are you?"

Grimes' face twisted so angrily that Tenrael flinched. "I am Lieutenant Charles Grimes, a field agent with the Federal Bureau of Trans-Species Affairs."

Tenrael had heard of the Bureau. It was created shortly before he was captured, but he'd never feared it. From what he understood, the agency concentrated on bigger threats, while he did nothing worse than bring unease to people's slumbers—although he'd prided himself on being very good at it.

Then he'd lost his freedom, and next his will, and finally his dignity. His pride had been the last thing to go, struck down like a tree felled by an ax. Now he had nothing but a faint hope for an end.

"Destroy me," he pleaded. He dropped his head.

Grimes came closer, until he was near enough to tightly grasp Tenrael's chin and pull it up. Tenrael's eyes were swollen from the beating he'd received, and he blinked to clear his vision, examining Grimes as the man inspected him.

Grimes was tall and lean. He wore grubby farmers' clothes like the rest of the rubes, but Tenrael could easily imagine him in a suit—not a flashy one like Donovan's, but one with clean, spare lines. Grimes' face was narrow and angular, his mouth paradoxically wide and lush-lipped, and his striking eyes were topped by eyebrows almost too light to see. Although the hour was late, his pale cheeks were as free of stubble as Tenrael's.

"You don't have to shave, do you?" Tenrael blurted.

With a low growl, Grimes gripped his chin hard enough to hurt. But he didn't deny the words either. "You stink of them."

For the first time in decades, Tenrael felt shame. He wished he could have washed himself. Which was ridiculous. Grimes had come to destroy him, hurt him, or abandon him. None of those required that he be clean. But despite the absurdity of it, he wanted to please Grimes. Wanted Grimes to take him and fill him and make him feel alive again. He hadn't wanted anything in years except to die. This felt good, even if he knew he wouldn't get what he longed for.

Shocking even himself, Tenrael wrenched away from Grimes' hand and lurched to his feet. He put his hands on the back of Grimes' head—knocking his hat off in the process—and tugged him close for a kiss. He'd never done such a thing before and was surprised he was able. But then Davenport had never specifically forbidden it.

Even more surprising, Grimes didn't move away. The opposite, in fact. He grabbed Tenrael's horns hard and invaded his mouth with a passion and ferocity that made Tenrael weak in the knees. None of the marks ever wanted to kiss him.

When Grimes finally broke the kiss, Tenrael braced himself for a blow. Instead, Grimes breathed raggedly in his ear. "Thought you'd taste bad. Corrupt. You don't."

Grimes himself tasted wonderfully bittersweet.

Then the long-fingered hands were all over Tenrael's skin, dragging, prodding at bruises, the nails scratching at lash marks. It hurt very nicely, especially paired with Grimes' teeth on his nipple.

In all the years of his captivity, all the thousands of times he'd been used, Tenrael had never once been aroused. But now his cock grew as hard as the iron bars of his cage, and for once, his moans were of pleasure rather than pain. He plucked at Grimes' shirt. "Please... skin."

Grimes backed away, but only long enough to shrug off his jacket;

then he pulled his shirt impatiently over his head and tossed it aside. He was thin but sinewy, his hairless skin the color of fresh milk—except for his pink nipples. Unlike Tenrael, he had a navel. Without really intending to, Tenrael fell to his knees, grabbed Grimes' hips, and tongued the neat little divot in his belly. Slightly lower down, Grimes' erection was clearly visible through the fabric of his thin jeans. Tenrael wanted to lick that too, so he fumbled at Grimes' belt, only to have his hands batted away.

"No," Grimes rasped. With unforeseen strength, he hauled Tenrael to his feet; then he kissed him again, driving him back and back until Tenrael was pinned against the wall, his wings grinding into the rough wood. More importantly, though, Grimes was grinding against him, providing sweet friction to Tenrael's aching cock. All the degradation and agony he'd experienced that night—and hundreds of nights before—faded away; even his torn skin and bruised bones became meaningless as he bucked his hips and tasted sugar and acid on Grimes' tongue.

But when he laid his palms on Grimes' back and felt the two long scars along the shoulder blades, Tenrael froze.

Grimes stilled too, and then took a step back. His jaw was clenched so tightly the tendons of his neck stood out, and his eyes sparked green fury.

"Please," Tenrael whispered.

Very slowly, Grimes turned. The scars were vivid red against his white skin. Angry.

"They took them away?" asked Tenrael, feeling the anguish in his own wings.

Grimes spun, lunged forward, shoved Tenrael back into the wall. "I got rid of them," he snarled.

"Why?"

"Useless."

For a long time, Tenrael's wings had been useless too, except as proof to the marks of what he was. Sometimes he'd almost wished they were gone, because they seemed to taunt him, reminding him of lost freedoms. But sometimes they gave him comfort as he lay curled in his cage, the feathers his only insulation against bitter cold.

Tenrael carefully reached behind himself, plucked a single feather, and presented it to Grimes on an open palm. He expected Grimes to refuse it, perhaps even beat him for offering. Grimes did neither. His face twisted oddly before he grabbed the feather and stuffed it into his pocket.

The kiss that followed was tender. Grimes pulled him against his chest and stroked a furled wing with one hand, smoothing Tenrael's sore ass with the other. Tenrael let his weight rest against Grimes, and oh, that was lovely—having someone hold him up, just for a few minutes.

With his head swimming and his tears leaking onto Grimes' shoulder, Tenrael barely noticed when Grimes moved his hand to Tenrael's cock, gave a few firm strokes, and stopped kissing long enough to whisper, "Come."

For just a few moments, Tenrael felt as if he were flying.

When he came back to earth, he was sagging in Charles' arms.

Charles eased him to the floor and stood looking down at him, the corners of his mouth turned slightly down. On impulse, Tenrael took his hand and licked it clean. His own spend tasted different from that of all the human men who'd used him, and he liked the way Charles shivered at the touch of his tongue. He wondered what Charles' come tasted like.

Almost gently, Charles withdrew his hand. "I came here to kill you."

"All right," Tenrael said. And it was. A better end certainly than he'd hoped for. He moved to his knees and let his head fall in submission. Even from that position he could see Charles retrieve his shirt and jacket and put them on before reaching into a pocket for a small iron brand and a lighter. When Charles came closer, Tenrael saw the shape of the branding head: a stylized sun with a single letter in the center. The letter was from an alphabet invented millennia ago for a language long since dead, but Tenrael knew what it stood for: the beginning of the Highest God's name. Burned or carved into his body, it would destroy him.

"Thank you," he said quietly, not looking up.

But Charles didn't heat the brand. He stood looking at it for a very long time; then he tucked it back into his pocket.

"Give me your feet," he ordered gruffly.

Tenrael was deeply confused and wanted to question him, but he'd been commanded and his will was not his own. He lay on his back—uncomfortable due to the wings—and raised his legs.

"Watch me," said Charles, and of course Tenrael did.

Tenrael saw Charles produce a switchblade and flick it open, saw him heat the knife in the flame of his lighter. Then Charles grabbed Tenrael's right ankle, lifted the leg a little higher, and cut repeatedly into the sole with the burning blade.

Screaming, Tenrael tried to move away, but Charles held him fast. "Be still," Charles growled, and Tenrael was. He'd been branded on his feet before—each new owner marked him to seal the incantation, to make Tenrael his own—but this was worse, because he was being both burned and cut. And he didn't understand.

With a grunt, Charles dropped the foot, reheated the blade, and took the other foot. The trailer had already smelled of Tenrael's blood, but now it also reeked of scorched flesh.

Charles cut a few more careful marks before releasing Tenrael's ankle. He muttered several sentences so quietly Tenrael couldn't understand them. They weren't in English, and they had the feeling of incantations.

"Look at it," Charles said.

It's an awkward thing to examine the bottom of your foot while lying flat on your back, but Tenrael had to obey. When he did, he saw the Davenport mark was gone. The new wounds were already healing, but the scars were vivid—two overlapping arcs, the bottom one with a small line intersecting the lower end. *C* and *G*, he realized. Beside them, a few red strokes forming a rudimentary feather.

All the breath left his lungs in a long *whoosh*. "Y-your sign." Even though he spoke the words aloud, he couldn't believe them.

"My sign. Kneel, Tenrael."

Tenrael clambered clumsily to obey, and his heart—for so long dead in his chest—hammered so hard he was almost deafened.

Charles' face was grim, but his eyes were soft. "You're mine now. Do you feel it?"

And yes, Tenrael did. He didn't have a soul—no demon did—but there was *something* deep inside him, something that had once soared high but had long since festered in chains. It had hurt him even when his body was whole, and it had made him feel ill, as if it were rotting. But now... now the chains were still there, but the putrefaction was gone. Instead, his not-soul felt cool and clean and good.

"Master," he said.

Charles closed his eyes and gave a brief shudder. When he looked at Tenrael again, he seemed to be in the midst of some internal struggle Tenrael didn't comprehend. Then Charles took a deep breath and let it out with a sigh.

"You belong to me now. But...." Again he mumbled a spell, all harsh consonants mixed with liquid vowels. He nodded when he was done. "I command you to retake your will."

The invisible chains within him flamed, melted, disappeared. Tenrael cried out and fell onto his side, convulsing as his skin burned and his wounds bled and his mind whirled.

When the storm subsided, Tenrael rose shakily to his feet. He looked at his hands, turning them over as if he'd never seen them before. Realizing that, like the rest of his body, they were once again his instruments to use as he wished.

"Why?" he asked, the word almost a sob.

"Don't know." Charles opened his mouth as if he might say more, but then closed it again. He licked his lips. "Wouldn't blame you if you killed them." He jerked a thumb in the direction of the door. "But if you do, the Bureau will send someone after you."

"Not you?"

"No. The Bureau won't send me next time."

Tenrael didn't want vengeance. He felt too *new* for that. Too clean. "I won't kill anyone."

Charles nodded. He came closer, and Tenrael thought Charles might kiss him again. But Charles just reached to caress a wing. "Fly, Tenrael," he said.

And without another word, he turned and left the trailer.

CHAPTER 4

⊗

*C*HARLES COULDN'T see the ocean from his little front porch, but he could smell it; and with his shirtsleeves rolled up, he could almost feel the tingle of salt spray on his skin. The sun, as it dropped below the red tile roofs of the houses across the street, stained the late summer sky with delicate pinks and oranges. If he could drink booze, this was the sort of evening for sipping good whiskey and slowly emptying a pack of cigarettes. Instead, a glass of water sat on the little wooden table, with a book splayed open beside it.

A black sedan turned onto his short street, moving slowly until it rolled to a stop in front of his house. Charles wasn't especially surprised when Sam Leonard got out. Sam wasn't quite a friend, but he came closer to that than anyone else Charles knew. He'd worked for the Bureau almost as long as Charles, and he was... well, Charles didn't know quite *what* Sam was. Not human, entirely. He moved faster than any man Charles had met, and his round yellow eyes had vertical pupils, like a cat's. He always smelled slightly musky, but not in an unpleasant way. He and Charles never discussed the things that set them apart from other people, but their differences helped them bond.

Sam wore gray trousers and white shirt. As always, he was hatless. He refused to wear the things; maybe they didn't sit well on his thick blond hair. Light-footed, he ascended the front steps, crossed the porch, and sat in the vacant chair, just as if he'd been invited. He and Charles remained silent for several minutes, both staring at the sky above rooftops.

"Want something to drink?" Charles finally offered.

"Nah." Sam had an odd voice, very deep and rumbly for his compact frame. He leaned back in his seat. After another minute or two, he turned his head. "You don't look hurt."

"I'm not."

"Chief says you're out on medical leave."

Charles snorted softly. "I resigned."

Sam nodded a few times as if he'd suspected that already. "What happened in Kansas?"

"Nothing."

"That's not what I heard. I heard there was a demon and it got away."

The guys in the Bureau were more gossipy than housewives. "Yeah," Charles said. "That's what happened." He rubbed his fingers along the smooth wooden armrests.

"So... you failed and that made you quit?" Sam turned slightly to face him. He was smart—too smart for the Bureau, really—and nothing much slipped past him. Now his head was cocked slightly and his eyebrows were raised. "That's not like you, Charlie."

Nobody else called him that. Even his mother had always referred to him as Charles. The diminutive cracked his defenses a little bit.

"I'm tired," Charles said. "I was with the Bureau almost fifteen years. I have so much blood on my hands." He held them up as though the gore might be visible.

Sam's answer was quiet, measured. "You've saved a lot of lives."

"Maybe. Does it balance out? And in the end, does it matter?" His eyes prickled, and for a brief moment he hated Sam for bringing this out of him. He took a calming breath. "I've killed all these monsters just because they weren't human, but I'm not sure they

31

were all worse than the people I saved. Gods, Sam—the things men do!"

Sam nodded and patted Charles' knee. Nothing sexual about it—Sam liked dames. Solely a bit of consolation. "I know. I've seen. But there are innocent humans too."

"Maybe there are innocent monsters. Or... I don't know." He covered his face with his hands. He couldn't drink booze, but maybe drugs would work. He'd never tried them. He knew places where he could buy opium or heroin. Even if the dope worked for him, he was aware the chemical peace would be brief. But it would be something.

He pulled his hands away and caught Sam's gaze. "Why did you join the Bureau?"

Sam shrugged elegantly. "I wanted to be a hero."

"Not me. They recruited me, you know? When I was still just a dumb kid thinking a college degree would get me somewhere. I admit it, I was flattered. And I thought the Bureau was somewhere I could finally belong. A place where it wouldn't matter so much that I was.... But it *did* matter. It does. In the end, everyone.... The more people look at me, the more they realize I'm not one of them."

Gravely, Sam stared. Charles knew what he saw: dyed hair showing white at the roots, unsettling green eyes, skin unnaturally pale for anyone, especially a man who lived in Southern California. And because Sam was smart, he might even have guessed at the things he couldn't see. The long scars along Charles' back. The deep yearning for other men.

Sam had family out in San Bernardino—a big clan of aunts and uncles, brothers and sisters, cousins, nephews and nieces. He had a steady girl whose blue eyes had vertical pupils like his. He had a home. But he understood Charles' grief, and he patted his knee again. "You can't just give up, Charlie. Every living being has a place where they belong."

"I belong here," Charles replied, waving his arms to indicate his house.

"Yeah, okay. But also, every living being has a someone."

Charles shook his head. "I don't think so."

With a small sigh, Sam sat back in his chair again. "What will you do? For dough, I mean?"

"I've got some saved."

"You never were much of a spender. How long will it last?"

"Dunno. I'll probably.... I've been thinking eventually I'll do some PI jobs. Catch enough cheating husbands to pay the bills." He'd been mulling over that idea for a few weeks. Basic investigative work like that was a piece of cake, and he had some contacts in the LAPD who would probably help throw a little work his way as he was getting started. And he could pick and choose which cases to take. None of them would involve demons.

"That's a good idea," Sam said. "You'll make a great private dick. Hell, maybe I should consider it myself. I'm real tired of getting almost killed." He rubbed ruefully at parallel scars on his left cheek. Harpy claws. Charles had been with him on that assignment.

They were both silent for a good ten minutes as the sky turned indigo and the stars began to appear. Sitting quietly with a companion and listening to crickets chirp wasn't such a bad thing.

Eventually Sam groaned slightly and hauled himself upright. "Have to go. Got a date with Anita tonight. She wants to try that fancy steak place in Beverly Hills. I keep telling her I can make good steak at home and it won't cost me a week's salary, but she's being stubborn. Wants to wear her new dress, I bet."

"She's a nice girl." Charles had met her only twice, but she'd smiled at him and didn't make him feel like a freak.

"Yeah, she is. I want to ask her to marry me, but I'm not sure I have the balls for it. What if she says no?"

Charles felt his mouth stretch into an unfamiliar grin. "She won't."

"If you're so confident, maybe I oughtta get you to ask her for me." Sam chuckled as he pulled a small notepad and pen from his pocket. "I know you have my phone number, but I'm going to write it down for you anyway. I want you to call me, okay? Invite me to do something with you. Even just coffee or whatever. We'll have a good time, and then the next time I'll call *you*, right? And you know that little hot rod

I've been working on? We'll take it out to El Mirage and drive so fucking fast we'll feel like we're flying."

Charles took the little piece of paper containing Sam's scrawl. He tucked it into his pocket—along with the black feather he always kept there. "I'll call," he promised.

With a satisfied nod, Sam clapped Charles on the shoulder. He left the porch and walked to his car, but before he climbed in, he paused to wave. Charles could barely see him in the darkness, but he waved back.

Long after Sam was gone, Charles remained on the porch. He hadn't bothered to turn on the outside light, and there was no moon, but he could see passably well anyway. He had good eyesight. As he'd been doing for weeks now—ever since Kansas—he let his mind wander. He thought about flying and sex, about monsters and heroes. He thought about the call of a man's heart.

He almost dozed, and he knew he should go to bed. When he left Kansas, he'd expected nightmares to plague him. But they hadn't—not a single one. His sleep was filled with visions of bronze skin, glowing eyes, and black wings. He dreamed of a creature bowing naked before him and begging him for... for everything.

Sometimes he woke up angry, convinced Tenrael had somehow bewitched him. Sometimes he woke up happy for the freedom he'd given the demon—a freedom Charles himself would never quite have. But always he woke up achingly hard and alone.

Maybe he wouldn't sleep at all tonight. Perhaps he'd go for a walk instead, pad barefoot along the wet sand and listen to the waves endlessly crashing.

Gods, his back *itched.*

He had almost decided on a course of action when his sharp ears caught a strange, soft sound like something battering against air. And then something landed in his front yard. It was large but nearly silent, and all he could see in the darkness were its burning eyes.

As Charles sat frozen, wondering if he really had fallen asleep,

Tenrael ascended the porch stairs to stand before him. He wore nothing but a white cloth wrapped around his loins, and with a few impatient tugs he removed even that and tossed it aside. He sank to his knees and bowed deeply. "Master," he whispered.

For a long moment, Charles couldn't say anything. His throat was completely stopped up. But he swallowed a few times and managed a choked sort of noise. "No. I gave you yourself."

Tenrael rose up on his knees. His hair had grown down to his shoulders, and although there wasn't enough light to tell for sure, Charles would have bet it was clean and silky, and that it was as glossy as the feathers on his wings. Tenrael's skin was unmarred. Perfect. And, oh gods, his beautiful cock was fully erect.

"I want to give myself back," he said.

"Why?" Before Tenrael could answer, Charles heard a car rumbling a block away, and it occurred to him that even at night his neighbors might notice a naked demon on his porch. So Charles closed his book, stood, and picked up the empty water glass. "Come inside."

Tenrael followed as obediently as if he'd been summoned; then he stood, looking around the living room curiously while Charles placed the book near his favorite armchair. Charles took the glass into the kitchen, and when he came back, Tenrael still waited, his hands folded in front of him.

"Why?" Charles repeated.

"I want to be yours."

"You don't owe me a debt for freeing you. You don't—"

"That's not it." When Tenrael trembled slightly, his furled wings shook. His erection had subsided, making Charles long to stroke the soft flesh back to life. "Please," Tenrael said.

Charles fought to control himself, but that single word almost broke him. He surged forward, pressing Tenrael back against the closed door, and he kissed those lush lips he'd been remembering in his dreams. Tenrael whimpered softly and opened his mouth, eagerly allowing entrance to Charles' tongue. He tasted wonderful.

But Charles wasn't satisfied. He moved his mouth to Tenrael's jawline, licking and sucking, and bit the cord of his neck. He left tooth marks on Tenrael's shoulder and along his collarbone, and he dug his thumbs into Tenrael's hips hard enough to bruise. In spite of the pain —or maybe because of it—Tenrael clutched Charles' shirt, keeping him close, and moaned jumbled pleas: "Yes... more... please... please...."

Charles teased Tenrael's nipples until they were peaked, red, and tender; then he nibbled at his flat belly. Although Tenrael's cock was hard again, the head red and shining, Charles didn't touch it. He mouthed Tenrael's balls instead, and stroked the tender skin behind them. Charles had never been so hungry for anyone, so desperate to taste him, possess him, to—

That last thought made Charles freeze; then he rose back to his feet. He yanked himself from Tenrael's grip and stepped back. "Why?" he asked for the third time, wiping his mouth with the back of his shaking hand.

According to the Bureau's mages, repeating an incantation three times made it stronger. Maybe they were right, because now Tenrael took a deep, shuddering breath. "I changed. I don't know whether it's my years with humans that did it or my minutes with you, but I'm not what I was. I'm... I'd say I've been corrupted, but I'm a demon, so I suppose the opposite is true. There's no joy for me now in bringing bad dreams and stirring bad thoughts. And when I fly, I don't feel free."

"But why come to me?"

Tenrael began to step forward, but then slumped back against the door. "I'm nothing now. An empty shell. But all these weeks, I've still tasted your kisses and felt your hands on my body. I've dreamed of you—and demons never dream. I want to serve you. I want you to fill me. Be my heart and soul, Charles, and I will be your wings."

The agony within Charles' chest was terrible, but it was nothing compared to the pain throbbing along the old scars on his back. He moved closer to Tenrael and traced a fingertip over the bite marks on his collarbone. "I'll hurt you."

"I know."

That wasn't the response Charles expected, and he shook his head. "I'm not a demon. I'm not anything. And I want to be good. Part of me does. But another part.... Maybe I was corrupted the moment I was conceived." He licked his dry lips. "If I had you, I'd want to mark you. I'd want to make you cry out."

Tenrael pushed forward until Charles' palm was flat against his chest. "But would you also want to kiss me? To stroke me and hold me and *want* me, instead of just using me?"

"Yes," Charles whispered.

"Would I be yours here?" Tenrael placed his hand over Charles' thudding heart.

"Yes."

"When you hurt me, would it be to degrade me? Or to please us both? Because I am still a demon, and for me pleasure and pain are very much entwined."

For a moment, Charles was silent. "I would never degrade you," he answered honestly.

Tenrael blinked as droplets of water slipped from his eyes. "Would you value me? Because, please, if you'll let me, I would like to value you."

In response, Charles reached into his pocket and pulled out the feather. "I would treasure you."

Tenrael dropped to his knees and smiled up at him. "Master," he croaked.

The word was surprisingly sweet.

Charles set the feather on a shelf. He took Tenrael's hand and towed him to the bedroom, where he spent over an hour tormenting his demon deliciously until Tenrael couldn't even say *please*. Then Charles finally took off his own clothing and with a single, hard thrust sank into Tenrael's tight, welcoming body. He drove hard and fast, shaking the bed, clutching tightly at the legs slung over his shoulders. And when Tenrael arched his back and came, his scream might have been from ecstasy or agony, or maybe from both. It didn't matter, because his eyes were wide and grateful. When Charles reached his own climax a few moments later, he remained silent so he could hear Tenrael's voice: "Yes... thank you... yes, master... yes."

Charles dropped off to sleep that night to the sound of waves, faint but audible through the open bedroom window, and the warmth of Tenrael, curled around his back. Tenrael had placed soft kisses along Charles' wing scars, and the eternal itching was gone. A PI, Charles thought, might find it useful to have a partner who could fly silently in the night.

He fell asleep smiling, and he dreamed very well.

PART II
BOOK TWO: CLAY WHITE

CHAPTER 1

I KNEW what he was as soon as I saw him. He'd likely fool the
fresh meat, the half-zonked kids who writhed around us.
To them he was just a smoking-hot guy, a few years older, whose pale
eyes reflected oddly in the dancing light of the disco ball. But I knew
what he really was.

I went to him anyway.

He must have seen the truth of me too. It wasn't just that I had
some years on the boys around me; a few other men in the club were
also old enough to remember MySpace and flip phones. But I'm...
rough around the edges. I can scrub myself clean, shave the dark
stubble from my face, and tame my curls into something respectable. I
can wear jeans that are not threadbare and frayed at the seams, a shirt
still crisp with the manufacturer's starch. But I can't do anything
about the tension that sits so deeply in my muscles that it'll be there
after I die. Or the hardness in my gaze. I can make my lips curl
upward, but I'm only baring my teeth. It'll look more like a sneer than
a smile.

He saw all this, but he didn't move away.

Instead he cocked his head slightly and parted his lips, revealing the slightest flash of fang. And he held out his hand, palm upward. Inviting me.

That surprised me. I expected him to run away, or maybe to attack. Yet there he stood, asking me to dance.

My legs carried me toward him, and my left hand—without my volition—rose to clasp his. He pulled me close enough to smell his odor of old smoke and copper pennies. My right hand proved just as willful as its mate and found purchase just above his tautly denimed ass.

I don't know what music was playing. No doubt something fast, mostly rhythmic with very little melody, the meaningless lyrics lost beneath the pounding electronic beat. We ignored the music, swaying in time to nothing but my heartbeat. He was graceful, dammit. They all are, as if they've forgotten altogether the meaty drag of a mortal body, as if gravity has no more influence than do the passing years.

I had been a clumsy boy, always tripping over feet that had grown bigger overnight, always dropping things from fingers that were slower than my mind. My father beat me for it and called me stupid, but the whippings didn't make me more agile—just scarred and enraged. When I grew up and joined the Bureau, I worked hard to learn control of my body. Long, sweaty months of punishing work, and eventually I could wield weapons with deadly force and accuracy or, if need be, use my fists and feet and bulk as handily as any demon. But I still couldn't dance worth a damn. This vampire's facile movements made me angry, even as he managed to pull me along in his shadow.

"You're tall," he said, as if he'd just noticed. He was too, but at six foot five, I had a few inches on him. He had to crane his neck to whisper in my ear. "And strong."

"I eat my Wheaties."

His laughter was a rumble against my chest. "And you're not wearing any of those awful colognes. Good." He had a very faint accent, one I couldn't place. Something European, I supposed. His skin looked as if it had been light even when he was human, and his hair might have bordered on ginger in the sunlight. I wondered how long it had been since he'd seen the day. Fuck, it might have been weeks since *I'd* been out between dawn and dusk. I'd become a night-walker too.

The song ended and another began, indistinguishable from the first. Boys gyrated around us, but we were an island. He was slimmer than I am, his tight jeans and tighter T-shirt accentuating his lean frame. His mouth would have seemed too wide if it hadn't been balanced by a long nose and flared cheekbones, and I wondered whether he groomed his eyebrows or if the arches were naturally perfect. I could feel his strength through his hands, one on my hip and the other midway up my back. I wanted to lean my full weight against him because I knew he could hold me.

Halfway through the third song—or maybe it was the fourth—he pulled me closer. Now we fit so closely together that his hard cock fit into the hollow near my hip. I was hard too. Aching. Had been since he first touched me.

We rocked against each other in a slow pantomime of sex, his cool breaths as jagged as my own. "What's your name, agent?" he asked me.

"I'm no agent," I growled.

He huffed, unbelieving, but I wasn't lying. It had been three months since I left the Bureau— Fuck. Since the Bureau left me.

My body must have stiffened, because he stroked my back as if I were a nervous pony. "I'm Marek," he said. "I use many names, but I'd like you to know my real one. The one my father gave me." I couldn't tell if his tone was mocking or wistful.

I wanted him to know my real name as well. I'd always figured a certain honesty was owed between hunter and prey. "Clayton White."

"Do your friends call you Clay?"

I shrugged in his embrace. They might if I had any. The other agents had just called me White. A color rather than an identity.

Marek undulated against me and sniffed at my neck, and my right hand slid slightly lower to grip his tight ass. The fabric of his jeans was thin enough that I could have torn it if I'd tried.

Two boys bumped into us. They were pretty, one dark and the

other blond, each of them delicate enough to snap barehanded. They smiled in hormonal, pharmaceutical bliss and spun away.

"So much more freedom than when I was their age," Marek said. "I never touched another man while I was alive. Or woman. I died a virgin. Such a waste."

"Not even the vamp who turned you?" I couldn't help asking.

"Not even. I was intended simply as a meal. Accidents happen."

Again his tone was light, but there might have been an undercurrent of sorrow. I didn't want to acknowledge the answering twinge in my own heart. My parents had needed a shotgun wedding, and my father never forgave me for it.

"How old were you?" I asked, not intending to. It seemed I had little control of myself tonight.

"Twenty-four. Old for a virgin, even in my time. I'll bet you didn't make it through high school untouched."

Untouched—such an old-fashioned way to put it. I shrugged again. My first was a wild girl two years older than me. She'd set her eyes on me the first day of my sophomore year, and although I'd already been fairly certain I played for the other team, the offer had been too good to refuse. I hadn't fucked a man until college.

Marek huffed with irritation or laughter—I couldn't tell which—and snaked a hand between us to squeeze my erection. "It's a pity when youthful lust goes to waste," he said.

"I'm not youthful." Hadn't been for a very long time. Hell, possibly never was. Sometimes I looked in the mirror and concluded that I'd been born old. My body was only now catching up to my real age.

"I was old before your grandparents were born. *You* are youthful."

He massaged my cock a moment more, and I didn't reply. I was wondering exactly when he'd been turned and what that meant to me. New vampires are impulsive, prone to biting before thinking. Makes them easy to destroy. The ones who survive for decades have learned caution and self-control.

The song ended. When another began, Marek remained unmoving against me, his mouth inches from my neck. "Will you follow me, Clay?" he asked.

"Yes."

He took my hand and led me across the floor. A few dancers leered our way and others reached toward us, but I glared and they pulled back. Instead of going to the front of the club, which was crowded, Marek took us to a side door. He pushed it open, and we exited into a narrow alley that reeked of garbage and cat piss.

I thought he might pause there. Darkness bathed the alley, nobody else was nearby, and the thump of music from the club would have muffled any sounds. But he kept a gentle tug on my arm, sometimes turning his head to give me a small smile as we left the narrow space between brick buildings and turned onto the sidewalk. I knew it was my imagination, but it almost seemed as if his footsteps made no sound while my own boots clomped heavily enough to crack the pavement.

The calendar showed us well into September, and yet San Francisco baked in an early-autumn heat wave. Even now, hours after sunset, sweat beaded on my skin. Marek's dry palm absorbed the moisture, as if his body would take in any of my fluids. Perhaps it would. Sweat isn't so very different from blood, both being cousins to the seawater that birthed us all.

A few blocks away, the neighborhood turned seedier, although several newly refurbished buildings proved that gentrification was creeping in. Nowadays even falling-down shacks fetched a million dollars or more from tech company employees. I couldn't afford to live in the city, not even with my severance package from the Bureau, which I called "fuck-off money." Just enough to send me on my way quietly. Just enough for a shitty apartment in the East Bay, where the cockroaches resembled some of the demons I'd killed when I was an agent.

Marek finally stopped at the door to a defunct Chinese restaurant. Brown paper lined the inside of the windows that still sported painted lettering offering lunch discounts on beef chow fun and wonton soup. The red awning had faded to pale pink and was tattered at the edges.

To my considerable surprise, Marek pulled out a key and unlocked the door. Then he bowed deeply and gestured me inside. "Please. You're invited," he said.

I scowled at his little joke. We both knew that the old saw about vamps needing an invitation to enter was horseshit. As was most of the other crap people wrote about the monsters. They are damned hard to kill, but you don't need to stake them or drag them into sunlight. The Bureau issued special bullets—silver with tiny wooden particles—and as long as you aimed well, they'd do the trick for vamps, shifters, and most other species. They'd work just fine on humans too.

I don't know how long ago the restaurant had closed, but the interior still carried faint odors of soy sauce and oil. Several yellowish lights cast a dim glow, revealing the few tables and chairs that remained on the scuffed tile floor. A thick layer of dust shrouded the long counter, and discolored walls showed lighter patches where pictures had once hung.

"Why here?" I asked, kicking at a pile of stained tablecloths.

"Privacy." Marek had closed and locked the door as I was looking around. Now he approached me with his hands loose at his sides and the corners of his lips curled upward. Even his walk was graceful, as if music were playing and only he could hear it. Maybe there was music. Vamp senses were better than human to begin with, and too many years of shooting firearms had dulled my own ears a bit.

"Okay," I said when he was almost within reach. "But why here specifically?"

His smile faded and his gaze shifted to the floor. "It's where I'm staying. For now."

I wondered whether desiccated corpses lurked in a storeroom or somewhere in the kitchen.

When Marek looked at me again, he somehow looked both very young and exceedingly ancient. "Are you ready, Agent White?" he asked quietly.

"I'm not an agent!" It had been a long time since I raised my voice, and I startled myself a little. I'd thought myself no longer capable of true anger. I'd been picturing my amygdalae—the almond-shaped spots in the brain that process emotions—as withered and shrunken. But Marek's words made my hands shake and the blood churn through my head.

He didn't back away from my fury. Stone-faced and soft-voiced, he said, "Not anymore."

I bent and reached into my right boot.

The rules are clear. When the Bureau terminates an agent, there's paperwork. Mounds of it. Then the agent—the *former* agent—turns in his badge, his ID, his gun. He's escorted to the door by grim-faced men in dark suits. And fuck-off money is deposited into his bank account.

Although most of the details were gray and blurry in my memory, there had been one important deviation. When I'd set my gun on Townsend's desk, he gave me a long, narrow-eyed look before downing the generous shot of scotch he'd poured himself when I sat down. Then he slowly pushed the weapon back toward me. "Keep it," he said.

"But the Bureau—"

"Rules. There's ways around them, White. You worked here long enough to know that. When a guy's spent some years rounding up monsters, killing some of 'em, he collects enemies. I'm not cold-hearted enough to send him back into the world unarmed." He moved the gun a little closer to me. "Take it."

And I had. He hadn't asked for my Bureau-supplied bullets either.

I'd had to buy a boot holster, since they weren't standard-issue for the Bureau. And I wasn't licensed to carry the thing. But that hardly mattered to me.

So in the overly warm wreckage of that Chinese restaurant, I pulled my old gun out and pointed it at Marek.

His smile reappeared, brittle as old glass, but he didn't move.

"I'm a good shot," I informed him. "Always have been."

"Doesn't matter much at this distance, does it?"

"Not really." I kept my hand steady and hoped my confusion didn't show. "You got a death wish or something?"

That made him laugh. "That wish was fulfilled nearly three hundred years ago, my friend."

I was too shaken to respond to that last part. Three centuries. I'd heard of vampires that old but had never met one. "Forget the semantics. You're lively for a dead guy—are you aching to be a bona fide corpse?"

His expression went somber. "No. I'm not sure why, but even after all this time, I'm not eager to depart this plane."

"You'll depart real quick when I pull this trigger."

"Yes," he said. And then he moved so fast that my eyes couldn't track him. Before my instinct to shoot could even kick in, my gun was skittering across the floor and Marek's arms were wrapped around me in a python-like embrace. I couldn't lift my hands to defend myself, and although I tried to kick him, he held me so still that I couldn't get enough momentum to do any harm. His fangs scraped my neck as delicately as a razor.

But he didn't bite.

I should have been struggling, even if I knew he was stronger. I could have shouted and screamed. I could have spit empty threats of retribution from the Bureau. But I didn't do any of those things, and my heart continued to beat slow and steady. Despite the sharp teeth pressing against my skin, I wasn't afraid.

"Who has the death wish?" Marek whispered. He sounded amused.

"I don't want to die."

"Perhaps." Still holding me, he moved back a little so he could look me over. "You'd make a wonderful vampire. Beautiful and quite terrible. Is that what you're hoping for?"

I growled my denial and he smiled. "Good, because I won't do it," he said.

"Then just fucking kill me."

As the words left my mouth, I realized the truth. I did not honestly want to die. But life was a heavy burden, and ever since I'd been a small child, I'd expected one of the monsters to finally win. No waiting any longer—which was some sort of relief.

But Marek released me and took a step backward. "If I wanted to murder you, I would have done so before you pulled your gun."

"Then what do you want?" I shouted.

He stood looking at me. Something in the way the light hit his eyes, something in the way he held himself... I don't know. Maybe it was just the goddamn fangs. At that moment he appeared completely inhuman, a creature as alien as a space dragon from Mars. Distant and inscrutable.

But he didn't frighten me, and in that strange alien face, I recognized something familiar. Something I saw every time I looked in a mirror.

"I need to warn you," he said.

Instead of listening I moved toward him and grabbed the back of his head. And I kissed him, fangs and all, feeling the sharp pricks on my tongue and tasting the hot metal of my own blood. He could have broken away—he'd already shown his strength—but he pressed closer and laced his fingers behind my neck. I didn't know if he wanted me the way I suddenly wanted him or if he only craved a light meal, and I didn't really care. For that moment I had him against me, hard and solid, and he gave his mouth to me freely. Nobody ever gave me anything.

We fell, Marek and I, landing on the dirty floor in a tangled pile. I was on top. Our mouths never lost their connection, but now his hands roamed over my shoulders, my back, my ass. Sometimes he squeezed me hard enough to hurt, as if reminding me what he *could* do if he chose. The little bursts of pain spurred me on, and I ground against him.

I'm not a thinking man. Never have been. I do things, sometimes rashly, sometimes to great detriment—yet my recklessness has saved my life more than once. I pawed at Marek's clothes, heedless of consequences, wanting only to touch him, to penetrate his body as I was penetrating his mouth. If he killed me in the process, well, there are worse ways to go. I've seen them.

With his shirt in tatters and his jeans pushed down his thighs, Marek suddenly went very still beneath me. He pushed my head back a little and held my face with surprising gentleness. My blood smeared his lips and chin like poorly applied lipstick.

"I need to warn you," he repeated.

"Kill me or don't. I don't give a fuck about warnings."

"But you still give a fuck about something, don't you?" Soft voice, soft hands, pale eyes showing warmth—a monster with a façade of tenderness. At least he could manage the façade. I never could.

"I give a fuck about fucking." I pushed my groin—still clothed—against his naked one.

"Is that why you came to the club tonight? For sex?"

I remembered my original mission then and, ashamed, disentangled myself from him. I stood and backed away several steps, but he remained sprawled on the floor, his pale cock hard against his belly. *How the hell do vampires get hard-ons?* I dragged my focus back to more important matters.

"I came looking for you," I said.

"Me?"

"I know about the murders."

His expression went blank. Moving gracefully, he rose to his feet. He pulled up his jeans but let them hang unfastened and low on his hips. "You know better than that, Agent White. I didn't kill them."

I ignored the *Agent* and shook my head. "Five young men, dead. Every one of them drained dry."

"So you assume a vampire did it."

"Seems a safe assumption." Uneasy about where the conversation was going, I crossed my arms and narrowed my eyes. As I said, I don't like to think—and questioning my actions leads nowhere good.

Marek gave me a look that a schoolteacher might bestow on a dim student. "You've seen what my kind does to people. Have you ever seen corpses like these?"

"I haven't seen these victims at all. The Bureau isn't exactly in a sharing mood." I'd heard rumors and read between the lines of the news reports, but I hadn't viewed the bodies. Hadn't even gotten my hands on any photos.

Marek prowled closer. There was something disturbingly near to pity in his gaze. It clashed with my blood on his skin. "They were dried-out husks," he said. "Not just their blood gone, but *everything* liquid. Nothing left but bones and hair, and skin like old leather. Mummies."

"How would you know that if you didn't kill them?"

"They were left for me to find."

None of this made any sense—least of all that I simply stood there, still hard from his touch, my gun far out of reach. But the orderly house I'd made of my life had begun to crumble months earlier, and perhaps all semblance of logic had crumbled with it. "Left by who?" I asked. "And why?"

He searched my eyes. "Will you believe me if I tell you?"

I shrugged.

After a long pause, he nodded. "Let's go somewhere else for this conversation. Coffee?"

I may not be an intellectual man, but I have some share of curiosity. So I agreed.

CHAPTER 2

*B*EFORE WE left, Marek washed the blood from his face and buttoned his jeans. He dampened a scrap of his now-ruined shirt and, grinning, cleaned my face too. Then he reached into a plastic bag and pulled out a plain black T-shirt. I wondered if he'd deliberately acquired one that was a size too small—it showed off every line of his lean torso and exposed a strip of pale skin below the hem. If you didn't pay too much attention to his eyes, he could have been mistaken for a human boy interested in nothing more than sharing his body. But I knew better.

He didn't say anything while I retrieved my gun, put on the safety, and tucked it into my boot holster. He even turned his back to me as he led the way out of the restaurant. Maybe I could have shot him before he turned around. I didn't try.

The temperature had cooled while we were inside but not enough to make me wish for a jacket. The fog hadn't settled into this part of town, probably due to the light breeze that sent bits of paper skittering along the sidewalk. Although the air reeked of piss, the wind brought a hint of salt from the Bay, that damp, piscine odor that I imagined the whole world had smelled like, once upon a time.

Marek walked quickly and I had to hurry to keep up. But we didn't go far. Three blocks from his restaurant, we came to a donut shop with brightly lit windows. Inside, the scent of coffee was thickly overlaid by the aromas of frying dough and sugar. I ordered for us at the counter—two coffees and a glazed old-fashioned—then joined Marek at a booth in the corner. The table was scarred and sticky, the vinyl upholstery cracked. But the coffee was decent and the donut freshly made.

Since Marek seemed disinclined to speak right away, I looked around. Working for the Bureau meant I'd spent a lot of time in places like this one, trying to stay awake through the night hours when those I hunted tended to appear. Because this was San Francisco, the late-night crowd was a little different from those in other cities. Fewer truck drivers and more drag queens.

In the harsh fluorescent light, Marek's skin was nearly translucent and his eyes glowed as if lit from within. I stared at him shamelessly, wondering whether he'd been as beautiful when he was alive, wondering what he'd witnessed over the decades.

"Monsters come in many guises," Marek said quietly. His hands were wrapped around his mug as if for warmth.

"You think I don't know that?"

"Some of them are human."

"A lot of them are."

He lifted his cup and took a small sip, which fascinated me. I'd heard vampires could consume things besides blood if they chose, but I'd never sat down with one and witnessed it myself. He put down the mug and ran his sharp, pale tongue over his lips. "Why were you in the club tonight?"

"Told you."

"Right. Looking for whoever murdered those men. But you say you no longer work for the Bureau."

I lifted my lip, showing my teeth. "Call it a hobby."

"So hunting is your entertainment now? I don't think so. I'm guessing... penance. Why are you no longer an agent, Clay?"

This time I actually growled, and I turned my head away. I didn't owe him an explanation. It was none of his business—none of anyone's goddamn business.

After waiting a few moments, Marek sighed. "All right. You will remain a man of mystery. But let me assure you of one thing—I was looking for the same thing as you tonight. Looking for the person responsible for those deaths."

"Why the fuck would you care?" I demanded, turning to face him again. I realized as the words left my mouth that I was implicitly acknowledging that he was not the murderer. It was a stupid thing to believe, yet I believed it. After all, had he intended to kill me, he'd already had plenty of opportunity.

He leaned back in his seat, making the vinyl squeak. "Would you believe I am a principled fiend? Probably not. I have the feeling such a shade of gray doesn't exist in your black-and-white world." He leaned forward and dropped his voice. "Let me explain it this way. I learned very early that if I snacked lightly on humans instead of draining them, I'd be much less likely to come to the attention of men like you. I abstain from murder out of a desire for self-preservation. Do you believe that much?"

Slowly, I nodded. It wasn't the first time I'd heard a story like that, although it had never come to me straight from the vampire's mouth. But there were vamps I'd been instructed by the Bureau to ignore. Townsend had compared it to feral cats. If you removed them from the neighborhood, more would move in to take their place. But if you neutered them and returned them to streets, they'd keep any newcomers away and few new kittens would be born. As I had recently experienced, Marek was far from neutered. Yet perhaps the principle still applied.

Seemingly satisfied that I wasn't arguing with him, Marek reached over to my hand, which clutched my mug, and used one finger to trace a vein. It made me shiver.

"There's more to it than that," he said. "Not only do I leave my victims alive—and really, few would consider themselves victimized by what I do with them—but I also keep my eyes open for... more lethal predators."

"Vampires with fewer scruples?"

"Sometimes, yes. And all kinds of other beasts. Human and otherwise." He seemed to consider a moment before continuing. "Do you remember that serial killer in Boston a few years ago? The media called him the Harvard Horror."

The case hadn't been mine, both because it was on the East Coast and also because everyone believed the perp was human. But the FBI often shared information with the Bureau—sometimes we even cooperated—and like most of my fellow agents, I'd followed the case out of professional curiosity. "He was never caught," I said.

Marek's teeth shone very white. "Not by your people, no. But the murders stopped, didn't they?"

"Yes."

"That's because the Harvard Horror lies in many small pieces in a landfill. He tasted good." He looked smug.

"So you don't *always* abstain from murder."

"I indulge when the situation calls for it."

I didn't point out that a vampire's notion of a justified killing might be skewed. Sometimes humans had twisted views of their own. "If he wasn't a vampire intruding on your territory, why would you bother with him?"

"Because I'd generally rather not have federal agents poking around. Generally." He gave my hand another quick caress. "Because I *could* kill him without any twinges from whatever remains of my conscience. And because you are not the only one who wishes to perform penance."

I drained the last of my coffee, stood, and returned to the counter, where I paid for a refill. I thought about buying another donut too, but I wasn't in the mood for sweets. Truly, I hungered for something more substantial. Marek waited patiently, watching me instead of allowing himself to be distracted by the noisy teenagers a few tables away or the colorfully dressed people sitting at the counter.

"You said you had a warning," I reminded him, after I'd resumed my seat.

He ran quick fingers through his hair—a shockingly human action.

"I was at the club looking for whoever—whatever—killed those men. But then I saw you, and I thought I might make sure the Bureau was aware of what's going on. I had other thoughts about you too. Those had nothing to do with murders or federal agencies." The predatory look he gave me made me shiver again, and not from fear.

"So if you're not the killer, who is? Or what?"

"I don't know."

"That's not very helpful."

He shrugged. "Maybe. I can tell you that it is not one of my kind, which at least narrows your field of suspects a bit, yes? I can tell you that I believe there are undiscovered victims—perhaps discarded in the Bay or elsewhere. There are rumors among the boys in the clubs. They know something is stalking them, yet they are not afraid for themselves. The young always think themselves invulnerable." His smile suggested he might have been referring to foolishness he'd once possessed himself.

I could have countered that even as a small child, I'd known exactly how susceptible to harm I was. In fact, some days I'd gone to bed mildly surprised I'd survived thus far. Some days I still did.

"Anything else?" I asked.

"I think whoever is doing this knows I am here and is trying to lure me closer, but I do not know why. I believe the murders will continue unless someone catches him."

"What do you want me to do with this warning?" I asked.

"Tell the Bureau."

"Which no longer employs me."

"They might listen nonetheless. I'd appreciate if you'd ask them not to hunt me. This time, at least, we're on the same side."

I snorted. "I thought you didn't like it when agents come poking around."

His expression went momentarily bleak. "I also don't like it when young people end up dead. I know you don't believe that, but it's true. And this killer is more elusive than the Harvard Horror." The ghost of a smile flitted across his face. "Policemen sometimes call for backup, yes? This time, I believe I need backup."

Grimacing at the mental image of vampires in blue uniforms, I drained my mug a second time. I dug in my pocket and pulled out a pair of wrinkled singles, which I left on the table for whoever had to clean up after us. Then I stood. "I'll tell 'em," I said. "Can't guarantee they'll listen."

His answering nod was regal. "Thank you."

The darkness wrapped around me like a cloak as soon as I left the donut shop, and despite the caffeine I'd just consumed, I was suddenly exhausted. If my wallet had been fatter, I'd have considered a hotel room for the night. Someplace with clean white sheets, sparkling granite and chrome in the bathroom, tiny bottles of shampoo and conditioner smelling of lemongrass, and where the only ghosts were polite, corporate ones. But since my cash reserves were low, I trudged in the direction of the nearest BART station.

I'd gone four or five blocks when I heard his light footsteps behind me.

When Marek grasped my wrist and dragged me away, I didn't resist. He took me down a narrow alley between a laundromat and a housing clinic, and then through a tiny parking lot to a loading dock behind a bodega. In a tight, closet-like alcove, he pushed me back against the concrete wall.

"Long ago, I was taught to finish what I'd begun," he whispered. And then he kissed me fiercely.

This space was so utterly dark that I was nearly blind, so I closed my eyes to concentrate on the taste of him—bitter coffee—and the feel of his body against mine. This was better than my imagined hotel. The exhaustion drained from me at once, replaced by passion that had been suppressed while we sat in the donut shop. Moaning into his mouth, I grabbed his ass and pulled him closer. I was as hard as I'd been in the Chinese restaurant, and his cock was equally stiff. I spread my legs and bent my knees a bit to equalize our heights, the building supporting my back as we rutted together.

I could have come like that, quick and dirty and desperate. But Marek pulled away, dropped to his knees, and opened my jeans, then used one cool hand to pull out my cock.

A wise man knows that a vampire's mouth is an imprudent place to put his dick. But I'm not all that wise, and when it came right down to it, there were worse ways to die. In fact I almost laughed at the irony of it. I imagined what the guys at the Bureau would say when they found out—those men and women I'd worked with for years but had never become close to. They'd shake their heads. Call me names. But I think some of them would be envious, deep inside their hardened hearts. Every agent expects to die at the hands of some monster; few picture themselves enjoying the process.

And I was enjoying indeed, nearly delirious with the pleasure of Marek's tight throat around me and his soft hair between my grasping fingers.

He didn't bite me. Well, not quite. Sometimes he drew his head back, releasing my cock with an obscene *pop*, and then with infinite care and delicacy, he drew a fang across the tender skin of my glans, my shaft, my scrotum. It didn't hurt. The opposite, in fact. That sharpness sparked my nerve endings so deliciously, I had to grasp his hair tightly to keep from convulsing and collapsing.

Marek seemed as caught up in the experience as I was. Vampires don't need oxygen, yet when he wasn't sucking me, his breaths came harsh and rapid. And sometimes he paused to press his nose against me and inhale.

My cock was deep in his throat when I came, and I had to stuff a fist in my mouth to muffle the cry. I leaned back against the building, gasping, and Marek stood. He took my hand and chuckled as he licked it—I'd bitten myself hard enough to draw blood.

Before I could fasten my jeans, he kissed me again. Slowly this time. Tenderly. Still tasting of coffee but now also of my fluids—blood and semen, salty and warm.

"Keep yourself safe," he whispered in my ear. "Don't give up. Don't let the darkness overwhelm you. There's still light within you." He kissed my cheek. And then he was gone.

CHAPTER 3

THE BUREAU'S West Coast headquarters occupied one of those ugly urban buildings that had sprouted up during the late fifties and early sixties. No effort or money had been wasted on ornamentation, and passersby paid it so little attention that they likely didn't even remember it was there. This particular edifice was four stories of graying concrete in a nondescript neighborhood in one of the many communities that made up Los Angeles, and for several years, it had been more of a home to me than any of the dull apartments where I'd slept. It still felt like home now, even as I entered through the door marked *Visitors* and stepped into the cool sterility of the lobby.

Every surface there was hard and smooth; it was a space completely devoid of warmth and life. The smallest noises echoed, and my footsteps sounded like an advancing army. Liz Biggs sat behind a tall reception desk, her back straight and hair as perfectly coiffed as always. "Can I help you, sir?" she asked crisply, as if she hadn't known me for years.

"Need to see Townsend."

"You may email his assistant to set up—"

"Now."

"Associate Director Townsend is in a meeting."

Almost certainly bullshit, but I didn't call her on it. "Then he can take a break. I need to talk to him. People are dying."

A flash of irritation showed on her face, which I considered a major victory. I continued to stare her down, even though both of us knew there wasn't a damn thing I could do if she turned me away.

Biggs blinked first. She spent a moment working her tablet before looking up at me. "You may go ahead, Mr. White. He's in—"

"I know where he is." I took the plastic card she held out and stomped past her. When I reached the elevator bank, I flashed the card at the scanner. Although Townsend was only three floors up and I certainly could have taken the stairs, the card wouldn't let me into the stairwell. The Bureau was careful about which parts of the building visitors could access.

The elevator doors whispered open, I stepped inside, and the doors closed. There were no buttons to press, but thanks to the card, the elevator knew where to take me. I wondered who was watching on the security cameras. Tipping my face upwards, I gave a mocking little salute.

The elevator released me into a long, nearly featureless corridor. None of the metal doors showed any markings, and they all had scanners rather than knobs. As I walked by, I imagined I could feel the invisible hexes on each threshold, meant to repel certain magics and unwanted inhuman visitors.

As an agent, I'd spent almost all my time in the field rather than at HQ. I hadn't even had an office here, although they gave me a temporary space whenever I'd come in to work. Still, I'd walked this hallway countless times. It felt odd to be doing it again, without the weight of my badge in my pocket.

Townsend's suite lay at the end of the hall, accessible through wooden double doors rather than metal. They opened as I approached, then shut behind me. His reception area was carpeted, the walls hung with landscape paintings, and the faint odor of lemon furniture polish tingled my nose. His assistant, Victor Holmes, smiled placidly from behind his enormous desk.

"He'll be with you in a few minutes, Mr. White."

Holmes was a tiny man, his face and body twisted from a brutal encounter with an ogre in Montana. But although he was confined to a wheelchair and appeared barely strong enough to lift a pencil, everyone except Townsend was terrified of him. Including me, to be honest. Something about the peculiar glint in his eyes. If I had to choose to fight either him or an ogre, I'd go with the ogre.

But today I didn't have to fight Holmes.

"Would you like some coffee?" he asked.

"No." I didn't sit in one of the heavy leather chairs either, instead choosing to pace the room and inspect the paintings as if I aspired to become an art critic. Holmes watched me.

It was interesting that nobody had searched me or asked me to hand over my weapons. Surely they knew I was armed. In fact, somewhere between the building's front door and Townsend's office, I'd undoubtedly been body-scanned, and my gun would have been easily visible inside my boot. Also the knife I kept as a backup in the other boot. Either they didn't believe I was a threat or they were confident I couldn't harm anyone.

I was peering at a scene of snowy mountains flanking a meadow when Holmes called my name. "You can go in now."

The furniture in Townsend's office was big and utilitarian—several battered gray filing cabinets, a cluttered bookshelf, an immense metal desk. He'd stuck newspaper clippings haphazardly on the walls, and everything reeked of cigarette smoke. Townsend himself stood behind the desk, overflowing his expensive suit, his smiling face an unhealthy ruddy color. As usual, a half-empty bottle of scotch perched on the surface in front of him, along with stacks of papers and an overflowing ashtray.

"This is a surprise, White." He shook my hand with a heavy grip, collapsed into his oversized leather chair, and gestured at the low chair intended for visitors. Then he poured himself a glass of scotch. "One for you?"

"No thanks."

"Given it up?" he asked, eyebrow raised.

I simply shrugged. After being severed from the Bureau, I'd spent a month or so drunk. But booze has never suited me, and I decided I wanted to spend whatever time I had left with a clear head. Besides, there are better ways to die.

"I hear you're living up in Frisco," Townsend said, despite knowing that nobody really called it that.

"Yeah."

"Nice city, if you don't mind freezing your balls off all summer. You staying out of trouble?"

"I guess."

He lifted his glass, drained it in one swallow, then refilled it. Some of the guys used to say Townsend's veins ran with nothing but scotch, and I'm not sure they were joking. If he'd ever become drunk, I'd never discerned it.

"You been seeing a shrink?"

"No."

"I figured." He tugged at one ear. "Psychologists. Sometimes they're worse than wizards, you know? Least wizards get shit done. But sometimes a good headshrinker is what a fellow needs. Helps with the nightmares." He tapped his forehead.

"I sleep fine," I lied.

"You're still a kid. I know you don't feel like it, and you figure your glory days are behind you. But there's plenty of work you can still do—good work, important work—if you get your head together."

"If you're trying to tempt me with a job offer, that's not why I'm here."

Townsend's bark of laughter shook his entire body. "No, I didn't think so. Anyway, your days with the Bureau are permanently over. But there are many other doors waiting to open. I'll even be a reference. I have positive things to say about you."

"Gonna tell them about the little kids I killed?"

"I'm going to tell them you're a good man who sometimes acts with his heart and guts instead of his brain. The same could be said of most heroes."

"I'm no hero," I muttered, looking away. Then I firmed my jaw and turned back to face him. "I didn't come here for job counseling either."

"Of course not. I threw that in for free." He drained his glass a second time and didn't pour more. "What can I do for you?"

"You can send some agents up north to catch whatever's been murdering young men."

Townsend showed no surprise at my statement. He took a cigarette package out of a desk drawer and flicked a silver lighter to life. When he exhaled, he blew a perfect smoke ring. We both watched it drift to the ceiling.

"This isn't any business of yours," he finally said.

"Just because I'm not on the Bureau payroll doesn't mean it's not my business."

"And why do you think it is?"

I had to think about that for a moment. "They're people who don't deserve to die. If I can do something to stop that—"

"It won't bring back those children."

I winced, not so much at the reminder of what I'd done as at the echo of what Marek had said about penance. I hated feeling I was so transparent that anyone could see my feelings and motives. "I know."

After a deep sigh, Townsend took several long drags from the cigarette and then stubbed it out. "So, what can you tell me about the situation?"

"Not much. A bunch of dead young men—more than the cops are aware of. Kids who liked to hang out in clubs. Every one of them drained."

"Anything else?"

"It's not a vampire. At least I don't think so."

"What makes you say that?" he asked, chin lifted.

"Condition of the bodies. Not just bloodless, actually desiccated."

"You don't think a vamp can do that?"

"No."

"What makes you so sure?"

I looked down at my hands, sitting uselessly on my lap, then up at him. "I spoke with a vampire."

I gave him a cleaned-up version of my encounter with Marek. Townsend listened expressionlessly, but his eyes told me he wasn't surprised to learn about Marek—and he knew perfectly well we'd done more than chat. When my brief narrative was finished, Townsend refilled his glass but didn't yet drink it. "So you believe in an ethical vampire?" he asked.

"Maybe. If he was the perp, why would he have let me live? Why send me here with a warning?"

"Dunno. Because he hopes to deflect attention from himself?"

I'd considered that possibility, but it didn't feel right. Of course my instincts had been wrong before, with lethal results.

Townsend heaved his bulk out of the chair and took a few steps toward a wall, where he inspected a yellowed newspaper clipping. The headline was about a congressman from Modesto who'd been caught in a Bureau sting operation a few years back. The bastard had tried to sell his soul to the devil in return for being elected governor. I hadn't worked on that particular case, but I remembered it well.

Still facing the wall and with his scotch glass in hand, Townsend spoke. "I appreciate you sharing this information."

"And? You'll send agents?"

"No."

"But—"

"I believe what you've told me, White. You've never been a liar or an alarmist, and frankly, you don't have the imagination to make this shit up."

I shook off the small dig. "Then why won't you act?"

"San Francisco police are already on the case."

"SFPD!" I snorted. "Yeah, that's fine if the perp speeds or parks with his wheels angled wrong." Actually, I have a fair amount of respect for local law enforcement agencies. They do a tough job under challenging circumstances, and I'd always relied on them for information while working a case. But they were neither trained nor equipped to deal with nonhuman criminals. That's what the Bureau's for.

"It's their ballgame," Townsend said.

I hopped to my feet. "But why, dammit?"

He tapped the newspaper article and then turned to face me. "Politics, my boy. The Bureau's priorities lie elsewhere. And that's all I'm gonna tell you. Anything else is above your pay grade." He chuckled at his bad joke.

"Politics. And how many people will die because of it?"

"Everyone dies. Eventually." He laughed again, although I didn't know why. He pointed at me with the hand holding his glass. "They die even if they've never sinned. They die despite love and medicine and good intentions. It's the first rule of the world, son. What goes up, must come down. What lives, dies."

"Your job is to delay that." I wanted to shout, but I dropped my voice to a gravelly rasp instead.

"It is. And I do. But I can't save everyone—none of us can—and I am not exempt from outside pressures."

"Dammit, Townsend! You can't—"

"Enough. The matter's settled—the Bureau's not involved." He softened his tone. "You've done your duty. You can rest easy over this one."

I growled, turned on my heel, and headed toward the door.

"White!"

I stopped but didn't turn around.

"If you get yourself in the middle of this, you're going to end up dead," he said.

"Everybody dies."

"But there's no reason to hasten the inevitable. Take this."

Looking over my shoulder, I saw him holding out a small piece of paper. "What is it?"

"The contact info for a former agent. He retired... oh, some years back. Does private-eye stuff. If you're gonna throw yourself into the mess, he'd be a good man to have at your side. Him and his partner both."

"I can't afford a private eye."

"Talk to him. Maybe he'll take the case pro bono." When I hesitated, Townsend moved closer. "*Think*, White. No need to throw yourself on the sword. At least try for help."

I didn't point out that I'd come to his office for exactly that reason. Instead I grabbed the paper, and without saying another word, I left. I didn't speak to Holmes either. Had there been a trash can along the way, I would have tossed the note. But there wasn't, and curiosity got the better of me by the time I was in the elevator. Scrawled in black ink was an address in Santa Monica, along with a name: Charles Grimes.

CHAPTER 4

I TOOK the train down to LA and then rented a car. I hated navigating Los Angeles, I hated crawling down the freeways, I hated breathing the exhaust. All while folded into a tiny death trap the size of a clown car.

I'm not a big fan of LA.

But I managed to reach Santa Monica in one piece just as the sun was falling into the Pacific, lighting sky and water with carnival colors. I was momentarily tempted to abandon my mission and walk barefoot on the beach instead, with the breeze ruffling my hair and gulls calling from the pier. Maybe I'd even buy an ice cream cone and eat it while watching the Ferris wheel and roller coaster.

Instead I parked in front of a stucco bungalow with a Spanish tile roof. Two rocking chairs on the front porch flanked a small table; colorful tiles hung on the wall. The ornately carved front door had a decorative metal plate covering the peephole. I rang the doorbell and waited.

The door opened quickly, but just enough for a figure to fill the gap. "Charles Grimes?" I asked.

He scrutinized me instead of answering, and I stared back. He was tall and lanky, with pale skin, straight white hair, and irises that were an odd pale green. He wore khaki trousers and a blue dress shirt and could have been anywhere between thirty and sixty years old.

"What do you want?" he finally asked.

"Townsend gave me your name."

That bit of news made him pinch his mouth. "Show me your badge."

"Don't have one. Not anymore."

More staring, this time with his nearly invisible eyebrows drawn into a V. "What's your name?"

"Clayton White."

"You were the agent in that Redding mess."

"Yeah." I tried to unclench my jaw. "That's not why I'm here."

After a brief pause, he opened the door more widely and stepped aside. I followed him into a room that, while in excellent condition, looked as if it hadn't been changed since the house was built in the thirties. The floor, window frames, and ceiling beams shared the same dark wood, while tiles ornamented the stuccoed fireplace. The furniture was substantial and somewhat worn—three overstuffed armchairs, two large bookcases, and an old-fashioned rolltop desk.

While I stood in the center of the room, Grimes gave me another long look before he seemed to reach a decision. "Ten," he called.

That confused me briefly, but puzzlement was replaced by astonishment and fear when a creature strode into the room. He wore nothing but a pair of briefs, but that wasn't what made me gasp. Against his back were furled an enormous pair of black wings.

"Demon!" I shouted, reaching for my gun.

Grimes moved as swiftly as Marek and grabbed my arm before I could draw my weapon. "Don't," he snarled. "He's mine."

Had I been thrown into this situation a few weeks earlier, I might have struggled. But my recent encounter with Marek had taught me that not all monsters were as dangerous as I'd assumed. So I relaxed and let Grimes remove my gun from the holster. He checked to make sure the safety was on before tucking it into the back of his waistband. The entire time, the demon stood impassively nearby, his hands folded in front of him.

68

"Sorry," I rasped.

"Tenrael sometimes has that effect on those who don't expect him. Especially Bureau agents."

The demon's name was familiar from my training. "Tenrael. A bringer of nightmares?"

"Not anymore," said the demon with a slight smile.

"I don't understand."

Grimes walked to Tenrael and settled a hand on his shoulder; Tenrael leaned a bit into his touch. "You don't need to understand," said Grimes. "You came here on your business, not ours."

Fair enough.

"All you need to know is that Tenrael is my partner and nobody may harm him."

I nodded, and some of the tension in Grimes's body eased.

"Sit down," he said, waving at a chair.

I did so, wondering if his furniture was custom-made to fit his height. For once I didn't feel as if I dwarfed my seat and didn't worry whether it would hold up under my bulk. Grimes took the chair opposite me, and Tenrael knelt gracefully beside him. Without even looking—seemingly well accustomed to such movements—Grimes reached over and stroked one of Tenrael's glossy wings. It was clear from their postures that these two cared deeply for each other. Instead of being disgusted by the idea of someone loving a demon, I found myself slightly envious of their relationship.

"What really happened in Redding?" asked Grimes, sharp-eyed. "I've heard rumors, but not the truth."

"I don't...." Don't want to talk about it. Or think about it. Don't want to remember. But if I was going to ask a favor and I couldn't pay them, didn't I owe them something? I cleared my throat. "I fucked up."

"You led a raid on a necromancer."

"Yes."

"And during the strike, the necromancer murdered five children he was holding captive."

"Yes." I pretended I couldn't hear the ghosts of their screams, but the all-knowing gazes of Grimes and Tenrael stripped my secrets bare.

"Why did you endanger children?"

"I didn't know they were there." Since my audience waited expectantly, I continued. "I'd been told that only the necromancer was there. I didn't take the time to verify." Too eager to act, too eager to neutralize the enemy.

"So you had bad intelligence and poor judgment, and people died."

"Children died," I whispered.

"And you were drummed out of the Bureau."

"Yes."

Despite having their steady gazes trained on me, I didn't feel unfairly judged. Maybe they were weighing my soul, but not with hostile intent and perhaps not without finding some good there as well. I tried not to squirm, not even when I realized that Grimes wasn't quite human and I had no idea what he might be.

"I thought I was doing the right thing. But I was stupid, and God, I'm so sorry. It haunts me." I don't know why I felt compelled to confess here and now. I hadn't revealed any of my feelings on the matter to anyone else. It felt good to unburden myself.

Still stroking Tenrael's feathers, Grimes gave a small nod. "Sometimes our courage exceeds our wisdom. When things turn out all right, they call us heroes. When things turn to grief, they call us villains. Either way, we're just people with some foolish ideas."

"I didn't come here for sympathy or absolution," I said, although in all honesty his words comforted me somewhat.

He laughed. "Good, because I have no power to absolve anyone. Why *did* you come?"

Simply as that, I told him. As I unspooled the tale, I found myself being more open than I had been with Townsend. I didn't divulge the precise details of what had transpired with Marek, but I made it clear that our interaction had not been platonic. I'm not sure why I felt drawn to such honesty, but I suspect it was because Grimes—whatever he was—and his demon were so obviously in love.

When I finished, Tenrael spoke. "Do you know why Townsend won't act?"

"Politics, he says. I don't know what he means."

"Could mean anything," said Grimes with a scowl. "It's a handy excuse. But the explanation doesn't matter. If he doesn't want to do anything, he won't. Nothing can change that. What I'm more interested in knowing is why you're pursuing this. It won't bring back those dead children."

"I know."

"It won't even stop the nightmares. I... I did some things I'm not proud of. A long time ago. And although I like to think I've done a lot of good since then, it never balances out. There's no holy scale to tip." As he spoke he petted Tenrael's wing, and Tenrael nodded in agreement.

"You're the third person to accuse me of seeking penance. I'm not."

"Then why?"

The answer came to me at once. "Because it's the right thing to do. Not to benefit me—I'm irrelevant. But those young men, they shouldn't be murdered. They should be safe." It wasn't well articulated, I was aware of that. But it was true.

After exchanging a look with Tenrael, Grimes nodded. "We'll see what we can do."

I WAS GOING to spend the night in a cheap motel—the rental car being far too small to sleep in—but Grimes unexpectedly offered to host me for the night. Since I was exhausted, I headed into the bookshelf-lined spare bedroom, leaving Grimes and Tenrael talking softly in the living room. The mattress was comfortable and the darkness surrounded me like a warm cloak, yet I had trouble falling asleep. My closed eyes couldn't stop the images of all my wrong decisions and the people who'd been hurt by them. Not just those children. I'd had a lover once, when I was in college. He was a fellow student, a slightly chubby boy who thought of himself as undesirable, but I'd seen beauty in his quick mind and warm smile. By the time we graduated, he'd begun to speak of the future, of building a life together. But I'd been so certain of my destiny—an agent bound to die young—that I'd abandoned him, breaking his heart in the process. All the years since, I'd refused to speculate on what might have been. Yet tonight, in this little bungalow by the sea, I caught myself wondering.

"No," I mumbled and turned to face the wall. There was no point in torturing myself. And that long-ago lover? No doubt he'd recovered and found someone kinder, smarter, better. Someone who was happy to daydream about mortgages and gardens and children instead of skulking through nighttime streets in search of monsters.

Monsters. How could I properly identify them, even define them, anymore? Yes, I'd encountered—and often slaughtered—a great many creatures that undoubtedly qualified. Ghouls that stalked graveyards and morgues in search of fresh flesh, relatively speaking. Revenants mindlessly seeking revenge. Shifters that let their animal impulses control them. Demons far more terrifying than the one currently hosting me. All manner of things that went bump in the night. And vampires, of course. Quite a few of them.

But as one of those vampires had recently pointed out, humans were fully capable of monstrous acts, of attacking their own kind—sometimes even their own families—with unmatched ferocity. Or, more often, making stupid decisions that got other people killed.

How to judge a living being? By his species? His actions, past or present? His intentions? I didn't know. And as I lay there, I realized it was hubris to even try, especially when I couldn't fairly judge myself.

I imagined I heard the soft *shush* of flapping wings, and I fell asleep thinking of Marek and the tender way he'd touched me.

CHAPTER 5

HEN I walked into the kitchen, Tenrael was cooking breakfast—a surprise since demons don't need to eat. But he hummed happily while he fried bacon and eggs in a cast iron pan, his wings moving slightly to the rhythm of the song. He was naked this morning. Nothing sexual about it, simply a creature comfortable in his own skin. Grimes, wearing black trousers and a burgundy shirt, sat at the small kitchen table with a glass of water and a newspaper. The morning light coming in through the windows gave everything a lemon-and-butter tint. It was a cozy scene, far more domestic than anything I'd witnessed in my own family, and I had to fight hard to strangle a new tendril of hope. This would never be me. The only time a guy like me gets a white picket fence is when he's using the pickets to stake things.

Without looking up from his newspaper, Grimes pointed at an empty chair. Then he got up and poured a mugful of coffee from the old-fashioned percolator on the stove. He brought it to me and sat down again. "Ten and I did some research on your problem," he said.

"Yeah?"

"Didn't find anything useful. Went on a wild goose chase after chupacabras, though."

"That's a mixed metaphor," Tenrael said from the stove.

Grimes shot him a look of annoyance and fondness in equal measure, then turned to face me. "We're fairly certain it's not a chupacabra."

"Well, I guess that narrows it down." I sipped my coffee—bitter and strong—and sighed. "Is it a vampire?"

"Are you looking for verification that you didn't fuck the perp?"

"No, not really. I only.... I've jumped into things blindly before. Don't want to do it again."

Grimes gave me what I hoped was an approving look. "We don't think it's a vamp. Neither of us has heard of one doing this to its victims, and we've been around for a while."

"A while." Chuckling, Tenrael brought over two overflowing plates of food and set them in front of us. Mine had the expected bacon and eggs, but Grimes got pancakes nearly drowned in syrup. I never imagined I'd be served breakfast by a naked demon, and damn, the food sure smelled good. I thanked him and dug in. Before I knew it, I'd cleaned my plate and drained a second cup of coffee.

Grimes cleared away the dishes and washed up while Tenrael dried. They moved easily together in the cramped space, a well-practiced dance punctuated by quick smiles and caresses. After all the breakfast things were tucked away and Grimes had wiped down the counter, he sat again at the table and Tenrael knelt beside him. I didn't understand why he knelt, but they both looked entirely comfortable with it. It was probably hard to sit in chairs with those big wings.

"How are you paying your bills now that you've left the Bureau?" Grimes asked.

"Didn't leave—they canned me. They gave me severance and I had a little bit saved up."

"And when that's gone?"

I shrugged. I guess I hadn't expected to outlive my savings. But now, for no reason I could articulate, I *did* want to survive. Well, I'd worry about my finances later, if I got that far.

Grimes rubbed his chin. "What about signing on with a local police force?"

"Don't really picture myself as a boy in blue." I'd never been a team player. One of the good things about the Bureau had been the degree of independence I'd had. "Anyway, you don't need to give me career advice. That's not what I came for."

"I know. Let's talk about what you did come for."

"You said you couldn't find anything out."

There was a flinty aspect to Grimes's smile. "You think we give up that easy? I used to be an agent, once upon a time. And my Ten? He endured horrors you can't imagine and came out of it strong as hell."

Looking at Tenrael, kneeling placidly and leaning slightly against Grimes's side, I wondered about those horrors. What would terrify a demon?

"What else do you have in mind?" I asked.

"We're going up to San Francisco with you. We'll see if we can help you find your perp."

THE TRAVEL PLANS were slightly complicated. Grimes would follow me in his vehicle to the car-rental place, where I would return my shoebox on wheels. Then he and I would ride north together. Tenrael? He was going to fly, apparently. Fuck.

"Is there a reason you won't go in the car?" I asked him.

"It's not very comfortable for me. And I like flying."

Simple enough. If I had wings, I'd chose them over the freeways too.

Before we left, Tenrael and Charles embraced, and then Tenrael plucked a feather from his wing and handed it over. Smiling, Grimes tucked it into a pocket. It was such an intimate scene that I found myself blushing. I hadn't thought myself capable.

Grimes owned a 1960s GTO, light blue and in pristine condi-tion. Even the pale vinyl upholstery looked straight out of the show-room. The exhaust rumbled thrillingly, like an angry rhino, and the seating was comfortable even for a man as big as me. It turned out that zooming up the 5 was a lot nicer in this car than in an econobox.

"I wouldn't have pegged you for a car guy," I commented as we were passing over the Grapevine.

"I'm not. I found this one, I liked it, and I take good care of it."

"Did you do the restoration work yourself?"

Grimes shot me an inscrutable grin. "I bought her brand-new."

That raised a basketful of questions, but I couldn't think how to phrase them. *What the hell are you?* seemed a rude thing to ask a man who was doing me a favor. I deflected my questioning to another topic. "How did you and Tenrael, um...."

"Become partners?"

"Yeah."

"Seems unlikely, doesn't it? Bureau man and a demon."

I thought about it. "Dunno. Maybe not. Probably have more in common than if you'd hooked up with an insurance salesman or waiter or something."

"Probably." He drove silently for a few miles, neatly accelerating past some semis and an RV. "I was supposed to destroy him. I freed him instead."

"Why?"

"I don't think I could have lived with myself if I'd done any differently."

I nodded in complete understanding. "What did you free him from?"

The corners of his mouth turned down. "You're imagining monsters, aren't you? Things with talons and fangs and scales?" He snorted. "It was humans. Just ordinary *Homo sapiens*."

"Fuck." I believed him. While I had specialized in other species, I'd seen what my own was capable of.

"You want to know something funny? After I freed him, I left. The men who'd been torturing him for years were right there, and he could have torn them to pieces. Nobody could have stopped him, and I wouldn't have thought any less of him if he'd done it. But he simply flew away."

I might have had trouble swallowing a story like that before, but now that I'd met Tenrael, I found it entirely credible. "So the demon is better than the human?"

"Maybe. Sometimes. He came to me of his own free will and desire. And the more he got... under my skin, the more I thought about tracking those motherfuckers down and giving them a taste of the pain they'd inflicted on him. Ten talked me out of it."

"An ethical demon?"

"A practical one," Grimes answered. "He didn't want me to go to prison. Anyway, for a long time now I've had the satisfaction of knowing they're moldering in their graves while Ten and I are still kicking. Kicking together." He smiled.

Grimes stopped twice to get gas and once for a late lunch. While I had a burger and fries, he ate apple pie. I didn't ask him about his unusual diet.

Without offering to stop at my place—and I didn't ask him to—Grimes crossed the Bay Bridge into the city, which he seemed to know well. He had no trouble maneuvering through heavy traffic and down meandering streets, and he finally pulled into a garage beneath a little hotel across the street from Sutro Heights Park. I waited in the garage, leaning against the warm metal of the car, while he checked in. He came out glancing at his watch. "Ten'll be here soon."

I hadn't been a part of the discussion about where Tenrael would meet us, and I was frankly curious as to how he'd flap down unnoticed. I understood better after I'd followed Grimes across to Lands End and up a trail that overlooked the Pacific as it entered the Golden Gate. Eucalyptus and other trees grew tall there, and a foghorn made its mournful calls. We sat on a bench and watched as a fog bank swallowed the sunset and crept forward to engulf the city. I was glad for my jacket.

Tenrael's approach was silent, perhaps muffled in part by the sound of the ocean beneath us. I startled wildly when he landed, but at least I didn't go for my gun. He wore dark pants, and with his bronze skin and black wings, it was hard to see him clearly. But Grimes didn't hesitate to fold him into a quick, hard embrace. "Good flight?" I thought Grimes sounded wistful.

"Hmm." Tenrael nuzzled at Grimes's neck.

I found myself wondering where Marek was.

The darkness camouflaged Tenrael's wings as we walked back to the motel, but since it was San Francisco, perhaps nobody would have found them remarkable. I saw strange things in the city nearly every day, and that wasn't even counting the supernatural residents. Tenrael sat in the front passenger seat, his wings squashed awkwardly, while I took the back seat and gave directions to the club where I'd met Marek. There was no particular reason to believe our prey would be there tonight—the city had a lot of clubs—but it seemed a good place to start. Several of the murder victims had last been seen alive there.

Grimes parked the GTO in a lot nearby. We made an odd trio as we marched down the sidewalk, Tenrael barefoot.

Interestingly, the bouncer seemed more eager to let Tenrael into the club than to admit Grimes and me. Tenrael was certainly intriguing and exotic, while Grimes and I looked like disgruntled dads —and not in a good way. Still, after sizing us up and perhaps deciding either one of us could best him in a fight, he allowed us inside.

A mixed crowd jammed the bar and dance floor. Young people mostly, but some in their thirties and forties. Although the majority were male, the entire gender spectrum was represented. The one thing almost everyone had in common was a scarcity of clothing. While they must have been comfortable in the oppressive heat, I felt distinctly overdressed, and the mingled scents of cologne, alcohol, and sweat nearly overwhelmed me.

The three of us fanned out, each threading his way through the throngs in search of anything unusual. I was groped, jostled, and pawed, although my glare persuaded even the drunkest to back off quickly. I had a few pangs of longing over the beautiful naked flesh and the joyful way these people moved their bodies. I'd never experienced such casual pleasure, not even when I was their age.

An hour or so later, I stood outside the club with my companions, none of us much wiser after our expedition. "There are ghosts there," Tenrael announced as he shifted his ruffled feathers into place. "They float along the edges of the room looking forlorn."

I hadn't noticed them, but then I had no special gifts for seeing the incorporeal dead. "I've never heard of a ghost killing people like this."

"Nor have I. They're not who we're looking for. I doubt they want to harm anyone. They just long for what they've lost."

Because conversation inside the club had been nearly impossible, we decided on an alternate tactic. Tenrael and Grimes stood several yards down the sidewalk, shadowed from streetlights by a shop awning, while I skulked inside a recessed doorway half a block in the other direction. We stopped anyone who came out of the club and questioned them briefly about whether they'd seen anything suspicious. Some of them were too intoxicated to give coherent answers, and the rest had no idea what we were talking about.

The flow of departing clubgoers had slowed to a trickle when Grimes and Tenrael rejoined me. "This isn't getting us anywhere," Grimes said with a scowl.

Tenrael patted his shoulder. "We can try other places."

"Do you know how many bars and dance clubs there are in this city?"

"We have time."

"The potential victims don't."

Realizing I was famished, I rubbed my belly. "Let's give it up for tonight. Maybe we can think of a better plan during the day." I wasn't as optimistic as I tried to sound, but I didn't want to simply stand on the dirty sidewalk, feeling defeated.

We walked to the same donut shop where Marek and I had gone. The women behind the counter weren't happy with Tenrael's shirtless state. But after they scolded him in Vietnamese and he replied calmly in the same language, they hesitated only a short time before giving in. I wondered what he'd said to convince them. He sat at a booth near the back of the room while Grimes and I ordered coffee and donuts, along with a ham-and-cheese sandwich for me. Then we ate and drank silently, each lost in his own thoughts.

"Will you stay at our motel?" Grimes asked after we were done. "Our room has a couch."

I shook my head. Trying to settle my substantial body onto a couch was an exercise in anatomical origami that never ended well. Besides, I'd have felt as if I was intruding on their intimacy. "I'll take BART to my place. I need a shave and a change of clothes."

We agreed on a meeting time, and I watched as they moved away, their bodies so close that their shadows merged under the streetlights. I didn't head for a BART station. Instead I walked to Marek's Chinese restaurant. It held the same desolate air as before, the edges of the brown paper curling inside the windows. I couldn't see any lights on inside, and there was an unambiguous emptiness to the place, a conviction that nobody was home—not even a vampire.

Still, I hesitated to knock. I ended up going around to the back of the building, an alley crowded with garbage bins and reeking of old food and cat piss. The green paint on the restaurant's service door was peeling badly, and the flimsy lock was no match for me. Picking locks was one of the many useful skills the Bureau had left me.

I was in a storage room, dark and dusty, strewn with papers and cardboard. A part of me expected to discover bodies with their throats torn open, but the only corpses were tiny ones—several cockroaches, some flies, and a rat. Next I came to the kitchen, cramped and mostly empty aside from dented stainless steel counters and a large, corroded cooktop.

Only one small space remained before the dining room. It had probably served as the restaurant's office, but now it nearly broke my heart. Marek had set up a pallet on the floor, nothing more than a pile of sheets and blankets. Three shirts hung from a hook on the wall, and two pairs of jeans sat neatly folded beneath them. Within reach of the makeshift bed was a little stack of paperbacks, their covers battered. He might have picked them up from one of the giveaway bins outside a bookstore, or perhaps they'd been abandoned on buses or in coffee shops.

Marek had existed far longer than I had, yet this was all he had to show for it—a lonely little squatter's nest made of discards. I'm not sure what I'd expected, but I guess I'd hoped that Marek would have established more substance to sustain him.

I buried my face in my hands and considered whether to sleep here. I was just about to remove my boots when somebody—or something—made a small noise behind me. I tried to spin around to confront my assailant, but even as I turned, something sharp sank into my back just below my shoulder blade. A fierce coldness rushed through my veins. Too paralyzed to even cry out, I began to fall. I was unconscious before I hit the floor.

CHAPTER 6

Y FIRST awareness was of chains that bound me upright to something hard and solid. I immediately tried to strain against them, but they were strong. The second thing I noticed was the agonizing pain in my head, as if someone were scraping the inside of my skull with a rusty file. And third, I felt the cold.

I was naked, my hands shackled tightly around the back of a concrete pillar and my ankles tethered in place at the sides. A ball gag stuffed my mouth, making my jaw and teeth ache. A stream of drool ran from my lower lip down my chin.

I wasn't used to feeling fear, and it didn't overwhelm me now. Rage churned fiercely within me, however, along with a sickening pit of hopelessness. With a muffled roar, I struggled until my body ached and my skin was torn, but I couldn't loosen my bonds.

Breathing hard through my nose and urging myself to be calm, I surveyed my surroundings. I was in a large basement—slight smell of damp, but otherwise clean, without even stray cobwebs. Concrete floor painted gray, several pillars like the one I was chained to, a low unfinished ceiling criss-crossed with beams. Light fixtures were mounted on the ceiling, but right now the only illumination was from several small windows high in the wall. The glass was frosted, letting in only a dull glow. Although three of my prison walls were cast concrete, the fourth was made of cinderblock and inset with a metal door. Aside from the windows, which not even a child could have fit through, the door was the only escape—and it was out of my reach.

There were no shelves in this room, no furnace or washer and dryer, no cardboard boxes marked *Xmas*. None of the usual basement accoutrements. Just a naked and gagged former agent chained to a pillar.

With my head still throbbing, I decided the best course of action was to rest, to conserve my strength, to allow whatever drug I'd been given to work its way through my system. My captor obviously didn't want me dead, at least not right away. I wasn't sure whether to be comforted by that thought, since a great many fates were far worse than a quick death. But what the hell was I being saved for? A vampire's meal?

I might have dozed. It was impossible to track the passage of time, and I kept on shivering. When I became fully aware again, my head was clear and most of the pain had receded. Of course it had been replaced by a variety of maddening aches, most a result of the chains —but my full bladder made sure to get in on the game too.

I eventually gave in to the inevitable and pissed, then spent some time watching the little river of urine make its way to the drain in the center of the room. Handy, that.

Fuck, my mouth and jaws hurt. It was funny how agonizing a small ball gag could become over time. Nobody was ever going to croak from having his mouth propped open, yet the pain could eventually become bad enough to make a man wish for death. The Bureau had taught me a great many methods to hurt a being without truly *harming* him. I knew a thousand small ways to inflict exquisite torture. Although that didn't help me right now, not one fucking bit.

I tried to distract myself by picturing what I'd do to Marek if I got my hands on him, but even in my imagination I couldn't harm him. *Idiot*, I chided myself. I wondered whether I'd feel any better if I could curse myself out loud. I was no genius, but I'd always been smarter than this. I knew better than to think with my dick.

Still.... Those long strong fingers. That sweet cool mouth. His soft hair.

For the first time, I wondered about the absence my death would create. Who would notice it? My family was a distant memory, and the Bureau no longer cared. My landlady? Well, she'd notice when I didn't pay next month's rent, but her only sorrow would be having to discard my few possessions and find a new tenant. I had no idea how Tenrael and Grimes would feel. We barely knew each other. When I didn't show up at the appointed time, they'd probably conclude I flaked out, and they'd return to their cozy little bungalow by the sea.

Yeah, self-pity was definitely going to help.

Metal clicked loudly—the turning of a lock—and I focused sharply on the door.

As a figure stepped through, the overhead lights came to life, forcing me to squint against the brightness. No, not one figure. Two.

The first was achingly familiar, although I'd met him only once. Tall and slender, paper-pale, reddish hair, and eyes so light they were nearly colorless. Marek wore jeans, a white shirt, and a black jacket, and I noticed he stood well away from the windows. His face held no expression at all.

In contrast, the stranger beside him was grinning widely. I suddenly realized that while I'd never met him, I knew exactly who he was. His name was McArthur Buckley, and I'd seen that smile shining from newspapers, magazines, and television screens. Somebody famous often stood beside him, a rock star or actor or socialite. He was a whiz-kid tech zillionaire who'd recently given up app development in favor of political ambitions. Handsome, smart, charismatic. Everyone said he had a serious shot at the Senate during the next election, and after that, who knew?

Now, dressed in jeans and a Stanford T-shirt, he beamed as he looked me up and down. Although I was naked, his appraisal didn't feel sexual. "Older than my usual," he said, directing his remarks at

Marek, "and not as pretty. But he's strong. He'll do nicely. Thanks for the gift."

"I didn't mean him for you," Marek replied, sounding petulant.

"Eh, you can feed off anyone; it won't make any difference to you. If you're hungry I can have a couple whores brought in. But this guy…. Can you feel his energy?" He held his palms toward me as if he was warming them at a fire.

"He's with the Bureau of Trans-Species Affairs. If he goes missing, they'll—"

"They canned him. I looked him up." Buckley pulled a small card from his pocket and pretended to peer at it. My driver's license, I assumed. "Had to poke around quite a lot and ended up hacking into the Bureau's database. Seems our pal here fucked up and got some kiddies slaughtered, so he's out a job. He's single, broke, no social media presence, nada. Nobody cares that he's gone."

Despite how Buckley's reasoning mirrored my prior thoughts, it didn't make me like him any better.

"Anyway," Buckley continued, "I've got pals in Washington. The Bureau leaves me alone."

I desperately wanted to pound that smug face to a pulp.

Apparently deciding the villain exposition time was over—yet leaving me sadly lacking in understanding—Buckley tucked my license away. Then he took out a round object, a little like a pocket mirror or makeup compact, and placed it on the floor about four feet from me. It was shiny silver, with figures scratched into the metal. I couldn't tell if they were drawings or an alphabet I didn't recognize. In any case, I didn't like the mystery thing at all. It sat there unmoving and silent yet emanated a field of power that made my hairs stand on end.

Buckley backed up several feet and, ignoring me and Marek, began to poke at his phone. Hell of a time to tweet.

Behind him, Marek stood with arms crossed, his hands in tight fists and his mouth open enough to show his fangs. Sometimes he shot me a quick look as if he were trying to communicate something. But I'm no psychic. I just narrowed my eyes and glared. My hands were numb from the chains, but they tried to ball up too, and I bit that fucking gag nearly hard enough to break teeth.

Then Buckley put his phone in his pocket and looked expectantly at me.

I felt... something tight. At first it was only mildly uncomfortable, as if I'd been wrapped in an elastic casing. But then, still invisible, it constricted until I could barely draw oxygen, the breaths coming through my nose in thin, desperate draws. I began to feel lightheaded, the edges of my vision going gray. Just before I passed out, the constriction disappeared as suddenly as a popped bubble.

My relief was brief, however, because within seconds every cell in my body felt as if it had been turned inside out. I think I screamed into the gag, but I didn't hear it. Didn't sense anything at all except agony so pure that I lost all notion of self and time. It could have lasted a moment or a century. I couldn't identify the type of anguish—burning? tearing? crushing? sharp? It was simply the quintessence of pain, and it was all I had.

Eventually, and slowly, the agony receded. I came to myself and realized I was sobbing. My eyes were too bleary to see, and my body ached where I must have pulled against the bonds. Worse than that, though, was the overwhelming weakness within me. I couldn't have remained standing if the chains hadn't held me up. Even lifting my head was too much, so I let it droop.

Then cool hands were framing my face, lifting it, and Marek was holding a scrap of soft fabric to my nose. "Blow before you suffocate yourself," he said softly.

I was too feeble to do anything but obey. I had a bright flash of memory—me young and very small, with a terrible fever just broken. I was curled up in soft quilts, and my mother held a damp washcloth to my head and smoothed sweaty hair back from my face until I fell asleep. She'd died not long after that. A night out drinking with her friends, a curve in the road taken too fast. I would have given anything to be back in that childhood bed.

But I was in McArthur Buckley's basement, and a vampire was licking my face.

"Don't bite him!" Buckley called sharply.

"I'm not. Tears are almost as good as blood." When his tongue reached the edge of my ear, he whispered as softly as a light breeze in the treetops: "Sundown."

Marek released me and backed away, carefully avoiding the metal object on the floor. I didn't blame him. No promise in the entire world would have induced me to touch that thing.

Buckley was grinning again, his eyes crinkled at the corners. He had an air of satisfaction, like a man who'd just accomplished something especially clever. He took a few steps forward, scooped up the round thing, and stuffed it into his back pocket. But as he moved, my vision cleared enough for me to see him more distinctly—and what I observed made me start shivering again.

He was glowing. Not visibly, but that was the only way I could describe it. Energy radiated from him so strongly that I believe his touch might have killed. He was the most stunningly *alive* creature I had ever seen and a stark contrast to the undead man behind him. But there was no beauty to his vitality, not when I realized that the energy was stolen. From me, from the dead boys. It was far worse than if he'd simply drained my blood.

I didn't know what he did with what he'd taken from us. Perhaps it made him live longer and increased his health. Perhaps it gave him the charm that captivated journalists, millionaires, celebrities, and politicians.

Without another glance in my direction, Buckley left with Marek hard at his heels. The lights went out as they left, and the lock clicked into place.

I sagged in my chains and waited for the next round.

CHAPTER 7

HE LIGHT through the windows dimmed and disappeared, leaving me in darkness. Although my jaw continued to hurt and my bruises ached, the worst devil I faced now was thirst. It didn't help to remember the desiccated corpses of Buckley's previous victims.

Since my situation wouldn't sustain life for long, I assumed Buckley would return soon to finish draining me. The thought of going through that pain again almost made me retch, but I fought it back and struggled not to choke. Then I wondered why I bothered. Not only would choking be a gentler death than what awaited me, but in my last moments I'd have the grim satisfaction of knowing I'd cheated Buckley out of some of his plunder. Of course that meant he'd probably kidnap his next victim sooner. Some innocent kid who had done nothing wrong and had plenty to live for.

Dammit, I was no innocent, I'd done of plenty of wrong, and my life amounted to nothing much. But I wanted to keep it anyway. I wanted to live.

The door clicked open, but this time the lights stayed off. The space beyond the door was dim, but I recognized Marek's tall, slim outline and then his rapid, light tread. He carried something, but I couldn't see what.

When he reached me, he set down his burden without a sound and pulled something from a pocket. "We don't have long," he said as he moved behind me. A slight rasp of metal, and the chains at my wrists were gone. They clanked as he set them aside. My muscles and joints had locked up during my captivity, and I groaned as I tried to move my arms forward. As Marek worked on the other chains that still held me upright, I managed to lift my hands and fumble the damned gag out of my mouth. Closing my jaw, at last, was a sweet relief. I didn't yet try to speak—and my tongue might have been too dry to manage it anyway.

Marek, however, talked fast and low while he worked. "I'm sorry. You won't believe me but I am. I didn't mean for this to happen to you. I thought... I thought I might find a way to defeat him if I let him lure me close and I pretended to befriend him. He thinks a vampire minion is a lovely idea. But I led him to you. I'm so sorry." He kept on like that, but I couldn't make sense of his words. I was too confused, too sore, too drained. I'd lost track of whether I trusted him.

After he unlocked the last of the chains, I crumpled, but he caught me and held me up. "Clothes," he said. "Not yours. Sorry." Hurriedly, despite considerable fumbling, he helped me into a pair of sweatpants. Once on, the legs reached only to midshin. We couldn't get the T-shirt on at all and just gave up.

With what were likely expletives in his native language, Marek supported me as we shuffled out of the room and into the adjacent one. That space had a more traditional basement appearance—fewer chained captives and more household detritus—although it was still clean and neat. Just crossing that expanse of floor exhausted me, and I looked up at the stairway in defeat. "I can't. Just kill me and be done with it. Feed from me, break my neck, I don't care, as long as you don't let that fucker near me again."

"I'll carry you."

But as he attempted to reposition me, likely to heave me over his shoulder, a crash resounded above.

Marek swore again. "He's home already."

"Why don't you kill him?"

"I can't even touch him."

Another bang, this time accompanied by shouting. Marek looked puzzled, but the ruckus above wasn't my immediate focus. "Shoot him. There was a gun in my boot. The bullets—"

"Are harmless to him. He showed me. He held your gun a few inches from his skull and pulled the trigger. The bullet just bounced off. And that was before he... fed from you."

Shit. Even in top condition I'd have been no match for someone who could resist a vampire and withstand bullets. And right now I was far from my top condition. I could barely stand on my own.

Marek grunted. "When we get upstairs, I'm going to take us to the front door. It's not far. If Buckley sees us, I'll distract him while you get out as fast as you can. I'm not sure how long I can keep him occupied."

"He'll kill you."

"I've been dead a long time. Let me have a small chance to be a hero." He kissed me then, very sweet and gentle, careful not to let descended fangs nick me. Then, as the tumult above continued, he lifted me and hauled me up the stairs.

We emerged into a vast kitchen, dark except for a small light over the stove. Marek set me down and, with some support from the counters, I was able to walk unaided. I wondered how many rich and famous people had eaten food from this this place, perhaps even while a young man was bound and dying beneath them.

Unfortunately our route appeared to be taking us closer to the noises. "A back door?" I whispered to Marek.

"Leads into a walled garden. You'd never get out. If you go out the front, you'll be right on the street. Turn either way and there are neighbors. Get one of them to call the police."

I continued to follow him, but I doubted the success of his plan. Even if I did make it to another house and convinced someone to call 911, it would be too late to save Marek. I wasn't even confident the police would stop Buckley from preying on others in the future. With his connections and preternatural charm, he would undoubtedly find a way to convince them he was innocent. And why should they listen to the claims of a disgraced former agent?

We passed through a narrow passageway lined with cupboards—a butler's pantry—and into a dining room with a table long enough to seat at least twenty. Thick rugs cushioned our footfalls and large paintings hung on the walls, but it was too dark to discern any details. When Marek pushed on the double doors at the end of the dining room, the noises of a fight grew louder. And I thought I recognized the voices.

"Fuck," I said, stepping into a short hallway.

"What?"

I never got a chance to answer. We rounded the corner and there were the front doors, one of them slightly ajar. But Buckley stood in the center of the grand foyer with his phone in one upraised hand, his teeth bared in a furious snarl. Grimes faced him, his expression a mask of fury. A handgun lay at his feet, but he held a knife in one hand. A short distance away, Tenrael sprawled prone and motionless, his arms reaching toward the other two and his wings sickeningly mangled.

"Run!" Marek shouted, pushing me toward the door. It was foolish of him. With Marek's speed and with Buckley otherwise engaged, Marek could easily have made his escape. But instead he rushed at Buckley with a roar. When Buckley waved his phone, Marek jerked as if he'd been shocked, and then he crumpled to the floor. He staggered to his feet and attacked again. He got a little closer this time, and Grimes was able to advance nearer Buckley with his blade. But another hand wave sent them both staggering back. Marek appeared to have taken the worst of the assault, because when he fell again, his body convulsed and blood flowed from his mouth.

I was weak, I had no weapons, and there was no way I could harm a man who so easily felled Marek. But damn me if I was just going to stand there and let Buckley destroy... my friends.

I threw myself at him.

All things considered, it wasn't much of a throw. More a

lumbering followed by a collapse. But I'm a big man, and my weight was enough to bring Buckley down beneath me. Pinning him in place, I tried to choke him. My hands found their way comfortably around his neck, but nothing was working properly and my grip was unsteady. Buckley screeched a string of noises that sounded entirely inhuman.

Excruciating pain racked me as he began drawing energy from me again.

Even unbound, there was nothing I could do to fight him. I couldn't even manage to scream. I just lay atop him, paralyzed, and felt my self—my psyche, my soul, my life essence—pour out of me like blood geysering from a severed artery.

Not a bad death despite the agony, I thought dimly. At least I'd tried to do what was right. At least I had allies. And oddly enough, as I slipped away I felt at peace with myself. In the end I'd acted with honor.

CHAPTER 8

A SHRIEK, horrible to hear even in my barely-there state.

THE SMELL OF HOT BLOOD. Not, I thought, my own.

THE PAIN STOPPED ABRUPTLY, a bubble popped. My eyes too heavy to open. My heart too weakened to beat.

A slightly accented voice, thousands of miles away. "He's dying. Please, I can't— He's *dying*!"

Another voice. "Do it."

"What if he doesn't want this?"

"Then he can reject your gift later. When he's capable of choosing." A pause. "Now, or it'll be too late."

A few seconds later, blood in my mouth. Cold and metallic, but I was so very, very thirsty, and it was liquid. A faint sparkle of sharpness at my neck. Long fingers gentle in my hair.

Swallowing.

So tired.

Nothingness reached for me. But not the anguishing kind Buckley had thrust at me. No, this was soft and warm. Like my sickbed when I was five, with the quilts pulled up to my chin and a loving touch on my skin.

I welcomed it like a lover's embrace.

CHAPTER 9

I AWOKE consumed by hunger—so much hunger that I couldn't think at all. I lunged to my feet and stumbled toward the door, focused entirely on finding sustenance. But something moved rapidly to intercept me, and it bore me to the floor and kept me pinned there, no matter how viciously I fought.

"Feed," commanded a familiar voice. An arm appeared in front of my mouth and I sank my fangs into it, then swallowed and swallowed the delicious fluid.

I wasn't sated when the arm was taken away, but at least I was coherent enough to become aware of my surroundings. Marek knelt on my chest, licking delicately at his torn wrist, his expression a mixture of excitement and apprehension.

"The Chinese restaurant," I said. Because that's where we were, in the small office Marek had used as a sleeping space. The room where I'd been captured.

He nodded. "It's secure and there are no windows."

"Buckley?" I asked when my sluggish mind made a shift.

"Dead. While he was busily murdering you, Grimes was able to stab him in the eye." I couldn't blame Marek for looking pleased about that. "We hacked his corpse to pieces and scattered them, just in case. I think Grimes burned the head. Buckley's gone for good."

"And…. Fuck. Tenrael?" I remembered him in a heap on Buckley's floor. "Is he dead too?"

"It's very difficult to kill a demon. His wings will take a few weeks to mend, but he'll be fine."

"How did they find me?"

We both knew I was dancing around the elephant in the room, but Marek humored me. "Tenrael did it. You didn't meet them when you were supposed to, and he…. Something about tracking you through your dreams. You'll have to ask him about it. They're at a motel. Giving you some space until you're ready to… face the world."

I didn't take the obvious opportunity to discuss the obvious. "And you? You're all right?"

Still atop me, Marek spread his arms. "I am in excellent condition. Although right now I'm hungry. And I imagine you still are as well." He looked at me. Waiting.

I couldn't ignore the inevitable any longer. "Vampire," I whispered. I explored my mouth with my tongue, which caught on my fangs. I liked the taste of my blood, but it wasn't as good as Marek's.

He climbed off, but only so he could kneel beside me. When I sat up, our faces were close. "You were fading. It was either this or I'd lose you forever." His expression was so solemn, his strange eyes burning with emotion. "I'm stronger than you. But if you wish to destroy me, I won't resist."

I didn't answer. I stood instead and looked down at myself. I was naked, my skin clean and whole, my frame as substantial as it had been before Buckley caught me. No sign of bruises or other souvenirs from my captivity. But when I laid my palm against my chest, my heart was still, and my lungs didn't work unless I willed them to. I was cool to my own touch. I guessed I'd no longer be able to see my reflection in a mirror, but my fingers told me that someone had cleaned and combed my hair, and that I had a couple of days' worth of stubble on my face. I wondered if I'd carry that unshaven look for the remainder of my existence.

I flexed my muscles. Strong—very strong. As if I could move a mountain. I saw every detail of the room sharply despite the darkness, heard the rustle of rodents and insects in the walls, smelled soy sauce and hot oil and steaming rice. I smelled Marek too, an intoxicating aroma of blood and sorrow and strength that made me want to tear off his clothing and sink into his body.

Assessing my internal self took more courage. Yes, I was ravenous, longing to chase something and feed on the hot essence of life. Yet I still felt like me, Clayton White. A person with many regrets and more than a few old grudges, a person who possessed more than his share of flaws. Also a person who wanted to protect the blameless, not harm them. Who wanted love and companionship and respect, and who wanted to give those things to another. Funny. I'd always assumed those were purely human needs.

While I was evaluating myself, Marek had crossed the little room and taken something out of a desk drawer. Now he stood in front of me, offering me the object. My gun.

"It's loaded," he said. "With your special Bureau bullets."

I took the weapon and weighed it in my hand. It had always felt like such a powerful thing, but now it was only a small metal object of little importance.

"Why am I... calm?" I'd seen newly risen vampires before, and they'd seemed like nothing more than mindless fiends. No more humanity to them than a rabid beast possessed.

"Your first waking meal was from your maker. That helps a great deal, especially when your maker is quite old. Few of us are granted that when we are new."

I nodded slowly. "Your blood." I could still taste it, but even better, I could *feel* it within me, granting me strength and a comforting solidity. I imagined that this is how a junkie must feel after a long-awaited hit, except I was clearheaded.

Marek granted me a tiny smile. "It helps that you are who you are. This change you've undergone, it alters a great many things but not your essence. Your core self remains. When someone with a faulty core is suddenly given immense power and a hearty appetite, he will use that power to hurt humans. But when the core is sound....” He shrugged. “Then so is the vampire.”

“I've become the ethical monster? Is that what you're telling me?”

“What you are is still within your own control, just as it's always been. You simply have different parameters on what you can do.”

“Parameters.” The room was too small for pacing, especially with the bedding taking up most of the floor space, so I opened the door and walked into the kitchen. That room had a few small, high windows, much like the ones in Buckley's basement, but even in the office, I'd sensed that it was night. Still holding the gun, I padded around, catching the scents of every long-ago meal prepared here. Marek watched me from the office doorway.

Eventually I paused to lean back against a counter, its metal the same cool temperature as my skin. Looking down at the gun, I wondered how it felt when a bullet entered a vampire's heart. Not as painful as what Buckley had done to me, I was sure of that. But the vamps I'd shot in the past certainly hadn't enjoyed the experience. They'd reacted much the same way as humans would—shock and terror—before the bits of wood did their job and the vamps were destroyed.

I glanced at Marek. “What if I decide I enjoy murdering humans?”

“Because it's inevitable a monster will make that decision.”

Using my newfound speed, I rushed to him, but he didn't even flinch. “Don't you think I've learned my lesson by now?” I growled. “Humanity—or lack thereof—doesn't define whether someone's a monster. Buckley was human.”

He hesitated a moment before reaching to stroke my jaw. “Then why are you afraid you'll become a murderer?”

It was hard to find the right words, especially with him so close, touching me. Apparently becoming undead hadn't loosened my tongue. “I'm afraid because of that core self you were talking about. It's flawed.”

“They all are. Otherwise we'd be gods.”

“But there's darkness there. A lot. What if I act on it?”

Another light pass of his fingertips over my skin, making me shiver, but not with fear or cold. My entire body had become an erogenous zone. "Every sentient being on Earth has that darkness," Marek said, "and we all have the potential to act on it. I think there's not much likelihood of *you* doing so."

So Marek had faith in me. This was an interesting thing to know.

But I stepped away from him nonetheless. "How will I eat?"

"There are a dozen packets of blood in that cooler," he answered, pointing. "Enough to keep even the newly risen satiated for a few days."

"And when it's gone?"

"Your appetite will ebb soon to more reasonable levels. There are ways to obtain more packaged blood, but ultimately you won't find it satisfying. The same is true of animal blood. They will sustain you without truly filling you."

"So then?"

His response was quiet. "You could hunt. This city houses a great many homeless people, and those so far at the fringes nobody notices their absence. You could feed off them for a long time before the Bureau came after you."

"No."

"Good," he replied, smiling. "Then I can teach you to hunt the way I do. Nobody dies. No more harm done to them than if they'd donated to the Red Cross—and the rewards are better than cookies and orange juice. Or...."

"What?"

A slight hesitation before he spoke. "Or I hunt for us both, and you feed from me. If you're willing to remain with me, that is."

I realized I was licking my lips. "You want that?"

"Desperately," he whispered.

"Why?"

"I honestly don't know. I've been drawn to you since the moment I saw you in the club. I don't know why. It's never happened to me before. But I wanted you, and nothing since has diminished that."

There are enchantments that can cause instant attraction. They're illegal, and the Bureau arrests anyone who provides or procures them, but people use them anyway. It was possible someone had cast an enchantment like that on Marek and me. But I couldn't imagine who would do that, or why, or how. And in any case, that kind of false love always evaporates quickly. My desire for Marek hadn't abated even when I thought he'd betrayed me, and it hadn't faded away when I died. In fact, now that we were tied by blood, I never wanted to leave his side.

I set the gun on a counter. Perhaps someday I'd want it, but not now. "Yes," I said—to being drawn to him, to staying with him, to feeding from him. Yes to it all.

As if in a goth version of a corny romance, Marek and I flew into each other's arms.

Kissing when we both had fangs was... interesting. Erotic. Our blood mingled in our mouths, increasing our passion exponentially. When I imagined what it would be like to feed from Marek while he fed from me, while we fucked, I almost came then and there.

"I should probably eat first," I gasped after pulling back a bit.

Chuckling knowingly, Marek took my hand and led me to the cooler, lifting the lid and then handing me a packet. I used my fangs to tear it open and then chugged the contents. Cold and plasticky. It reminded me of those prepackaged sandwiches sold at airports and convenience stores—soggy bread, limp lettuce, the meat and cheese hardly more than tasteless paste. Those sandwiches had filled my stomach when I'd been hungry and without other options, and now the packaged blood would do the same.

I polished off six of them and Marek had two. My stomach was full and the need within me had faded. Well, *one* need. Because when I looked at Marek, an entirely different hunger consumed me.

This time I tore his clothes right off, and although he could have stopped me, he didn't try. He was too busy running his hands over my skin as if claiming my body as his own. I didn't try to stop him.

We didn't make it back to the bedding in the office but instead ended up rolling together on the hard tile of the kitchen floor. We kissed and caressed, nipped and scratched. My newly enhanced senses made everything so much *more*, but so did the knowledge that this wasn't just a quick fuck with a stranger. This beautiful, enigmatic, astonishing creature was mine if I wanted him—which I did—and I was irrefutably his.

Vampires need not worry about safer-sex practices, and I discovered that bits of fleeting pain made the pleasure even sweeter. He entered me using nothing but spit for lube, and I clutched his ass and bit the tender juncture of his neck and shoulder. We climaxed together, screaming our bliss so loudly that I believe the building trembled.

Then we looked at each other. Smeared with blood and semen and dirt from the not-especially-clean floor. Our skin dotted with bite marks. Our hair snarled into knots. And we laughed together. That felt as good as the sex. Better, even.

Afterward we cleaned each other at the kitchen sink, using the spray attachment like a shower head. We got water everywhere, and it was playful and silly and altogether wonderful. Still slightly damp, we retired to the office for a second round, this one slower and softer.

Cradled against Marek in our nest of blankets, I found myself believing in happy endings.

"What are you laughing about?" he asked, cool breath a whisper on my skin.

"The universe. I had to die in order to find what I'd been wanting all my life."

"If there's a God, she surely has a sense of humor."

I brushed my lips against his temple. "Do you have a plan for us, or do we play it by ear?"

"I have... an idea. It's not a plan yet, but we could make it that if you wish."

The idea of a shared scheme made me smile. "Yes?"

"Charles and Tenrael do private investigating. We could do something similar. Cooperate with them at times. They've mentioned the possibility, and they think we'd make good partners. But also...."

"Yes?"

"There are other situations like Buckley. Occasions when people are endangered and the Bureau can't or won't act. And there are occasions when those in danger are not human." Marek sighed.

"Are you saying we could be bodyguards to the supernatural?"

"Something like that."

I turned the concept over in my head and couldn't find a single fault with it. And then I thought of all the stories Marek must have about his long existence and how if luck was with us, we'd have many years for him to share them. I thought about how I'd never stand in the sunshine again. But then, I'd mostly been a creature of the night even when I was alive. And now, day or night, I need never be alone again.

I squeezed Marek tightly.

I'd spent years flirting with death. Now, wonder of wonders, I embraced the undead. And I wanted to do it forever.

PART III
BOOK THREE: CREATURE

CHAPTER 1

John was greedy.

Every time the first sliver of sunlight came through the high barred window, he'd crawl across the floor and lay sprawled on his back, waiting for the thread of heat to grow into a ribbon. Eventually it became a blanket, warming him through the thick layer of grime that coated his skin. He closed his eyes and spread his scrawny limbs, and for a short time he possessed a crumb of comfort. One small thing he could claim as his own.

But then the sun would recede, unraveling his blanket until nothing remained but darkness and cold and the unforgiving hard surfaces of the cell. During those bleak hours, he hated the sun with an icy rage that chilled him more than the stone floor on which he lay. But every morning when the first rays again snuck in the window, his love was rekindled. John gorged on the light as long as it was his.

John wasn't his real name. He didn't remember his name, didn't remember having a name. But a man needed a name, even if he was all by himself in a cell with inconstant sunlight as his only visitor. Sometimes he said it out loud just to hear the solid consonants echo against the walls. "John. I am a man called John."

Only... he wasn't at all certain that he *was* a man. He had all the parts a man ought to have, at least as far as he could tell. His legs were too weak to hold him upright, his arms as thin as broomsticks, and his cock hung flaccid and useless. Yet he did have legs and arms and a cock. Like a man. But within the long emptiness of his memories, he'd never once had food or drink, and men needed those things to survive. And in those days before he was in the cell—God, he wished he didn't recall those days—people had done things to his body that no man could have survived. He still had marks from those days, bumpy scars and puckered ridges that itched under the dirt but wouldn't heal.

And he had no heartbeat.

If he wasn't a man, though, he didn't know what he might be instead. So he called himself *John* and *a man*, and he greedily drank the sunlight when he could.

"John," he whispered today as the light slipped away. "I'm John. Come back to me soon, please."

In the settling darkness, he rolled onto his belly and began to drag himself back to the corner where he spent the nights. It wasn't any different from the other three corners, no softer or more forgiving against his thin skin, but somehow it soothed him to have a particular place to settle in. It was as if he had a daily schedule, an agenda: go bathe in the light, and then go rest in his bed. A variation on those men who went to the office and then returned home for a cocktail, dinner, conversation with family, perhaps some radio or a bit of reading, and then to their thick mattress with cozy bedding.

Were those real men as foolish as he? He didn't know.

Today as he made his slow commute to the corner, he heard a sound. Not the tiny scrape of his body against smooth rock, but something sharper and brighter. Metal rasping and squealing.

John froze. Before he could understand the new noise, bright light assaulted him from the ceiling on the opposite side of the cell. He cried out, cowered into a ball, and covered his eyes with his arms. A louder metallic screech, and a wave of warm air washed over him. Despite his own familiar stink, he caught scents of alcohol and smoke.

"Jesus *Christ*." The man's voice was rich with disgust and shock.

A cooler, more controlled voice answered. "Put your gun away, Simmons."

"But Chief—"

"Now. Act like an agent, not a little girl."

John heard the rustle of clothing and the slight creak of leather. "Is it…. Jesus."

"It's still… well, animate's the best word for it, I suppose. It's been a long time since the boys had a crack at it, but that doesn't much matter. It still moves around a little."

In the silence that followed, John gained enough courage to pry open his lids and take a peek around his arms. An opening had appeared in one of the cell walls—a door he hadn't remembered existing—and two men in suits stood just inside, blocking his view of whatever lay beyond. One man was young and would have been handsome if he hadn't looked so terrified and ready to bolt. The chief, older and larger, had a relaxed posture and an unlit cigarette between two fingers.

"We oughtta just burn it," said the younger one. Simmons, John presumed. "Something like that shouldn't even be here. You shoulda burned it a long time ago."

"We considered it, of course. But it's harmless enough, and we thought it might someday come in handy. Which, in fact, it has."

John tried not to hear the impersonal pronoun they used for him or the ease with which they discussed killing him. Maybe if he spoke they would realize he was just a man named John and they'd let him out of this prison.

"P-please," he stuttered, his voice hardly above a whisper. He wasn't accustomed to talking to anyone but himself. But before he could continue his plea—before he could even decide what to beg for —Simmons backed away.

"I can't do this, Chief. Not this one. Gimme another assignment. Anything."

"You are an agent with the Bureau of Trans-Species Affairs. You've known from the moment we hired you that creatures of many kinds haunt the Earth. Most of them considerably more dangerous than this pathetic thing."

I'm not a thing. But John's tongue wouldn't move.

Simmons was now outside the cell completely, invisible behind the other man's bulk. "Gimme one of them monsters. I don't mind. I'll go back to Idaho and hunt more of them werewolves if you want. But I ain't.... Not this one."

The chief, who had his back to John, sighed. "I'm disappointed in you." He turned slightly to look at John. "Well, that's a shame. But I'll get this straightened out."

He left, and the door slammed shut with a finality that made John groan. A few seconds later, the light went out, and he heard a more distant door close.

"No, no." His treacherous tongue had decided to work again. "Don't leave me here. My name is John."

Nobody returned, and the darkness remained. John dragged himself to his corner, curled into a tight ball, and sobbed without tears.

CHAPTER 2

$\mathcal{H}$ARRY LOWE nursed his coffee and wondered if he could get a fourth refill. When he'd arrived, the diner was nearly empty, so nobody had minded him occupying a booth. But now the breakfast crowd was beginning to fill the place, and the waitress—exhausted as she worked through the final hours of her shift—was casting him impatient glares.

The next time she neared, Harry pasted on his most charming grin and held up the mug. "Just one more for the road? Please?"

Her scowl didn't lift, but she poured anyway. She didn't leave room in the cup for his generous additions of cream and sugar, so he scalded his tongue as he drank the level down. Fifteen minutes, maybe twenty, and then her patience would end and he'd have to leave. But he'd enjoy the diner's life and activity while he could. And then... well, he'd face that when he came to it. In the meantime, the jukebox was playing Perry Como's latest hit.

Staring out the window at the slow parade of traffic, Harry caught movement at the corner of his eye and turned his head, expecting to find the waitress standing there. Instead, a man loomed over him, fedora in hand and suit buttons straining.

"Morning," the man said.

Realizing his mouth was agape, Harry attempted to pull himself together. "Ch-chief Townsend?"

Instead of answering, Townsend smiled, tossed his hat onto the empty seat, and sat down beside it. Harry wouldn't have thought Townsend's bulk would fit, yet he looked comfortable, as if the booth had been intended for him all along.

Before Harry could stammer out any questions, the waitress appeared. "You ordering?" she asked, narrow-eyed.

"Of course, sweetheart. Ham, two eggs over easy, toast, side of bacon—I want that lightly done, now—and coffee." Townsend thrust his chin toward Harry. "How about you, boy?"

"I, uh—"

"It's my treat."

Harry had eaten a hamburger when he first arrived at the diner, but that had been some time ago, and he wasn't sure when or how he'd find his next meal. So he nodded. "Oatmeal with milk, please," he told the waitress. "And orange juice." That would keep his belly full for a while.

The waitress's frown lifted slightly. Perhaps she was pleased with the unexpectedly large order and hoped for a good tip. Townsend looked as if he carried a lot more money than Harry did.

"So," Townsend boomed, "how have you been, my boy? It's been six months since your interview, hasn't it?"

Actually, it had been six and a half, but Harry didn't argue. "I'm fine."

"Have you kept yourself fit? I know you might not have much incentive for it without the Bureau in your sights, but…." Townsend shrugged.

Harry's anger, never buried too deep, rose at once. "Are you here to rub it in that you wouldn't hire me?"

Townsend's smile didn't fade. "Not at all, not at all. I just hoped we'd have a little chat."

That was a lie. Harry was certain that nothing Townsend did was unplanned or inconsequential, and the two of them had nothing to chat about. But Harry was getting a free breakfast out of it, not to mention an excuse to stay longer in the diner, so he decided to hear Townsend out. It wasn't as if Harry had spent much time in conversation lately.

The waitress brought an empty mug for Townsend and an OJ for Harry. She poured Townsend's coffee and gave Harry a refill before hurrying away. Townsend, sipping his coffee black, watched Harry add sugar and cream. "You like it rich and sweet, huh?"

Harry felt his cheeks heat. "Less bitter this way."

"Sure. The world is bitter enough already." Townsend took out a pack of cigarettes, shook one free, and set the package on the table without offering one to Harry. He lit the cigarette with a gold lighter, then tilted his head back to exhale a cloud of smoke.

The morning sun already shone brightly through the windows, because in Los Angeles the sun was always out, even if it had to fight the smog. One of the things Harry had hated about working the graveyard shift was that the sun made it too hard to sleep during the day. Of course, that wasn't an issue for him anymore.

"What have you been doing with yourself, my boy?" Townsend flicked his cigarette against the dirty glass ashtray.

"Nothing. Working."

"Let's see now. You had some kind of a job at the train station, didn't you?"

"I'm a janitor." *Was* a janitor. Now he was unemployed, broke, and about to be homeless. He'd been searching for something else—anything else—ever since he got canned, but although he'd had a few good leads, nothing had panned out. One guy had hired him to pump gas, but when Harry turned up for his first day of work, the man had sent him away. Decided he didn't need anyone after all, he said.

As Townsend took a few easy drags from his cigarette and swallowed some coffee, Harry tried to guess his age. Townsend had thinning gray hair, heavy jowls and a thick neck, and a nose and cheeks that carried the hectic glow of a long-time drinker. Yet despite the signs of age and excess weight, he moved with a younger man's grace and sense of power.

Just as Townsend stubbed out his cigarette, the waitress arrived with their food. Harry's bowl of oatmeal looked slightly pathetic compared to Townsend's feast, but neither man commented on it. Townsend spread butter and strawberry jam onto his toast, salted his eggs heavily, and then looked up and grinned. "Nothing like a good breakfast to start the day."

Harry, who had been awake for nearly twenty-four hours, simply stirred his oatmeal.

For several minutes, Townsend occupied himself with cutting, chewing, and swallowing, occasionally chasing bites with gulps of coffee. Harry's oatmeal was bland but filling, and he enjoyed the juice. He used to imagine that when he moved to California, he'd eat oranges straight off the trees every day. But orange trees were hard to come by on Bunker Hill, and juice had been outside his budget even when he was employed.

By the time the waitress reappeared, Townsend had emptied his plates, although Harry's bowl remained half-full. "I'll have a piece of pie, sweetie. You have coconut cream?"

If she was surprised that he was ordering dessert with breakfast, she didn't show it. "Yeah, we got that. One for him too?" she added, as if Harry wasn't capable of speaking for himself.

"I'm fine," Harry muttered, and she gathered the empty dishes and went away.

Townsend was watching him. "It's a funny thing. You're from where? Iowa?"

"Missouri."

"Yeah. So lots of kids like you come to the City of Angels from Missouri, Kansas, Ohio… wherever. And they're all looking to make it big in pictures. They want to be the next Montgomery Clift or Elizabeth Taylor. But not you. You didn't come here to be a movie star."

"I don't know how to act."

That made Townsend boom out a laugh. "That doesn't stop any of them, kid. They figure a pretty face is good enough. And yours isn't bad."

Harry's cheeks burned again. He wasn't sure if this was a backhanded dig at him and the secret he'd thought well hidden until his last meeting with Townsend. "I don't want to be an actor," he said quietly.

"I know. *You* wanted to be an agent in the Bureau of Trans-Species Affairs. An unusual ambition for a boy from Nebraska."

Ignoring the misplaced geographical reference, which he suspected was intentional, Harry finished his juice and pushed the glass away. He wiped his lips with a paper napkin and, despite the amount of coffee he'd consumed, felt weighed down by exhaustion. He was too young to be this tired. Maybe the California sun was to blame, or the smog. He ought to give it up and move somewhere else.

"What do you want from me, Townsend?" he asked.

"An honest answer. Why did you want to join the Bureau? And don't give me more of that claptrap about wanting to serve your country and help people. You could do that by becoming a dogcatcher back home in Cowshit Corners. What's the truth, Harry my boy?"

Sullen-faced, Harry twitched a shoulder. "What do you care? You already turned me down."

"That I did. Do you know why?"

Harry lifted his chin. "Because I'm queer," he growled softly. He thought he'd been discreet, avoiding the frequently raided bars and instead finding temporary company in places like Westlake Park. But he should have known that the Bureau would find out about his darkest secret. During the interview, Townsend had confronted Harry with details of his last few meet-ups, and Harry had known his hopes lay in ashes.

But now Townsend shook his head. "That wasn't it. In fact, I was impressed that when I asked, you owned up to it." He paused when the waitress arrived with his pie, and he took a big bite before continuing. "Some of my agents are homosexuals. One of them retired from the Bureau and began doing a private-detective gig with a male demon!" He laughed as if this was the funniest thing he'd ever heard.

"Male demon?"

"He's harmless enough, nowadays. I guess his partner keeps a check on him. Or maybe it's the other way 'round—Grimes can be quite a threat himself. Anyway, the Bureau doesn't disqualify homosexuals as long as they're honest about their proclivities and they keep their personal lives... unobtrusive."

Although it was possible Townsend was lying, Harry couldn't figure out why he'd bother. Just to torment Harry in some inexplicable fashion? Didn't make sense. Harry wasn't worth the effort.

"So why didn't you let me sign up?"

Townsend took two enormous bites and a swallow of coffee before responding. "'Cause you're not hard enough for it, kid."

"I'm—"

"Hold on! You've got fire in you, I'll say that. But anyone can get angry. I bet that little gal can throw an impressive tantrum when her ire's up." He gestured toward the waitress, who was taking an order three tables away. "But that doesn't mean she's cut out to be an agent. I need men with steel inside 'em. Men who won't fold when something mean and deadly pushes at them." He shook his head. "I see a softness in you, Lowe, and I can't afford that."

Nobody had ever accused Harry of being soft. Headstrong, yes. Stupid. And useless. But although Harry had always feared that a certain weakness lurked in his core, he'd thought the flaw was invisible to everyone else.

He finished the last of his coffee, cold and sickly sweet. "So you tracked me down to gloat?"

"No. But tell me if I'm right: the real reason you wanted to join the Bureau is because you can't destroy your own monsters—the inner ones—so you figured you'd kill some creepy-crawlies instead." He pushed away his empty plate and waited, eyebrows raised.

"What are you—an agent or a shrink?"

"A good agent needs to know more than how to fire a weapon. He needs to be able to read his target."

"I'm your *target*?" Harry hoped he came across as annoyed instead of afraid.

"In a way, in a way. But not for anything negative."

Harry had had enough of this conversation and of Townsend in general. He simply wanted to climb into bed and pull the covers over his head. He could still do that—his rattrap of a room was paid for two more nights.

The waitress came by and slapped a bill on the table, but when Townsend handed her a five and told her to keep the change, she almost smiled. She knew full well she'd never have gotten a tip that big from Harry.

While Townsend was occupied with lighting a cigarette, Harry abruptly stood and grabbed his light jacket. "Thanks for breakfast," he muttered before making a beeline for the exit.

He was halfway down the block when Townsend caught up, latching onto Harry's upper arm with a grip hard as iron. "Not done with you, boy."

Trapped in the middle of the sidewalk, Harry glared. "What? You ain't happy until I spill my guts? Fine. Yeah, I got some ugly stuff inside me, I guess. Dunno if it's any worse than what the average Joe's carrying. I figured if I joined the Bureau I'd maybe get to be a better man. That good enough for you?"

Judging by Townsend's wide smile, it was. But he didn't loosen his grip. "Very good. Now listen carefully. I have an assignment in mind. It's important. It's also a bit delicate in nature. And the agent who takes it on must be very young. I'd originally assigned it to one of my boys, then another, but it didn't work out."

"So? I'm not one of your agents." But Harry's heart danced a hopeful rhythm.

"This will be a trial run. I won't swear you in, not yet. But if you can pull off this assignment, well, that'll prove something, won't it? You can join the Bureau then."

Harry jerked his arm away—he'd have bruises there soon—and pretended he possessed pride and dignity. "But you don't want me, remember? I'm weak."

"Oh, son, don't be an idiot. You can pound the pavement looking for another shitty job, and you can spend your last couple of nights with the roaches at the March Hotel. You can fade into obscurity. You'll end up shriveled and dusty before you know it." Townsend held out a paw. "Or you can take this one last chance."

For a long moment, Harry considered running off, even though he knew that no bright future awaited him here in LA or elsewhere. He wasn't especially smart, he wasn't especially skilled, and his good looks would be gone after a little more hard living. Maybe he'd just fall into a bottle and never climb out, like his old man. He'd always figured that was his destiny anyway, so why fight it? And he sure as hell didn't trust Townsend.

But maybe it was true. Maybe he had one final shot.

"Okay."

Townsend grinned as he gestured at a gleaming red Cadillac parked across the street. "Come for a ride with me, boy."

CHAPTER 3

*T*HE BUREAU'S West Coast building hulked near the Four
Level Interchange just north of downtown. At one time the
headquarters might have boasted Art Deco lines like the nearby city
hall, but the grimy cement structure had been marred over the years
by asymmetric additions that stuck out like tumors. Townsend
steered his Cadillac into the gated parking lot, and a uniformed guard
waved as they entered.

"We're building a new HQ up in Sherman Oaks. We've barely
broken ground on it, but it'll be a lot nicer. Give us more room to
stretch out."

Unsure what he was expected to contribute to the conversation,
Harry remained silent. Townsend had refused to divulge any details of
the assignment during the short drive. He'd seemed cheerful, but his
demeanor hadn't calmed Harry, who didn't trust him. Every time the
car stopped at an intersection, Harry had been tempted to bail out.
Surely he could outrun a big guy so recently stuffed with breakfast
and pie. But Harry had nowhere to run *to*, at least nowhere that wasn't
a dead end, and anyway, he couldn't help but be curious about what
Townsend had in mind.

Instead of parking, Townsend rolled to the curb adjacent to the big front doors. A young man in a suit came dashing out, and when Townsend and Harry got out of the car, the kid hopped in and drove off without a word. Harry didn't get a chance to see where he drove to, because Townsend swiftly led the way into the building.

Harry had come here for his interview, and on that occasion he'd had plenty of time to take a look around the lobby. Not that there was much to see: well-worn marble floors, white walls empty of all décor except for a large sculpture of the Bureau's emblem, a few uncomfortable wooden benches, and a reception desk. Townsend whisked him through without even a glance at the woman behind the desk. He headed for the bank of elevators, but instead of pressing the call button, he took out a key and unlocked a slightly battered wooden door off to one side. "After you," he said, gesturing at the dimly lit descending stairway.

Obediently, Harry started down the steps. Townsend closed the door—the lock snicking into place—and followed close behind. Their footsteps echoed loudly. Although Harry could easily imagine Townsend giving one good shove between his shoulders to send him flying onto the floor below, he kept his pace measured.

The narrow corridor at the bottom of the stairway had scuffed walls and a few flickering lights. Although there was nothing overtly sinister about the space—which included several identical doors distinguished only by the black letters painted above them—the hairs on Harry's nape prickled and his stomach knotted tightly. Townsend unlocked door C and waved Harry inside.

A grizzled man in uniform, sitting behind a desk, rose to his feet as they entered. "Chief," he barked. His left arm was missing, the empty sleeve folded and pinned to the shoulder; deep scars etched his cheek and jaw on that side. He could have sustained those injuries in the war, but the marks looked suspiciously like they'd come from claws.

"Good morning, O'Keefe. You're having a quiet shift?"

"Always do, sir."

"Tell you what. Why don't you take a break? Go get yourself some coffee and a sandwich. My boy Lowe and I will just be visiting for a while."

O'Keefe turned his hard gaze to Harry and then nodded. "Yes, sir. If you need anything—"

"We'll be just fine."

Limping heavily, O'Keefe crossed the room, unlocked the door, and left, pulling the door closed behind him. Townsend walked to the other side of the desk and collapsed into the chair, which creaked in protest. After a few moments of leafing through the tidy stack of magazines—*Life, Boxing Illustrated, Home Craftsman*—he pulled out a cigarette and lighter. "O'Keefe could've taken retirement, you know. We take care of our men." He blew a cloud of smoke. "But he wants to stay on. A lot of guys, they get used to this life. They have a hard time giving it up."

"What about the agent with the demon?"

Townsend laughed. "Yeah, he was still young when he left us. I thought we'd keep him longer. Being a Bureau agent, that's what kept him on the right path. If he'd never signed on with us, well, let's just say there's a good chance we'd have met up eventually anyway—with a far less positive outcome for him. Anyway, his demon does that for him now."

"Does what?"

"Keeps him honest," Townsend said with a wink and a chuckle. He tapped his cigarette against a metal ashtray and leaned back in the chair. "Why am I here?" Harry asked. There was no place for him to sit, and he was tempted to pace the small room like a caged animal. Instead he stuffed his fists into his pockets.

"Death."

"What?" Harry hoped he didn't look as spooked as he felt.

"You're here because of death. I guess we all are, in a way, the whole damn Bureau, but in this case that theme is more apparent."

"I don't know what you're talking about."

"When you think about it, death is the master of every one of us. Doesn't matter how strong we are. You could be richer than Rockefeller, more famous than Jimmy Stewart, more powerful than Stalin, but in the end, death beats you. And none of us gets much say in how or when." He grinned as if he found this amusing. Then he leaned forward and pointed the tip of his cigarette at Harry. "So tell me, boy. If you wanted to be the most formidable man in all of history, what would you try to do? And don't say make money, because I told you already that isn't it."

Unsure whether this was a simple conversation or a test of some kind, Harry chewed his lip in thought. He'd always hated it when his teachers called on him—his mind never worked fast enough, and the other kids laughed at his bumbling responses. "You'd want to control death?" He couldn't help phrasing it as a question.

Townsend slapped the desk hard, making Harry jump. "That's right! I thought you'd say something about creating life, but that isn't it either. Every two-bit floozy who gets herself knocked up can create life. Nothing special about that. But death!" He nodded. "That's something else."

Although Harry was relieved to have landed on the right answer, he still had no idea where the conversation was going. He remained silent and looked around furtively as Townsend stubbed out his cigarette and lit another. The smoke hung heavy in the room, which had no windows or other sign of ventilation. Besides the steel door to the hallway, there was a smaller door, also of heavy steel. Although no sounds came from behind the smaller door, Harry sensed that something lurked there.

How did O'Keefe manage to spend hours here, alone, without losing his mind?

"Have you ever been to Portland, Lowe?"

Harry blinked at the change in topic. "Oregon? No."

"Rains all the time. Weird things grow in all that dampness."

"Mold?"

"Weird *ideas*, boy. A man spends too much time cooped up inside, looking out at the gloom, he starts thinking strange things. Like maybe he starts thinking he'd like to get the better of death."

Oh, so they were back to that again. "How does someone do that?"

"Well, necromancy for one. Or vodou. A fellow who learns one of those can raise the dead." He shrugged. "It has appeal for some, I guess. The kind that want slaves to do their bidding."

Harry shuddered. "That's... awful. Can people really do that?"

"Sure. We took down a bokor—a vodou sorcerer—last year, up in Bakersfield. The agents we sent after him had to burn their clothes afterward. They couldn't wash the stink of death out of 'em."

"Jesus."

Townsend laughed. "No, that's a whole other kind of raising the dead, and no mortal I know has managed it. Anyway, here's the thing. A necromancer or bokor isn't really besting death—he's only... well, partnering with it. Because those things he raises, they might be shuffling around, but they're still dead. A *truly* powerful man would do more than that. He'd take the dead and bring 'em entirely back to life."

Harry could have stayed in Missouri, maybe with a job at the grain elevator. He could have headed up north and found employment in a Chicago factory or a Detroit car plant. He could have come here to LA and looked for something at the port. Or he could have hidden that he was queer and joined the Army. In short, Harry's life could have taken another path, a path that didn't lead to this office, locked in a basement with a man who was talking about raising the dead.

"That sounds fucking horrible," Harry said.

"I'm glad you think so." Townsend smiled. "But there's nobody you'd be tempted to dig out of their grave? No beloved family members, for instance?"

"I don't even get along with the ones that are still alive."

"That's right. You're alone in the world, metaphorically speaking. Many of our best agents come to us like that." He stubbed out the second cigarette and seemed to consider lighting a third. But instead he heaved himself out of the chair and walked around the desk.

As he drew near, Harry braced himself and didn't back away.

"There's a man up in Portland," Townsend began, "who *is* interested in bringing the dead back to life. Or so our sources tell us. He's apparently been unearthing fresh corpses, stitching the best pieces together, and trying to make the resulting mess human again."

"Like... Frankenstein?" When he was a kid, he'd sometimes been able to earn enough to go to the pictures, and he'd seen the monster played by both Chaney and Lugosi. Those hadn't been his favorite movies, though; he'd preferred Bogart and Grant.

Townsend clapped Harry's shoulder. "You got it, kid."

"Frankenstein is *real?*"

"This guy's name is Swan, but yeah. He's real."

"And you want me to do what?"

"Nothing much, really. Gather more information. Because so far all we have are hints and rumors, and we need to know if Swan's really onto something. We don't give a damn if he's just going around digging up some stiffs. That's the Portland Police Bureau's problem, and we're not getting ourselves tangled up in some kind of jurisdictional cockfight. But if those stiffs ain't so stiff by the time Swan's through with 'em, that's *our* problem."

This made some sense but was only a partial explanation. "So I go up there and ask him if he's got a mad scientist lab or something?"

"A little more subtle than that. Swan isn't going to want to advertise what he's up to. But we hear he's got a taste for pretty boys, so maybe he'll let you get close enough to see what's what."

Harry's mouth tasted of ashes. "You want me to seduce him?"

"Something like that."

He shook his head. "I'm no whore."

"Didn't say you were, boy. But a Bureau agent has to be willing to play whatever role an assignment requires. And this one requires a pretty boy." He clapped Harry's shoulder again, harder this time. "You don't have to fuck him—just play nice enough that you can get close to him. Can you manage that?" Townsend's expression had gone serious and hard.

Could he? The idea turned Harry's stomach. But was it really any worse than whatever dim future remained for him if he turned Townsend down? Hell, a couple of men in the park had offered Harry money to suck their dicks, and while Harry had indignantly said no, he'd thought more than once about those offers as his cash ran low.

"I can do it." His voice was hardly above a whisper.

Smiling broadly, Townsend patted him again. "Excellent! Now let me show you the bait we're gonna add to the hook." He marched to the smaller door. The lock squealed as he opened it.

Harry had steeled himself to see something terrifying, although he had no idea what that something might be. But when Townsend switched on the light, Harry saw nothing but a dingy room not much larger than a closet. Only after he and Townsend entered—and the door slammed closed—did Harry notice the pair of iron manacles hanging from the ceiling and the brownish stains splattered on the concrete floor. The small space reeked of piss, sweat, and something that might have been pure fear.

Harry backed against the closed door, the handle digging into his lower back. "I don't—"

"Hang on. This lock sticks." With a cheerful little smile, Townsend put a key into yet another door. It protested loudly when he pulled it open. "Here we go!"

Curiosity—and a sense of inevitability—overcame Harry's sense of self-preservation. He peeled himself away from the wall and crowded next to Townsend in front of the open doorway. It took Harry a moment to understand what he was seeing inside the bare, dirty cell, but when comprehension hit, he had to clutch the doorframe for support.

"Fuck!"

CHAPTER 4

$\mathcal{J}$OHN BASKED in his little patch of sunlight and thought about grass. He couldn't recall ever seeing grass, but he knew what it was, and he could picture the precise fresh green of newly sprouted blades. He conjured the smell—vegetative and almost sweet—and the tickly sensation of grass tips against skin. The only surfaces he'd experienced were hard and unforgiving: stone, tile, and steel. Yet he knew that if he lay back in a field of grass, it would be soft and springy beneath him, like a living mattress, and small insects would buzz around him as he gazed up at the limitless sky.

Sky. No—that was something to think about tomorrow. He allowed himself only one such musing per day. Yesterday he'd meditated on coffee, and today was grass. He'd save sky for tomorrow. And then the day after that....

Despair sliced into him like knives, and the hopelessness of his existence suddenly overwhelmed him, as it sometimes did. If he was being punished for something, shouldn't he at least know how he'd transgressed? Weren't even the worst criminals granted small mercies? He had so very little, and he didn't understand why.

Vague notions about grass did nothing to chase away his anguish, so he comforted himself as best as he could. "John," he whispered. "My name is John. I *am*." He repeated it until the agony faded to its usual dull ache.

He settled back on the stone floor and tried to imagine he was grass growing in the warm sunshine. He would have thousands of bright blades, each reaching joyously upward. If someone stomped on him, no matter. He would bend for a time, but soon he'd stand upright again. He would find strength in his pliancy. He would—

Metal screamed.

John curled immediately into a tight ball, tucking his face into his chest and covering his head with his arms, so he wouldn't see the light when it flooded his cell. But unlike the few other times this had happened, he didn't crawl into a corner. He had the sun now, and he refused to give up that precious warmth for even a minute.

"Here we go!" The familiar voice of the chief. Even though the chief had never touched him—had never even come particularly close —John was terrified of him. John was certain the chief had the power to destroy him. Or worse.

"Fuck!"

John didn't recognize the second voice, but he'd heard others like it. Younger men would stand beside the chief, exclaim in horror, and then refuse whatever task the chief had asked of them. John didn't know whether he ought to feel relief at the refusals, but he hated their disgust and shock. He was just John. They ought to be repulsed by his situation, not by him.

"W-what *is* it?" the younger man demanded shakily.

Him, not it, but John didn't say it out loud. They never listened to him anyway.

"Did you ever read Shelley's book?" asked the chief.

"What?"

"No, I don't suppose you did. You're not the literary type. And the films obscured the original message, I'm afraid. In the book, the monster was rejected by his maker—and by society as a whole— because he was hideous. The dead aren't pretty, Lowe, not even when they regain the semblance of life."

"This is...." The younger man—Lowe—paused and cleared his throat audibly. "Did Swan do this?"

"No, no. Swan's not the first to have these aspirations. Several decades ago, a fellow in Oakland made similar attempts, and he was successful, as you can see. Fortunately we caught up to him before he could do much damage."

"What happened to him?"

The chief chuckled. "He's dead, and quite permanently so. We burned his body to ashes. But we seized a lot of interesting evidence as well, including this. We studied this creature for some time, gathering what information we could, and since then we've kept it in storage. I thought it might eventually prove useful. And it has."

In the silence that followed, John tried to understand what the chief had said. The only part that made sense, however, was *studied*. That raised memories of chains and straps, of hard hands and ruthless eyes, of scalpels and prods and fire. "No," he moaned into his own chest, even knowing it would do no good. "Please."

Neither Lowe nor the chief responded, but one of them took a couple of hesitant steps closer. John slowly uncurled himself enough to look. The chief remained just inside the open door, but Lowe was nearer, his body tense and handsome face drawn into a frown. Unlike the others who'd come with the chief, Lowe didn't wear a suit. Instead he had on denim trousers, a plain white shirt with no tie, and a pale blue jacket. His coal-dark hair was longer than the crewcuts the other men had sported, and despite his clear distress, his brown eyes held surprising warmth.

"Is it... dangerous?" Lowe asked.

"No, not at all. It's extremely weak, in fact. But that won't matter for our purposes."

Lowe cast a quick glance over his shoulder. "What *are* our purposes? I don't understand."

"I told you—bait. If Swan doesn't find you enticing enough, you can lure him closer by showing him this creature. However far he's come in his experiments, he'll certainly be intrigued by evidence of prior success."

"Oh." Lowe had relaxed slightly, and now he gnawed on a thumb-nail. "But... I'm supposed to convince Snow that I know how to... do this?" He waved at John. "'Cause I don't—"

"No. The only way you could do that is if you were aware of the processes, and that information will not be given to you."

Lowe scowled. "Right. 'Cause I'm not even an agent."

"But perhaps you can be. If this assignment goes well. In any case, we have a credible tale for you to give Swan. I'll give you the details later."

That must have satisfied Lowe, who turned his full attention back to John. He came two steps closer and stopped again. This was more than any of the previous men had done, and although Lowe was frowning, at least his lips weren't curled in repulsion.

Although John had no faith he'd be successful, he had to *try*. Otherwise, when he was alone in the darkness of his cell, he'd despise himself too. "I'm John. Help me, please."

Lowe's eyes widened and he backed off a pace. "It... he... he can—"

"The creature can speak," said the chief. "It's sentient to some extent, although I don't expect it'll be teaching at Harvard. But as I said, you needn't worry about it being dangerous."

"That's not—"

"Although it occurs to me we may need to find a way to silence it before you show it to Swan. We don't want it to ruin your cover story."

Silence. God, would they steal his voice as well? Then who would whisper his name late at night, when the sunshine seemed only a dream and the emptiness threatened to swallow him for good? John clamped his mouth shut and curled back into a ball. He wouldn't beg anymore; he wouldn't let them see him cry.

In the silence that fell, John felt Lowe's gaze heavy upon his skin. And then the chief's voice.

"So what do you say, boy? Are you man enough to take this on? Or should I drive you back to Bunker Hill? I'll bet the rats at the March Hotel are missing you."

After a long pause, Lowe answered. "I'll do it."

"Excellent! Now come with me. We'll go over the details."

John hazarded a peek before they left, and he discovered that Lowe still stared at him. Lowe's expression was deeply troubled, but John couldn't discern why. Then the chief grunted impatiently, and Lowe followed him out of the cell. The door slammed shut; the lights went out. John was left with his patch of sunshine and a new sense of unease.

HE SPENT a few days thinking about words and their opaque meanings. He didn't understand most of the conversation between Lowe and the chief, and the parts he *did* understand scared him. Like *studied*. The chief had referred to him as *the creature*. What did that mean? What sort of creature was he, if not a man?

He had no answers. Yet his mind stubbornly asked the questions again and again, even when John sprawled in the sunshine and tried to think about the sky.

Then one morning, just as the first tendrils of light came creeping through his window, the chief and Lowe reappeared. This time Lowe wore a lightweight collared sweater and khaki trousers. Although he still seemed nervous, he also carried an air of resignation, as if he'd made an uncertain decision but planned to stick with it.

"Put these on it," said the chief.

When John saw what the chief pulled from his coat pocket, he cowered back into his corner. Chains. The last time he'd been chained…. *Oh, no. Please.*

Lowe took them with a frown. "You said he's not dangerous."

"It's not. This simply makes transport easier."

Lowe took a deep breath, crossed the cell, and crouched over John. Although Lowe was grimacing, his hands were surprisingly gentle as he manacled John's wrists and ankles, but not tight enough to hurt. Then he stood and looked at the chief. "Okay."

"Pick it up. It shouldn't be too heavy for you."

After a brief hesitation, Lowe stooped. John attempted to push himself back against the walls, to *become* the walls, but Lowe rather easily scooped John into his arms.

And that was strange. Because although John was terrified, he found himself leaning into the solid warmth of Lowe's body. He felt Lowe's rapid heartbeat, saw a tiny nick where he must have cut his chin while shaving. John smelled coffee, soap, cigarette smoke, and the hint of something sweet, like sugar or syrup. He relaxed a bit and settled his head against Lowe's shoulder, feeling as if he was somehow scavenging a little humanity.

All right then. Whatever lay in wait for him, he could enjoy this particular moment. Could relish a man's touch that didn't hurt.

"Let's go," said the chief impatiently.

Lowe carried John out of the cell—good *God*, he was out of the cell!—and then through some rooms and a hallway and up a narrow flight of stairs. By the time they reached the top of the stairs, Lowe was breathing hard. So was John, but from shock rather than exertion. It had been so long since he'd seen anything but his familiar four walls. Tentative relief played through him, because when he'd been *studied*, it was in a large room just down the hall from his cell. At least that place didn't seem to be his immediate fate.

With the chief in the lead, Lowe carried John through a vast, high-ceilinged space with hard surfaces that echoed every footstep. John trembled at the openness of it all and fought the urge to hide his face against Lowe's shoulder. He caught a quick glimpse of a grim-faced woman standing behind a long counter, and then—

Good Lord.

Then they were outside.

That was the *sky* above him, gloriously high and endless, the exact color of a robin's egg. And it was real, not just something he'd conjured from his Swiss-cheese memory. His friend the sun looked down on him with its full glory, unencumbered by iron bars. "Outside," he rasped.

Lowe glanced down at him but kept on walking.

They didn't go far, just a few steps from the building's door. The chief had led them to... a vehicle. *An automobile,* John's head primly informed him, although this vehicle bore little resemblance to his notion of what an automobile was. This thing was lower, sleeker, with rounded edges that made it look more like an animal than a machine.

"In the trunk," said the chief.

"But—"

"If you get pulled over, do you want the cop to see *that* right away?"

Lowe sighed. "Guess not."

As John was set down into the small space, he felt bereft to lose the warm contact. Panic crept in when he realized that Lowe was about to close a lid, trapping him inside. But Lowe took a moment to gently rearrange John's limbs so he lay more comfortably and then bent down to quickly whisper, "Sorry. It's just till we get there."

Inexplicably reassured, John remained quiet and still as Lowe closed him into darkness.

CHAPTER 5

*H*ARRY HAD been uneasy for days—starting the minute Townsend slid into the booth in that downtown café. By now he should be feeling better. He had a decent wad of cash in his wallet, more money than he'd ever owned at once. Enough, Townsend said, to get him to Portland and to support him while he seduced Swan.

He had a car too, a taffy-colored '48 Ford. Not as nice as Townsend's cushy late-model Caddy, the Ford showed a few dents and scrapes, and its interior smelled like an ashtray. But it was his to drive, at least for a while. He'd never owned a car.

He even had new clothes, because Townsend claimed Harry needed something better than the well-worn denims and threadbare shirts he'd brought from Missouri. The old church suit he'd worn for his interview was too short in the legs and too tight in the shoulders, and he knew it betrayed him as a rube from the sticks. Now he owned several pairs of nice trousers, some new shirts and sweaters, and a suit jacket that made him look downright snazzy.

But despite all the material goods and the escape from the March Hotel, Harry was troubled. Maybe that had something to do with the not-corpse in the trunk of his car.

He hadn't expected the monster to talk, surely hadn't expected him to *beg*. And although the monster looked horrible—all skin, bones, and vivid scars—his blue eyes were as human as any Harry had seen.

Jesus fucking Christ, what had he gotten himself into?

After Townsend recruited him, Harry had spent a few days at HQ with some of the agents. They'd given him the story to use on Swan and then drilled him so thoroughly that Harry almost lost track of his real history. Was he any longer the unwanted son of a drunk from Missouri, a guy with one thin, final hope of a future? Or was he a would-be actor who'd had a brief but torrid love affair with an older man, a gentleman of some means who dabbled in the arcane arts before croaking suddenly in a car wreck, leaving his monster and some of his money to his protégé?

Townsend had him sleep in a hotel near HQ. A nice place, not a rooming house like the March. Harry basked in the private bathtub and the soft, clean linens. He ordered from room service—a luxury he'd seen in movies but never experienced himself—and had a few drinks in the swanky hotel bar. On a whim he wandered into a book-store and bought a copy of *Frankenstein*, as if the book might somehow help him make sense of his predicament. It didn't. In fact, always a poor reader to begin with, he'd especially struggled with the old-fashioned language. Still, he'd kept the book, and now it was tucked into his suitcase in the back seat.

The monster hadn't raised any fuss on the day when Harry had cuffed him, hauled him from the cell, up the HQ stairs, and out to the car. In fact, he'd sort of leaned against Harry's shoulder as if enjoying the contact. That should have been unsettling, but it wasn't—not exactly. It made Harry want to protect him, actually. Maybe because the monster was the first person in a long time who hadn't acted as if there was something wrong with Harry.

"Great, I have the approval of monsters." Now with the monster in the trunk, Harry frowned and stepped harder on the gas.

The Ford took him swiftly over the hills and into the Central Valley, which reminded him uncomfortably of Missouri. Dusty farms and little nothing towns. He frequently glanced at the Sierras to the east, just to confirm he was in California.

Was the monster uncomfortable in the trunk? Scared? Harry had no idea what range of emotions such a creature might feel, but he was certain he'd already seen the monster show fear.

Uneasy with this line of thought, Harry tried to focus on the road. Eventually, though, his eyelids grew heavy, and shortly after the sun set, he pulled into the parking lot of the El Rancho Motel. It was an L-shaped, single-story building with a red tile roof. A row of palm trees stood nearby, two of them with the crowns broken off. But what interested Harry the most was the nearly empty lot; it looked as if he'd enjoy plenty of privacy here.

The old man in the office didn't seem the type to enjoy chitchat. He took Harry's eight dollars, watched him sign a fake name in the register, and then handed over a key with a worn metal fob. "Check-out time's eleven sharp."

"I'll be gone well before then." Harry sauntered back into the crisp evening air.

Townsend had instructed him to leave the monster in the car overnight. Less chance of complications that way. But Harry doubted he'd get any sleep, knowing the monster was still cramped in the trunk, chained and cold and alone. So after carrying his suitcase into the little room, he opened the trunk of the Ford.

The monster blinked up at him and didn't struggle when Harry lifted him into his arms. Luckily nobody was around to see him carry what looked like a naked, shackled corpse. The monster uttered a single hoarse word as Harry crossed the short distance back to the room: "Stars!"

The room boasted worn carpeting, wood paneling, a seascape painting, and sparse furniture. Harry's first idea was to set the monster on the armchair, but he doubted the monster could remain upright. He couldn't bring himself to just dump him on the floor, where Harry would likely trip over him. That left the bed. When Harry set him there, the monster lay on his back, completely still, his eyes wide.

Only now did Harry realize how filthy the monster was. He didn't smell particularly bad, but grime marred nearly every surface of his papery skin.

Shit.

Soon Harry found himself on his knees beside the bathtub, running a soapy washcloth over the monster's body. The monster kept his gaze fixed on Harry and didn't make a sound, didn't object in any way as Harry moved his arms and legs around. Finally the silence became too heavy. "Do these hurt?" Harry asked, scrubbing gently at one of the larger scars on the monster's chest.

"Hurt," the monster breathed in response. Harry didn't know if that was an answer or just an echo of his own final word.

"I want to take the cuffs off. Will you fight me if I do?"

"No." The monster lifted his wrists. "I won't fight."

So he *did* understand speech, and he could carry at least a simple conversation. Harry pulled the keys from his pocket and unlocked the manacles and then the ankle cuffs. He set the restraints aside in case he might need them later and then winced when he saw the terrible condition of the monster's wrists and ankles. "Sorry," he mumbled. Should he bandage the wounds?

"W-will you study me?" The monster interlaced his sticklike fingers as if in prayer.

"What?"

"Study." The monster traced a thumb down the long scar bisecting his belly, then looked up at Harry with an anxious frown.

"I don't know what you're talking about." Although Harry had a sinking feeling he knew *exactly* what was meant. When the Bureau had first acquired the monster, wouldn't men like Townsend have taken him apart to see what made him tick? Swallowing bile, Harry shook his head. "I'm not gonna... hurt you."

The monster's smile should have been terrible—thin lips stretched over yellowed teeth like a death's-head image on a grave. But he didn't look terrible, not even with the few remaining wisps of pale hair trailing from his scalp.

Harry cleared his throat. "You said.... Your name...."

"John. Please, please call me John."

"All right, John."

The monster's—John's—smile stretched even wider and he breathed a long sigh. "Thank you."

"I'm, uh, Harry Lowe." Nobody had ever taught him proper etiquette for introductions with the undead. He didn't feel as awkward as might be expected, though, probably because John was staring at him as though Harry were something amazing.

By now John was relatively clean, and Harry's knees had begun to ache. He stood and wiped imaginary dust from his pants. "I need dinner." But he couldn't just leave John in the tub, so Harry pulled the plug from the drain and then wiped John down with a towel before carrying him back to bed. "Stay here and be quiet. I'll be back soon."

"Yes." John stroked the bedspread and gave another smile. "It's soft."

Harry nodded curtly and left the room.

Earlier, he'd spied a little diner a couple of blocks away. He decided to walk rather than drive since he'd had no exercise at all today, apart from carrying John. But while the short stroll helped stretch his legs, it did little to clear his head.

The place was called Hazel's Drive-In, and the big, brightly lit windows looked inviting. Judging by the number of cars and trucks parked there, the food was probably decent too—an assumption supported when Harry entered and inhaled the delicious scents of sizzling meat and frying potatoes. But the din of conversation made him wince, and so did Eddie Fisher crooning on the jukebox.

"Just one?" asked the waitress nearest the door. She slightly resembled Harry's mother, with her drawn-on eyebrows, too-red lipstick, and deep lines at the corners of her mouth.

"Can I, um, get something to take with me?"

"Sure, honey." She handed him a menu. "Whattaya want?"

He glanced at the offerings. "Cheeseburger with everything and french fries. And a bottle of Coke."

"How about a piece of pie to go with? Our apple's real good."

"Okay." He had plenty of cash right now; he could afford a small splurge.

"That's a dollar and five cents."

He gave her the money and then leaned against a pillar near the entrance, watching the other customers. Tables held young couples or raucous groups of teenagers or families with little children. Some men sat at the counter; maybe they were travelers, like him. Harry wondered what these people would think if they knew his errand. If they discovered what lay in his bed at the El Rancho Motel. Or if they learned any of his other secrets, for that matter. But none of them even glanced his way.

The waitress returned quickly with a paper bag containing his food. At the cashier stand, she added a few paper napkins, a couple of mints, and a book of matches. "Thanks," Harry said when she handed everything over. He gave her a quarter, which she tucked into her apron.

"You have a good evening, now," she said.

He returned quickly to the motel, eating some of the french fries along the way. He almost expected to discover John missing, but when Harry opened the door, there was John on the bed, exactly as Harry had left him. He probably couldn't have gone far even if he tried. As far as Harry could tell, John couldn't sit upright, let alone stand.

Harry plopped down in the armchair facing the bed, and John watched as he pulled out the paper-wrapped hamburger, the cardboard container of french fries, and the bottle of Coke. Then Harry set the bag on the adjacent dresser with the pie still inside. "You, um, don't need to eat, right?"

The answer came as hardly more than a whisper. "I don't."

"Okay." Thick, juicy, and a little greasy, the cheeseburger tasted great. But having John stare at him while he ate was weird, especially because John's nudity was suddenly very obvious. He'd been naked all along, of course, and Harry had touched almost all of him when John was in the tub. But Harry hadn't really been thinking of him as a person then, while now for some reason he did.

After finishing the burger, he wiped his hands clean with the napkins, stood, and proclaimed, "Clothes." John watched Harry lift his suitcase onto the empty side of the bed and shuffle through the contents. Nothing he owned would be a proper fit for John, who was little more than a skin-covered skeleton, but eventually Harry selected an undershirt and pair of tan trousers.

He closed the suitcase and set it aside. "You can put these on," he said, nudging the clothing toward John.

John's eyes widened, but he didn't budge. "I... put them on?"

"Yeah. We're going to need to jury-rig a belt somehow, but they're better than nothing."

Moving slowly, John reached over to stroke the undershirt. "It's soft," he said, voice filled with wonder.

"I guess."

Harry watched him for a few moments, but it soon became clear that John lacked the strength to pull himself upright. He also didn't seem to have any notion of how to get dressed. After he fumbled the shirt onto the floor, Harry sighed and stepped around to help.

John cowered when Harry neared him. "I'm sorry, master."

Shit. "Master?" That came out more harshly than Harry intended, so he forced himself to soften his tone. "I'm not your master. I'm Harry, okay?" He sighed. "Let's get these clothes on you."

Although the outfit was many sizes too large, John looked even more human when dressed. How old had he been when he died? Harry couldn't tell. After Harry helped him lie down again, John kept running his fingers reverently over the fabric of his shirt and pants. Something about those small movements twisted Harry's heart.

"Gonna turn in," he announced, more loudly than necessary. "Long drive tomorrow." He got ready quickly, then turned out the light in hopes it would make climbing in beside John less awkward. It didn't— although at least he didn't have to face John's startled gaze.

"You do, uh, sleep, right?" Facing away from John, Harry rearranged the thin pillow into a more comfortable position.

"Yes."

Morbid curiosity brought the next question. "Do you dream?"

"No," John replied after a long pause. "I don't think so."

Would that be a good thing or bad? Harry had been plagued with nightmares since he was young; sometimes he'd cried out, loud enough to wake his family and cause his father to stomp into the bedroom and yell at him. The man who rented the room next to his at the March once complained too. But now and then Harry dreamed wonderful things—of flying like a bird or triumphantly slaying dragons. Of dancing in the arms of a man who loved him.

"Harry?" The whisper came when he was almost asleep.

"Yeah?"

"Did I…. Am I bad?"

At first Harry thought he'd just ignore the question. But he could feel John's presence just inches away, and he imagined the disquiet on that ruined narrow face. Not to mention the shadows in John's bright blue eyes.

"What do you mean? You did what I told you today."

"Yes. I tried to be good. I won't…. You don't have to silence me."

Shit. "Okay."

"B-but did I do something bad? Before?"

"Before what?"

"Before I was… like this?"

Harry hadn't given any thought to John's memories or sense of self, and it hadn't occurred to him that John might not know who he'd been before he died. Harry certainly didn't know the answer. It hadn't occurred to him to ask Townsend, who in any case might not have known either. But this wasn't a line of examination that Harry wanted to explore right now. Or possibly ever.

"You weren't bad," he said, although that might have been a complete lie.

John sighed into the darkness. "Thank you."

CHAPTER 6

*J*OHN WASN'T certain he was sane. After all, his memories began with a black abyss, and his life had been steeped in misery. Sometimes in the cell, especially at night, he doubted his own existence. But he'd been suddenly whisked away and now faced so many things he'd previously only imagined: The sky and the stars. A clean body covered in soft clothing. A bed. And a man who spoke with him—called him by name!—and whose touches never hurt. Maybe these were the desperate fictions of a tattered mind.

If it was a delusion, John intended to relish it as long as he could. He lay in the darkness, feeling the warmth from Harry's body, listening to the symphony of Harry's even breaths. This was contentment, better than a brief pool of sunshine.

And Harry said John hadn't been bad.

He fell asleep smiling.

HE WOKE early and spent some time watching Harry sleep. He was a beautiful man, with a diamond-shaped face that tended toward frowns when he was awake but smoothed during slumber. John traced a finger over his own cracked narrow lips and envied Harry's, lush and soft-looking. Unlike John's skin, pale as a mushroom, Harry was a light tan with slightly ruddy cheeks.

Harry opened his eyes and startled so violently that he nearly fell off the bed. "Shit!"

"I'm sorry!" John curled into himself protectively. He hadn't intended to make Harry angry.

But after a long look at John, Harry rubbed his eyes and shook his head. "You're different."

"I...."

"You look...." Another head shake. "Never mind. We need to go."

It didn't take long for Harry to get dressed. He carried his suitcase outside and returned immediately for John, who settled comfortably into his arms. John felt oddly safe when Harry held him, although he had no assurances that Harry wouldn't harm him eventually. Fine. He'd enjoy the contact for now.

Harry grunted as he crossed to the door. "You feel heavier."

"I'm sorry."

"Not exactly your fault, is it?"

As he had the previous morning, Harry put John in the trunk. This time John wore clothing and wasn't in chains. Still, Harry seemed hesitant to close the lid. "Are you gonna be okay in there? We got a long way to go today."

"I'm fine."

Frowning, Harry shut him inside.

In truth, the trunk was uncomfortable. John could barely move and definitely couldn't straighten his limbs, and sometimes the car's sudden starts and stops slammed him into the metal walls. But he was well accustomed to solitude, inactivity, and darkness, and at least the trunk was warmer than his cell. Also, when the car moved smoothly—which was most of the time—the gentle bouncing soothed him. Although he couldn't see or hear Harry, John knew he was close by, and that was a solace as well.

The car stopped several times, but not for long, and John remained locked in the trunk. By the time Harry finally opened the lid, it was nighttime again, but the stars were shrouded by an overcast sky.

Without saying anything, Harry carried him into a room similar to the last, although this one had two narrow beds instead of a wide one. Harry set John down on one mattress—still without comment—and then took a quick shower in the adjacent bathroom. He emerged with wet hair, wearing boxer shorts and an undershirt, and after a long silent scrutiny of John, he turned out the light. Bedsprings creaked as he got into the other bed.

John wanted to ask a thousand questions, but he dared not risk angering his keeper. So he remained quiet, although he didn't fall asleep for a long time.

In the morning John discovered he could sit up by himself. He held up his arms, and in the weak light that crept around the curtains, he thought he discerned more substance to his body than he was used to. He was still terribly thin, but now weak muscles seemed to have developed, and his skin felt softer and more supple. More alive.

He brushed a trembling hand across the top of his skull and encountered... hair. Nothing like the thick brush Harry possessed, but far more than the few tiny wisps John was accustomed to.

He glanced at the other bed and discovered that Harry was awake and staring at him. "You look different. You're changing. How come?"

"I don't know."

"Have you done this before?"

"I... I don't know."

Scowling at John's unsatisfactory answers, Harry got out of bed and prepared for their departure.

In the trunk John noted that today's journey was shorter and that toward the end there was far more starting and stopping. Traffic noise filtered into his cocoon, and he eventually realized that the odd pinging sound must be raindrops hitting the metal above. When Harry popped the trunk open, John wasn't surprised to see that his hair and clothing were damp. Behind him was a neon sign for the Totem Pole Motel.

"Got us another room. I'll look for something better tomorrow. God, I'd love to have a real kitchen! I'm so sick of eating restaurant food. I haven't had a home-cooked meal since I left Missouri." His face scrunched up, as if that were an unhappy memory. Then with a loud groan, he hoisted John into his arms.

Two beds again. John's slight disappointment was ridiculous, because he ought to be deeply grateful to have a bed at all. This room was slightly larger than the others, with a desk, a small round table, and a few chairs. Several paintings of Indians adorned the walls. John sat on his bed instead of lying down as he watched Harry fuss around, getting settled.

He finally hazarded a question. "Where are we?"

"Portland."

"Oh." He knew in an abstract way that the city lay at the northern edge of Oregon. It had a port, he thought, and mountains nearby. A lot of trees. As always, he didn't know where this knowledge came from.

Harry stood at the end of John's bed, hands fisted on his hips. "I got some errands to run."

John nodded.

But Harry didn't leave. Instead he remained rooted in place, brow furrowed as he scrutinized John. "I don't understand you."

"I'm... sorry."

"You can talk. And feel things. And I guess you can think okay too, right?"

Although this conversation made John uneasy, he was also gratified to have these things acknowledged. It meant Harry wasn't viewing him as an object. "I can," John agreed softly.

"Yeah. I've thrown you in the trunk of a car and dragged you a thousand miles away, and you ain't complained even once."

John sat up straighter in bed. "I'm clean, Harry. I have clothing. Beds. I've seen the sky! And I'm not... not alone." That part was important. Maybe the most important of all. "Why would I complain?"

Looking grave, Harry shook his head. "You ain't mine. You know that, right? When this job is over, the Bureau's gonna want you back. I don't know what they'll do with you then."

Although John had suspected as much, the words were still painful to hear. He sought courage within himself and found a small amount.

"When they take me back, I'll have good memories to bring with me. I didn't have those before." He even managed a smile, hoping it didn't look too ghastly.

"What do you remember?"

"Pain. A room somewhere. It had white tile. A metal table. Straps and chains. A man with…." He shuddered. "With knives. He told me to call him *master*, but he never said my name. Then there was shouting. Gunfire? More men. And then my cell with my patch of sunlight, and more chains and knives and… and my cell again. Then you."

He'd never said so many words at once, and even though he knew he was far from eloquent, Harry listened closely, his usually ruddy face pale and his eyes wide. When John finished speaking, Harry remained silent. He'd trapped his lower lip between his teeth.

Gathering all his bravery, John asked, "Can you tell me what I am?"

After a pause, Harry nodded. "Yeah." Then he sighed. "Do you know how to read?"

"I… I don't know."

While John watched, Harry rummaged through his suitcase. He pulled out a paperback book and tossed it to John, who surprised himself by catching it easily. The lurid cover depicted a woman in a yellow dress sprawled on a bed, unconscious or dead. Behind her a brutish man stared at his oversized hands. But the words were more important than the image, and John discovered he could read them very well. "The greatest horror story of them all," he recited. "Frankenstein." Swallowing thickly, he looked at Harry for an explanation.

"Have you read it?" Harry asked. "Or seen the movie?"

"I don't know." If he had, the details lay in the missing parts of his memory. But he did know one thing. "A monster?"

"Read it." Harry put on his jacket and a flat cap and left the room, shutting the door firmly.

John picked up the book and began to read.

CHAPTER 7

⚜

*H*ARRY DIDN'T want to think about the creature in his motel room. About John. About how, back in his cell, John had looked like a prop from one of the Saturday matinees Harry had snuck off to see as a kid, the ones his mother forbade because they were the Devil's work. But as part of that long-ago audience— surrounded by screaming girls held tightly by their boyfriends— Harry had imagined himself as the hero who defeated the monsters.

He also didn't want to think about how John now looked different from when he was in the cell. More human. Maybe a human who'd been ill for a long time, but now his bones carried more flesh and his movements were stronger. His eyes looked brighter too, tracking Harry's every move, and the rustiness was fading from his voice.

Harry most definitely didn't want to think about the questions this situation raised. What was John? What would become of him when this Swan guy was caught?

Fortunately Harry had plenty of other matters to occupy his brain. He drove around Portland for a time, getting a feel for the place. It wasn't a big city—LA could have swallowed it whole—but it was much larger than his hometown. A wide river bisected it, and a range of green hills rose to the west, behind the bulky brick and concrete buildings downtown. Heavy mist hung in the air, making everything soft and gray. Harry wasn't sure if he preferred it to LA's smoggy sun, but at least it was a change.

Townsend had given him Swan's address, so Harry stopped at a gas station to buy a map, then went for a quick peek at the house. Reconnaissance work, right? But his delight at feeling like a real agent dimmed when he saw where Swan lived: a sweeping stone mansion with an expansive front lawn adorned with an enormous sculpture of a mermaid. Throw in a couple of palm trees and the house would have looked at home in Beverly Hills. How the hell was he supposed to impress a guy who lived in a place like that?

Frowning, he pulled away from the curb and went in search of a place to eat. Not in this neighborhood, though—it was far too rich for his blood.

He ended up at a turquoise-and-yellow diner advertising all-day breakfasts and special hamburgers. Not many customers at this time of day. He bought a newspaper from the box outside, then sat in a Naugahyde booth and perused it while eating hotcakes and sausage. He'd never had much interest in current events; they'd seemed irrelevant to his life, even after he moved to LA. But he figured he ought to have some idea what was going on in the world. Swan might expect him to know things. So Harry read the headlines and scanned the articles before moving to the classified ads.

There were a lot of Help Wanted listings. Good-paying jobs he was qualified for, like working on the docks or in a warehouse. Maybe if he applied for some of them, his bad luck from California wouldn't dog him. He could forget about the Bureau and start fresh. Yeah, he'd have to pay back the cash Townsend had fronted him, and he'd have to hand in the car, but with a decent salary he could manage well enough. The Bureau could find someone else to go after Swan.

But then what about John? The good meal suddenly tasted like cardboard, and Harry pushed his plate away.

What happened to John was none of Harry's damn business. John was just a prop, like Harry's fancy new suit—a way to get into Swan's good graces. It's not like John was a person.

Right?

Growling softly at himself, Harry shook the newspaper. He would find an apartment, finish this fucking thing for the Bureau, and then make a real life for himself. John might not be any of his business, but it sickened Harry to think that Swan might right now be making more creatures like him. Creatures with ugly scars and big, scared eyes.

THE PLACE WAS HALF of a duplex, a modest yellow one-story with lace curtains and a tiny shared front porch. It stood on a quiet street in the southeast part of town, between a stucco apartment building and a laundromat. Having seen the ad in the newspaper, Harry had called from a pay phone in the diner, so the landlady was ready for him when he rang the bell. She was a squat, gray-haired woman with a sweet smile. "Mr. Lowe? I'm Mrs. Reynolds. Come in, come in."

There wasn't much to see: a living room with built-in bookshelves, a kitchen and bathroom—both small—and a bedroom. Although not fancy, the furnishings looked comfortable, and the entire place was spotless. Not only was the place nicer by far than the March Hotel, but it was cozier and in better repair than the dilapidated old farmhouse where Harry had grown up.

"Well, what do you think?" asked Mrs. Reynolds. While he inspected, she'd waited for him in the kitchen.

"It's great."

"I've recently rented the other unit as well, to a very nice young man. He's quiet. You'll hardly know he's there." She tilted her head slightly. "It's just you?"

Cue some of the Bureau's cover story. "No, my cousin will be living here too. He's been sick. I'm taking care of him."

She tsked. "What a shame! But how kind of you to look out for family. If he's convalescing, you won't be noisy, right?"

"Not at all, ma'am."

"Good. I expect quiet, cleanliness, and prompt rental payments."

Harry didn't plan to be here long enough to pay more than a month's rent, but he nodded. "Of course. Forty-five dollars, right?"

"Yes, with lights and heat included."

He paid her, signed some papers, and listened patiently to her descriptions of when to put out the trash and where he should buy groceries and household goods. She also tried to angle for information from him, but Harry stuck to his bare-bones tale. He and his cousin had come to Portland on the advice of a doctor. The cousin had a little money, enough to pay their way for now. If the cousin regained his health, Harry planned to look for a permanent job nearby. Although Mrs. Reynolds seemed disappointed not to gather any juicier details, she eventually handed over the keys and wished Harry a good evening.

After she left, Harry collapsed into an armchair in the living room. His life suddenly felt too complicated, his burdens too heavy. But after a moment of self-pity, he shook his head. "At least you ain't in Missouri, Lowe. And you ain't being evicted from the March."

He'd already paid for the Portland motel, so he decided to stay the night there. He needed to pick up a few things for the house anyway—some linens, food, a few cleaning supplies. And some clothing for John. After a last look around his new home, he headed for the car.

AS IT TURNED OUT, Mrs. Reynolds had given an excellent shopping recommendation. Located just a couple of miles away, the store had everything Harry needed. He filled his cart with groceries, sheets and towels, and a few shirts and trousers that he hoped would fit John. When he passed an aisle with books and magazines, Harry impulsively grabbed a few paperbacks. Nothing about monsters, though.

He had to swing by the new house to drop everything off, and by the time he pulled into the parking lot at the Totem Pole, he felt exhausted. He knew he should be thinking about ways to meet Swan but couldn't concentrate on anything except wanting a long soak in the bathtub.

When he stepped inside the room, John looked solemnly at him from the bed. *Frankenstein* lay on the mattress beside him. "That is what I am?" John asked in a tiny voice.

Harry couldn't face him now. Just couldn't. Without saying anything, he marched into the bathroom and slammed the door.

The house in Missouri had only a single bathroom, which the whole family shared. When he was little, he and his brothers used to bathe together, and the huge clawfoot had been plenty big enough for all of them. The motel tub was much smaller, but at least he had it to himself. He filled it as deep as possible with the hottest water he could stand. Then he leaned his head back against the porcelain, closed his eyes, and tried to think of nothing at all.

Wrinkled, warm, and pleasantly melty-feeling, he eventually emerged from the bathroom with a towel wrapped around his waist. Although Harry had been in the tub forever, it looked as if John hadn't moved a muscle. Harry gave him a weary smile and dug through his suitcase for something to wear to bed.

"It's not my name," John whispered.

Harry looked over at him. "What?"

"I call myself John, but it's not my name. I don't have a name."

"If that's what you call yourself, I reckon you *do* have a name, and it's John."

But John shook his head and pointed at the book. "He—*it*—was nameless."

"Yeah, maybe, but that's just a story. You're real. If you want to be John, fine with me."

John seemed to relax a little, and Harry grabbed underwear and a T-shirt. He almost removed the towel right there, but John kept staring at him, and that was... uncomfortable. So Harry returned to the bathroom long enough to dress and brush his teeth, and after he came back to the main room, he climbed into bed and switched off the light.

He hoped that would signal John to go to sleep, but no such luck. Even though Harry couldn't see him—couldn't hear him either, since John seemed to breathe only when he spoke—Harry could sense John's alert presence. He sighed. "Found us a nice place to stay. We'll move in tomorrow morning. There's a big park only a block away, so we can go there if you get strong enough." He hadn't meant to add that last part; it just slipped out.

John's response sounded wistful. "A park. With trees and grass?"

"I guess."

"I'd like to see that. Please." A long silence. "Harry?"

"Yeah?"

"You knew from the start that I'm a monster."

"Yeah. Townsend told me."

"You haven't treated me like one."

Harry had to think that over. "I don't know how a monster's supposed to be treated. You're the only one I ever met. I mean, in the movies the good guys are supposed to kill 'em, but Townsend said you ain't dangerous."

"What if I am? What if I get strong and…. Frankenstein's monster killed everyone he loved."

"I don't love nobody, so no problem there. Anyway, you don't seem like you want to go around killing folks. Do you?"

"No."

"Okay then. We're settled." Harry rearranged the pillow beneath his head and pulled the blankets up higher. Portland was colder than LA.

He was almost asleep when John whispered once more. "Thank you, Harry."

CHAPTER 8

*H*ARRY HAD unsettling dreams, but that was nothing new. At least nobody came to complain that he'd been shouting in his sleep. And when he saw that John had again filled out overnight, his cheeks losing some gauntness and his yellow hair less sparse, Harry wasn't even surprised.

"You figure if I helped, you could walk to the car? It's just a few steps from the door."

John smiled broadly. "I can try."

As it turned out, Harry had to bear most of John's weight, but at least John remained upright, his bare feet moving slowly over carpet and then pavement. No way was Harry going to stuff him into the trunk again. They had only a short drive, and if anyone saw John in the passenger seat, they'd probably assume he was a sick man. He no longer resembled a corpse.

John was surprised and delighted to ride up front. "I can look out the windows?" he asked when Harry got into the car. As if it was a big deal. As if it required permission.

"Sure."

John remained silent during the trip, his gaze tracking their surroundings. By the time they arrived at the house, he looked stunned. "There's so much to see, Harry! I don't... I don't even have names for half of it."

To Harry, the scenery had been ordinary. Cars. Houses. Shops. Bushes. Some pedestrians splashing down wet sidewalks.

The journey from car to front door was longer at the house than at the motel, and Harry had to nearly carry John up the three steps to the porch. But they made it inside okay. Harry left John on the living room couch while he went out to fetch his suitcase. He returned to find John smiling as he stroked the salmon-colored fabric.

"Meets with your approval?" Harry asked.

"This is what a home looks like. I knew the word but I didn't... I didn't understand."

"It's just a few rented rooms." But Harry had an inkling of what John meant. Even though Harry had just arrived and knew he wouldn't stay for long, this little place felt as if it fit him. None of the boarding houses in LA had felt like that. Hell, neither had the house he grew up in.

"Look, I gotta do some things today. But hang on." He hurried into the bedroom, returning a moment later with one of John's new outfits and the book Harry had bought the day before. He set them on the couch beside John. "Those are yours."

John's eyes widened. "Mine?"

"Yeah. My clothes don't fit you. And I thought you might get bored while I'm out, so...."

"I've never owned anything."

Harry shifted uncomfortably. "Now you do."

"I can't express.... Thank you."

Were those tears glittering in John's eyes? Surely not. Monsters couldn't cry.

"You can stay on the couch if you want, or there's a bed in the other room. Can you make it there all right if I ain't here? You can lean on the walls." Harry hadn't given much thought to their sleeping arrangements, actually, but there was no reason why John should stick to the couch when Harry wasn't home.

"I think so," John said.

"Fine. If anyone comes to the door, don't answer. Pretend nobody's home. But if the landlady comes by—she shouldn't, but I guess you never know—I told her you're my cousin. I'm taking care of you while you're sick."

John reached up to gently stroke his own face. "She won't be able to tell what I am?"

"Not unless she looks real close. You're, um, looking more human, you know?"

"But I'm *not* human."

Harry shrugged.

IT WOULD HAVE BEEN nice if Harry could have simply knocked on Swan's front door and asked him where he kept the reanimated corpses, but of course that wouldn't do. Townsend and the other Bureau agents had coached him thoroughly. *Take a restrained approach,* they said. *Get him interested in you first, then pull the details from him.* Harry had been skeptical about this plan. For one thing, subtlety wasn't exactly his strongpoint; he didn't have the smarts for it. And for another, Swan was going to have to swallow some big assumptions. But in the end, the agents had eroded Harry's protests. They were the professionals. They knew better than some dumb kid from Missouri.

So today Harry began the roundabout plan by getting a better feel for the city. He parked his car downtown and spent hours tromping around in the light rain, stopping now and then to warm up with a cup of coffee. The Bureau had given him addresses of a few businesses that Swan frequented—a couple of theaters, some bars, a bathhouse— but they wouldn't open until evening. Harry strolled by them now, wanting to see the outsides and surroundings in the daylight.

When Harry had received the list, he'd been surprised that a city as small as Portland had so many businesses catering to queers and that they seemed to operate more openly than similar establishments in LA. Townsend had explained that Portland officials took a more guarded approach to homosexuals, preferring to have them out in the open rather than hiding from constant raids. Besides, Portland had long been a city where men—loggers, sailors, soldiers—came in search of a little company, and the town fathers must have figured there was good money to be made off of those lonely men.

What would it be like to live in a city where a guy could show his affection for other men openly—at least in carefully selected venues? Maybe if Harry had grown up in a place like that, he wouldn't have needed to flee. But queerness wasn't the only demon haunting him, so maybe he'd have run anyway.

And haunting was a good word. Wandering the streets of this gray city, Harry felt like a ghost. Nobody knew him. Nobody spoke to him or spared him a glance. When it came down to it, the only people in the whole damned state who knew Harry existed were Mrs. Reynolds and the dead man waiting for him at home. Wasn't that a gas.

Only when Harry's rambles took him to skid row did he feel any kinship to the people he saw. Here men and a few women, each layered in dirty clothes, huddled in doorways or came reeling out of taverns, drunk even though it wasn't yet dinnertime. The rooming houses looked familiar too. Crumbling buildings where you could rent a cramped, dirty room for a night or two. Maybe you'd consider yourself lucky to at least have a roof over your head.

Not long before the sun set, Harry returned home. John was on the couch, wearing the clothes Harry had bought him, and he greeted Harry with a sunny smile. "The books are wonderful. Thank you."

Before John, nobody had ever expressed gratitude to Harry. Nobody had ever seemed happy to see him. Harry didn't know what to do with the warm feelings that resulted, so he scowled and dropped a newspaper onto the couch. "Picked this up today. Guess you can read it too." Then he went to the kitchen to make himself some dinner.

He couldn't even remember the last time he'd fixed a meal, and now he found it comforting to putter around the kitchen, searching for the right utensils, chopping carrots and potatoes, cutting up and seasoning a chicken. As a child, the only time he ate chicken was when one of his mother's hens grew too old to lay. Even stewed for hours, those birds remained tough. But this grocery store chicken looked young and tender. Harry slid the roasting pan into the oven, licking his lips in anticipation of the impending feast.

While dinner cooked, he sat on a hard kitchen chair, sipping Nescafé and watching raindrops course down the window.

His chicken dinner was delicious—even better than he'd expected. But it felt odd to sit and eat alone, knowing John sat in the next room by himself.

After putting the leftovers into the refrigerator, Harry washed the dishes and put them away. Another nice, homey task, although slightly jarring to do by himself. Back in Missouri, washing up was the kids' group task, which sometimes devolved into battles with soap-suds and towels if his father wasn't around.

In the bedroom, Harry changed into his flashy new suit. He'd never owned anything so nice or so expensive, and he spent some time admiring his reflection in the mirror. If a stranger saw him dressed like this, he'd assume Harry was a successful young man. One with a high school degree and maybe even some college, with a steady job and lots of friends. It was a good disguise.

Before leaving, Harry stepped into the living room. John had moved to an armchair, where he sat in the darkness with a book in his lap.

"I might be home late," said Harry.

"All right."

Harry fidgeted just inside the doorway. "What'll you do while I'm gone?"

"What do you want me to do?"

"I don't care." Then Harry pictured him remaining unmoving for hours. With an unhappy huff, Harry marched across the room and switched on the lamp next to John's chair. "You can turn lights on and off, can't you?"

"If you permit it."

"I.... Shit. I don't care. Look, just don't leave the house and don't answer the door. Don't wreck anything. Don't be noisy. Other than that, do what you want."

Wide-eyed, John nodded at him. "Thank you."

Harry walked to the entryway, where he donned the nice coat and fedora he'd bought in LA. He should have been focused on finding Swan, but as he got in the car and drove away, his thoughts remained firmly on John. Could a creature like John feel boredom? Loneliness?

Maybe in the morning Harry would buy a little radio to keep at the house.

ACCORDING TO THE BUREAU, Swan often visited two downtown movie theaters. Each of them had a balcony where men met other men. Honestly, Harry was curious to see this, but those dark, cramped quarters were probably not the best place to look for his target. He'd try the bars instead.

The Harbor Club stood at the corner of First and Yamhill. Although a sign on the door proclaimed it off limits and out of bounds to armed forces personnel, the main floor didn't appear sordid. A long bar with stools ran most of the length of the room, and small tables dotted the tiled floor. The well-dressed men and women inside sipped cocktails and laughed easily. In the back corner near the stairway, a man played the piano. Nothing seemed unusual at first glance, although a closer look revealed that, for the most part, men sat with men, women with women. And many of them were just a *bit* too close. Here and there a man's arm lay draped over his companion's shoulders, or two women held hands.

Harry stepped up to the bar and caught the eye of a burly bartender.

"What'll it be, Mac?"

"Just a Coca-Cola, please." In response to the barman's lifted eyebrows, Harry shrugged. "I'm on the wagon." It was an excuse he'd used before, and it wasn't exactly a lie—if you ignored the fact that he'd never been *off* the wagon. In any case, it seemed good enough now. The bartender poured the bottle into a glass and handed it to Harry, who gave him a dime and told him to keep the change.

Glass in hand, Harry prowled the floor. The agents at the Bureau had shown him several photos of Swan, but none of the men at the Harbor Club resembled him. They didn't mind Harry's close scrutiny, though, and many of them eyed him back. Several smiled, and a few even beckoned, but Harry continued his slow circling.

He noticed a few customers—all of them men—going up and down the back stairs, some alone and others in pairs. Heart beating fast, Harry climbed.

There were few lights in the mezzanine, and cigarette smoke collected there, turning the dark air murky. Sounds rose from the corners and edges: moans, skin moving against fabric and skin, soft laughter. Many of the couples were too engrossed in what they were doing to notice Harry as he strolled by, but some of the men looked at him hungrily, their expressions propositioning and challenging. One or two even called to him.

He'd seen similar scenes at Westlake Park, but the activity there hadn't been as concentrated or the scents—booze, smoke, sweat, the musk of male sex—so evident. Harry moved through the mezzanine as if in a dream, his head swimming and his cock hard. Nobody he saw resembled Swan.

When he descended to the main floor, another circuit proved fruitless. He left his half-full glass on a table and hurried out the door, then stood at the corner and gulped the cold, clean air. Maybe Townsend was right; maybe Harry wasn't cut out to be an agent. He couldn't even keep himself together during a simple walk through a cocktail lounge.

The next place on his list was Kokich's Tavern up on Ninth, several blocks away. Instead of driving, he walked and was glad for it; the exercise helped refresh him. This bar turned out to be smaller than the Harbor Club and less upscale. Only men here, and they drank beer and shots instead of cocktails. They looked as if they spent their days hauling goods or building houses. Here the interactions were more subdued—just men talking quietly to each other across a table or on adjacent stools. There was no mezzanine, and although some of the men may have fucked in the bathroom, they were discreet about it.

Swan wasn't at Kokich's either.

The third stop lay a few blocks north, near Twelfth and Stark, in the lobby of the Willamette Hotel. The hotel had probably once been grand but now looked past its prime, with faded wallpaper and dusty chandeliers. The bar was nice, though. Dark wood and well-polished brass, the colorful carpet only a little threadbare, the bartender and waiters in tuxedos. Again, all the customers were male, but they were better-dressed than Kokich's patrons. Older on the average too. They smoked and drank and spoke in subdued tones.

Harry spied Swan almost at once. He sat at the bar, his coat and hat on the stool beside him. He wore a gray pinstriped suit with a white shirt and a gray-and-blue patterned tie. His light brown hair, slicked carefully into place, showed gray near the temples, and his thin face with high cheekbones was more handsome than the photos had implied. Swan rested his right elbow on the bar, a cigarette held between two fingers. His gaze caught Harry's, and Swan didn't look away.

Although Harry felt terribly awkward, he feigned casualness as he crossed the room. He even put an extra touch of swagger in his stride. *The best way to catch a perp is to make him want to catch you.* That advice was from one of the Bureau's agents, and Harry kept it in mind, imagining himself as desirable and hoping it showed through. He was like a male version of Lana Turner or Rita Hayworth, he told himself—sexy, a little dangerous. Irresistible.

Maybe the self-coaching worked, because Swan wasn't the only guy who kept his eyes on Harry.

After reaching the far end of the room, Harry hung his coat and hat on a rack and sat in a red upholstered chair at a nearby table. A waiter took his order for a club soda—Harry was tired of Coke—and brought the drink promptly. Harry nursed it, wishing he smoked, furrowing his brow as if he were solving all the world's problems.

When he glanced up, a smiling Swan stood beside the table holding two glasses of amber liquid.

Damn. As easy as that. *But only the first step,* Harry warned himself.

"May I join you?" Swan's voice was deeper than his slender frame suggested.

Harry shrugged. "Suit yourself."

"Thank you." Swan set the glasses on the table. Although he moved with delicacy and grace, his handshake was as firm as a teamster's. "Arthur Swan."

"I'm Harry Lowe." Townsend told him to use his real name. No real reason not to, and it was easier than remembering an alias.

"Delighted." Swan sat opposite him and pushed one of the glasses closer to Harry. "Please allow me to buy you a drink."

Harry wanted to tell him that he never drank. But if Harry refused, Swan might reject him, in which case Harry had no idea how to make the next move. So he nodded his thanks, clinked glasses with Swan in a silent toast, and took a sip.

"You're not a fan of bourbon?" Swan sounded amused rather than annoyed.

"I just ain't...." Harry winced. "I'm not used to it. I'm from a dry county." He was pleased with himself for manufacturing that lie on the spot.

"Then allow me to get you something that will go down more easily." Before Harry could protest, Swan was on his way to the bar, where he had a conversation with the bartender. Swan returned several minutes later with a stemmed glass containing a darker liquid topped by a lighter one.

"What's this?" The contents of the warm glass smelled like coffee.

"Just try it. Drink it right through the layer of cream."

Harry did, and... it wasn't bad. It tasted of coffee, sweet but with an underlying kick he assumed was the liquor. His second swallow was more confident.

Swan leaned back in his chair. "Ah. I see I've found the right note for you, Mr. Lowe. Or may I call you Harry?"

"Harry's fine."

Smiling, Swan finished his own bourbon, reached for Harry's rejected glass, and took a healthy slug. "So tell me, Harry. Where is this dry county from which you originate, and what brings you to the City of Roses?"

This line of questioning felt comfortable; Harry had practiced it with the agents. "I'm from Missouri."

"The Show-Me State." For some reason Swan seemed amused by this. "Excellent."

"I suppose. But I've been in California for a little while. Los Angeles."

"Let me guess. You migrated in hopes of obtaining employment in the motion picture business."

"Yeah. How'd you know?"

"With a beautiful face such as yours, it seems a natural choice." Swan tilted his head, reminding Harry of the hawks that perched on power lines at home, scanning the fields for prey. "You were not as successful as you'd hoped?"

"My goals changed. I... met someone."

"Ah. What sort of someone?"

Harry took a large swallow before answering. "A man. He and I were... like-minded, right? He had some money. He hired me as his personal assistant."

Swan was rubbing the heels of his hands together. He leaned forward. "How personal, Harry?"

"*Real* personal."

"I see."

While Swan regarded him, Harry finished his drink. The liquor still burned, but less so by now. When the glass was empty, Swan turned slightly and signaled to the bartender, then resumed staring at Harry. "You've answered only part of my question. How did you get from sunny California to the sodden Northwest?"

"The man, my... employer? He died. Car wreck." Harry bit his lip and let his head droop. His version of sorrow must have looked authentic, because Swan reached across the table to lay his hand over Harry's. An onlooker might have interpreted it as a sympathetic gesture, but it felt possessive. And Swan's hand was cold.

When the waiter appeared a moment later with another drink for Harry, he didn't show any surprise that they were touching. Harry immediately took a long sip, burning his tongue in the process, but he didn't pull his hand from Swan's grip.

"What happened after your mentor passed away?" Swan finally asked.

"He left me a little money. Not a lot—I guess his family got most of it—but some. Plus his most precious possession." Harry cut his eyes to the side slyly, as if he had a delicious secret, and then he forced a grin. "I decided to come up here for a fresh start. Too many memories in LA. Now I'm settling in a little. Hoping to get to know some people." He downed all the rest of his drink in one burning draught.

Swan squeezed Harry's hand and finally let go. "Well, look. You've succeeded at that already, haven't you? We're getting to know each other quite nicely."

"I don't know anything about you."

"Oh, there's not much to know. I was born and raised here. I attended college back East of course—Yale—but returned to my hometown. Portland is not a cosmopolitan city, but it has its charms. Now that you're here, it has one more."

Lana Turner, Harry reminded himself. He tried for the type of mysterious smile she'd have when pursued by a handsome older man. "What do you do for a living, Mr. Swan?"

"Please, it's Arthur. I have investments. But I like to fancy myself a scientist and inventor."

Harry widened his eyes and bent closer. "Really? Mr. Lord—my boss—he did that too."

"What sort of work did he pursue?"

"Um… biology?" He twitched as if he were nervous—which didn't take much acting, really. "I'm not supposed to talk about it. How about if you tell me about Portland instead?"

Although Swan looked slightly peeved, that expression fled quickly, replaced by a smooth smile. "I'd be delighted. But you need another drink first."

After that, Swan went on at length about restaurants and mountains, about the coast, about the best places to shop and his favorite theaters. Harry did a lot of smiling and nodding, but the words flowed meaninglessly over him, especially after he began his fourth drink. Irish coffee. That's what Swan said they were called.

"I gotta piss," Harry said suddenly, interrupting a monologue about Swan's travels in New York City. He stood on shaky legs, looked around blearily, and spied the sign for the gents. He managed to make it all the way without tripping, which he considered quite an accomplishment.

But after he'd zipped up his fly and as he held his hands under the faucet, the bathroom door opened and Swan sailed in. In this light, brighter than the bar, his pallor seemed as profound as John's and his brown eyes less human. He waited for Harry to dry his hands. Then Swan maneuvered Harry's back against the door and pressed against him, pinning him in place. Swan captured Harry's head between his hands and leaned down for a fierce kiss.

Harry had fucked other men, but he'd rarely kissed them; he'd never much wanted to. He didn't want to kiss Swan either, but the alcohol messed with his head and made him weak, so he didn't resist. Besides, wasn't it his goal to get close to this man?

Swan pulled away at last, then traced a thumb across Harry's lower lip. "Delicious."

"I... I...."

"No, no need to be alarmed. I only wanted a taste. For tonight, at any rate. I find that a meal is all the more savored when one must wait for it. But I couldn't help but sneak a bit of an appetizer."

"I ain't your dinner."

Swan stroked him again. "Of course not." He took a step backward and straightened his jacket and cuffs. "In fact, I propose we meet tomorrow evening for a shared repast. Have you been to Huber's yet?"

"No."

"I'll meet you there at seven." One last touch, this time to Harry's cheek, and Swan left.

Harry stayed in the bathroom for some time. He leaned against a wall and then, gathering himself enough to move, splashed cold water on his face. When he emerged into the bar, he saw no sign of Swan. But the man must have paid the bill before he left, because the waiter and bartender ignored Harry as he put on his coat and hat and then, weaving a little, left the Willamette Hotel.

During the walk back to his car—made longer by a couple of wrong turns—Harry had time to think. He should have been pleased with the evening's events. After all, he'd found his fish and hooked him with ease. But instead of happy, Harry felt dirty. As if he needed another long bath. As if some kind of corruption had taken hold the minute he'd agreed to Townsend's plan.

So he thought about booze instead, the way it heated his stomach and made his brain feel wrapped in layers of cotton batting. The way it made the world seem far away, as if Harry were one of the clouds floating through the night sky. The disconnection from reality didn't frighten him tonight; if anything, it was a comfort.

He found his car and, with great concentration, managed to steer it over the bridge to the east side of town. Before he reached his duplex, though, he spied a little grocery that was still open. He parked crookedly near the curb. At the pay phone outside, he made a quick call to the number Townsend had given and left a message with a woman, saying he'd found Swan. Inside he discovered that hard liquor was sold only in state-run shops and that none stayed open late. But since grocers could sell beer and wine, Harry bought a six-pack of beer called Henry Weinhard's. Then he got back into his car and drove home.

CHAPTER 9

*J*OHN SAVORED every page of the book, which told a story of soldiers stationed in Hawaii as a war with the Japanese began. He didn't know anything about such a war, so he couldn't tell whether the tale was true. And with *Frankenstein* as his only comparison, he couldn't tell whether this was a *good* book. But he enjoyed it very much because it was his and because he'd been granted the great luxury of reading it.

One luxury among many, of course. He also had comfortable surroundings, nice clothing over a clean body, and the joy of seeing a great many wonders he'd only imagined. And he had Harry, who'd never once hurt him or made him feel like anything less than a man.

Ah, but John was *not* a man. When he finished the book and sat in the comforting puddle of lamplight, he again faced some painful truths and their corresponding questions.

What use did Harry intend to make of him? What would happen to John once Harry was done? Those were the practical questions. But more fundamentally, he wondered what it meant to be a monster. When he wore clothes, read books, conducted conversations, was he only fooling himself? Did he actually possess human qualities? What if he, like Frankenstein's monster, turned murderous in the end?

And what did he *want*? What driving force kept him animate in a lifeless body? He thought he might know the answers to those questions, but the answers were far too uncomfortable to face. Perhaps that made him a coward.

Lost in contemplation, he startled when the front door opened. A moment later, Harry came stumbling into the room with his coat poorly buttoned, his hat askew, and a carrier with six brown bottles grasped in one hand. His cheeks looked ruddier than usual; his eyes, usually soft and warm, appeared dull and flat. "You're still here," he said.

"You told me to stay."

"Yeah."

Harry left the room for a few minutes, although John could hear him rummaging in kitchen drawers. When he returned, he'd shed the coat and hat, and he held one of the brown bottles. He collapsed heavily onto the couch before taking a long draw. "Blah," he said, face twisted in disgust. "The Irish coffee was better." But he drank more anyway.

After some time passed, Harry sighed. "What'd you do tonight?"

"I read one of the books you gave me. Harry, was there really a war with the Japanese?"

"Yeah. Germans too. My Uncle Jimmy died in it."

"I'm sorry."

"Yeah. I liked him." He sniffed. "You don't remember that war?"

"I know of... the Great War. That was against the Germans, I think."

"That was over forty years ago. World War Two ended eight years ago. Now we're fighting in Korea instead."

John shook his head in confusion. There was so much he didn't understand. During the silence, Harry drained his bottle. He left the room and returned to the couch with a full one.

"I'll prob'ly be sick in the morning," he said thoughtfully. "I used to think the word *hangover* was kind of scary. Made me think of a corpse hanging from a noose." He glanced quickly at John and then away.

"Is there anything I can do to help you?"

"No."

Maybe if John were a real person, he'd know what to do. He understood that something distressed Harry but had no idea what, or what actions he should take. It was possible that John himself was the cause of Harry's misery. Surely it was repugnant to spend time so close to a monster. John worried about Harry—and worried about himself as well. Harry had brought him so much freedom and happiness. What would become of John if Harry abandoned him?

Harry held his half-empty bottle aloft, peering into the liquid depths. "Do you s'pose there's demons in there?"

"Demons?"

"Townsend said that one demon keeps his ex-agent from going wild, so I guess maybe some demons ain't so bad. Unless Townsend lied."

Unable to make sense of this, John simply listened.

After taking another swig, Harry wedged the bottle between his thighs and stared down at it. "Mama used to tell us that Daddy was a good man. She said the Devil got into him during the Depression, when Daddy lost his job at the feed store and we were poor as dirt. When he— Those things he did, those weren't really him, she told us. They were the Devil's work. If we all prayed real hard, Jesus would chase the Devil away." He looked at John. "We went to church every Sunday and said our prayers every night. But Jesus never did nothing."

Those things he did. John's otherwise faulty mind easily supplied him with possibilities about what those things might have been. His memories, it seemed, included a catalogue of cruel actions a man might visit upon his family.

"I never drank before tonight," Harry said. "I didn't want to swallow the Devil. But maybe now I have."

John moved the Hawaii book from his lap to the little table beside him and slowly pushed himself to his feet. His legs felt unsteady, and although it required tremendous effort to walk the few steps to the couch, he made it without falling. After kneeling on the floor near Harry's legs, John looked steadily into his eyes. "I don't think there's anything evil about you."

Harry shook his head. "You don't know that. I'm.... Everyone's always said I'm worthless, but they ain't exactly right. I could do a whole lot of bad if I wanted to. Maybe if I keep drinking, I'll want to."

"Then don't drink."

Anger flashed across Harry's face, and John braced himself for a punch. But then Harry sighed and rubbed his own chin. "I lied to you."

"About what?"

"You asked me if you were good... before. And I said yeah."

"I wasn't?" John was grateful he had the strength to keep his voice steady.

"I don't know. I have no idea who the hell you were before you... before you died. You coulda been a mobster for all I know. A murderer. Maybe you deserve everything they done to you."

Although John swayed on his knees, he didn't fall. And he didn't pull his gaze away from Harry. "Maybe I do," he whispered. "But I doubt you deserve whatever your father did to you."

Harry paled and blinked his eyes rapidly. Then, moving slowly like a very old man, he stood. "Going to bed," he muttered. He shuffled away, the bottle still in his hand.

"Why the hell did you sleep on the floor?"

John tried to scramble away from the angry voice but was trapped against the couch. He curled into a ball instead. When no blows fell, he hazarded a peek; Harry was crouched next to him with a furrowed brow.

"I'm not going to hurt you," Harry said quietly. "And I can barely move without puking."

"Oh. I'm sorry."

"My own damn fault, isn't it? But why did you sleep on the floor? Couldn't have been real comfortable."

"It's better than the cell," John said, patting the rug.

"Yeah, okay, but wouldn't the couch be better yet? Or the bed?"

"You didn't tell me where to sleep."

With a low groan, Harry collapsed onto his ass. "I'm no good at this. I can barely take care of myself, let alone anyone else."

John uncurled and sat with his back to the couch. Despite sleeping on a hard surface, he felt better than the previous day. Stronger. More substantial. "Maybe I should ask questions when I'm unsure what you want of me."

"That is a capital idea. I'm not smart, John. I'm not gonna figure things out on my own." With another groan, louder this time, Harry got to his feet. "I need coffee. Maybe some toast." Mumbling to himself, he shambled from the room.

While John sat on the couch, reading the previous day's newspaper, Harry rattled around the kitchen, then spent some time in the bathroom taking a shower. *This sounds like home*, John thought, although he had no way of knowing the truth of that. He wondered if he'd lived like this before—when he *did* live. Perhaps he used to sit with the paper during a quiet morning, catching up on news and sports, maybe exchanging conversation with whoever was in the next room eating breakfast and washing dishes.

Had he once loved someone? And God, had someone loved him?

John sat by the front window and peered out through the lace curtains. Their street was a quiet one. Cars drove by occasionally, all of them strangely shaped to his eyes. A stout woman emerged from the house across the street and stood on her wide front porch to beat a small rug with a broom. A younger woman walked up the sidewalk pushing a baby carriage, a little girl skipping beside her. A mailman with a heavy-looking bag marched by but didn't stop at their house. The door to the attached unit shut loudly enough for John to hear; a handsome blond man emerged, got into a car, and drove away.

Such ordinary people doing ordinary things. What would they think if they knew a monster was watching them? What would they do?

He felt extraordinarily fortunate to be granted this glimpse of their lives.

When Harry eventually returned to the living room, his greenish pallor had been replaced by his usual healthy skin tone, and he had a pillow crease on his cheek. "Let me see your feet."

An odd request, but John held them up obediently and watched as Harry measured one of his own stocking feet against John's bare one. "All right. Yours are just a little bigger." Then Harry sat in an armchair to put on his shoes. "I'm going to run errands. Need anything?"

"I already have so much."

Harry looked surprised and then smiled. "Yeah. I should remember how good I have it too."

WITHIN TWO HOURS HARRY RETURNED, grinning, and set a large bag on the floor. "Be right back." He ducked outside and reentered the house with a box.

John watched with fascination as Harry unpacked a tabletop radio, a pair of black shoes, and several paperback books. Whistling cheerfully, he set the radio on a shelf, plugged it in, and spent a few minutes fiddling with the dial He smiled broadly when he found a station with a male singer. "Sinatra. He'll do." He winked at John. "I've never blown this much dough in such a short period of time. It's fun. Do you know this song?"

"No. I think I was in that cell for a long time, Harry." The newspaper had led him to that conclusion; very little felt familiar.

"Yeah. I forgot. Well, maybe you'll like Sinatra. He's good. But if you hate him, you can turn the station, okay? Anytime."

"Thank you for letting me know."

Harry barked a laugh. "I'm trying to remember to tell you things. Okay, but look what else I brought."

It looked as though he'd chosen the books with John in mind. Most of them were novels of various genres, but one was a factual discussion of World War Two and another was a volume of poetry. John reverently touched the covers.

The bag also contained several pairs of socks. "Put 'em on," Harry said. "And shoes. We can try that walk we were talking about."

A walk outside. John's hands shook so badly he couldn't follow

Harry's directions, but Harry didn't seem put out at having to help. Then Harry handed him the blue jacket he'd been wearing the first time John saw him. "It's a little damp out. I forgot to get you a hat. Sorry."

"I don't think I can catch a cold," John said, smiling to share the joke.

Harry helped him down the front steps, and then they walked slowly. Partly because John was still weak and unsteady, but also because he wanted a close look at everything they passed. The iron rings set into the edge of the sidewalk from when horses had been tied up on the street. The row of red-leafed trees dripping slowly. The slightly wavy glass in the apartment building's windows. A rosebush bare of all but thorns and a few ragged leaves.

If Harry minded the snail's pace, he didn't show it. He strolled along with hands in his coat pockets, whistling the tune from the radio.

The park was just around the corner, which was fortunate because John wouldn't have made it much longer. He collapsed onto the first bench, where he could gaze up at the branches of towering evergreens and the gray sky above them or look down a gentle slope to a playground where the swings sat idle. A few birds flitted and strutted about.

"That's grass," John said reverently. "I used to imagine it, but it's better in person."

Harry looked at him closely and then hopped to his feet. He scurried around, collecting small items: some needles from an evergreen tree, a twig he found on the ground, a bit of mossy bark, several blades of grass. He brought them over and set them on the bench beside John. "You can touch them. Smell them. You can smell, right?"

"Yes." The pine needles poked at his skin and had a sharp, slightly bitter odor. The moss was exquisitely soft and spongy. The twig smelled of the earth on which it had rested. And the grass was fresh and sweet. It tickled his palm and made him laugh.

"*Thank* you," he said, hoping the depths of his gratitude showed. "This is so precious to me. It's a grand gift."

"I'm glad I can do it." Harry looked solemn. "I don't think we'll have long together."

John fought to quell the sadness that wanted to rise inside him. *Don't be greedy*, he reminded himself.

"Then I'll treasure this all the more."

HARRY WAS QUIET THAT AFTERNOON. He seemed content to sit in the living room with John, listening to the radio while John read some very strange stories by an author named Asimov. But Harry grew more restless as evening fell. Eventually he disappeared into the bedroom, and when he came out, he wore a suit and tie and looked unhappy.

"I might be back late," he said. "If you get tired, go to sleep anywhere you want."

"All right."

John wanted to ask about Harry's plans but held his tongue. Through the window, he watched Harry walk to his car and drive away.

CHAPTER 10

*H*UBER'S, SWAN claimed, was one of the oldest restaurants in Portland. Harry didn't know or care if that was true, but it was certainly a beautiful place. The high arched ceilings had stained-glass skylights, the bar and walls gleamed in rich dark mahogany, and the tile floor, although well worn, still showed its pattern. Harry wondered if anyone else in his hometown had ever eaten in such a fancy place.

He ordered a turkey dinner, which was the house specialty. Since he still had the ghost of a headache, he intended to avoid booze. But Swan insisted, and Harry hoped the food in his stomach would help him remain sober. Swan ordered a bourbon for himself and something called Spanish coffee for Harry. The waiter served this with considerably more drama—flames and flashy pouring—than what had accompanied the previous night's Irish coffee.

"This place was a speakeasy during Prohibition," Swan said. "My father used to come here for meetings. He and his colleagues drank Manhattans from coffee cups and the police looked the other way."

"Cops were probably on the take."

"Perhaps. Even today, the Police Bureau chooses to ignore certain activities when doing so advances their own interests."

Harry shrugged. He figured that was the case just about every-where. He didn't know why this city seemed to tolerate queers so readily, but somebody probably profited from it—and the cops prof-ited from *that*.

"Tell me, Harry. What line of work were you hoping to pursue here?"

"I don't need a job right away. Like I said, Mr. Lord left me a little money. And, uh, something else maybe valuable." Harry didn't have to fake his discomfort at this last part; he didn't like discussing John as a commodity. And he was becoming increasingly unhappy about using John as bait. But that was the assignment, wasn't it? And without John, Harry might never get the goods on Swan, which meant Harry would fail. Again.

Swan nodded thoughtfully. "I see. But I assume you don't possess enough to sustain you indefinitely."

His mouth full of turkey, Harry shook his head.

"Perhaps I could assist," Swan said. He'd hardly eaten at all. "I have good contacts. What are your professional aspirations and experi-ences? Aside from films, of course. I'm afraid I can't help you there." He smiled like a crocodile, all sharp white teeth.

Harry wiped his lips with a napkin. "Look, Arthur. You see me. I'm just a hick from a whistle-stop town. I've shucked corn, pulled weeds, hauled hay and manure. I don't reckon that's useful to any of your contacts."

"Not terribly, no. But you had quite a different occupation with your deceased mentor, yes? Personal assistant, you said."

"Yeah."

Harry let that affirmation sit there, blunt and heavy, and Swan didn't reply. He did, however, angle his body subtly in Harry's direc-tion. Harry just continued eating.

The longer Swan stared at him, the dirtier Harry felt. It didn't help that after the Bureau had rejected him, when his hopes and cash had begun to wane, Harry had considered an arrangement similar to what he'd been hinting at with Swan. Find a rich older man—LA was full of them—and persuade the guy to take Harry on. As a gardener, maybe, or driver. Something that gave the man an excuse to keep Harry real close without anyone making a big deal of it. And if Harry's services extended from the flowerbeds or limo to the bedroom, well, that was better than living on the streets. Wasn't it?

If Harry had stumbled onto such a wealthy man, he might very well have swallowed his pride. Hell, he'd already had trouble looking at himself in the mirror anyway.

Swan changed the subject, going on about renovations he'd recently had done to his kitchen, the new car he was considering buying, and his excitement about television. Portland's first station was due to begin broadcasting soon. Harry nodded at the right spots, but it was clear that Swan didn't expect him to add anything.

After the plates were cleared and more drinks arrived, the predatory gleam returned to Swan's eyes. "Perhaps you and I might discuss potential employment opportunities for you. After we get to *know* each other a little better of course." Perhaps that emphasis on *know* was meant to assure that Harry caught his meaning.

"Told you. I'm not looking for a job right now."

"What *are* you looking for, Harry?"

Harry pretended to think this over carefully, choosing his words at length, even though he'd rehearsed this with the Bureau. "Can I be frank, Arthur?"

"I rather hope you will."

"All right." A heavy sigh. "I didn't exactly find you by accident. Least not if you're who I think."

"Whom do you think I am?"

Harry looked around as if checking for eavesdroppers, then leaned forward and lowered his voice. "Mr. Lord, he was an inventor and scientist. Those were his hobbies, I mean. His real job was a lawyer."

"Yes?"

"The particular things he was… studying…. Look, I don't know much about it. I'm no scientist, and he didn't tell me much. Secret, he said. But he gave me a couple of peeks, some hints, and that… that gift he left me. So I have a general idea what he was up to."

"Which was?" It was Swan's turn to lean forward. And now Harry felt every bit the predator—a fisherman slowly reeling in his catch.

"Can't tell you. Not now. But one night when he was drunk he said something interesting. Said that up in Portland, a fellow was doing work like his, studying the same thing."

Already pale, Swan's complexion whitened another shade. "Why would he think this?"

"Dunno, not exactly. But he was a lawyer, remember? He had access to all kinds of information. A couple of private dicks on his payroll too. He was good at finding things out."

Swan pursed his lips so tightly that it looked painful. A thousand different thoughts seemed to be flashing through his eyes as he kept his gaze on Harry's face. Oddly, Swan's discomfort relaxed Harry, maybe because making someone else feel ill at ease was rare for him. It was kind of powerful, really.

"This has all been a swindle of some kind?" Swan spat the words fiercely.

"No, I'm just being careful. I don't know if you're the right man. Mr. Lord didn't tell me the fellow's name. After he died, I had a look at some of the notes Mr. Lord took after he talked to his private dicks. They didn't give a name either, but they described him. Named some of the bars he goes to. You fit."

Townsend had been very clear about this—Harry couldn't let on that he'd known Swan's name from the start. *Too direct, my boy. This game needs more smoke and mirrors.* It hadn't made any sense to Harry, but then, he wasn't the Bureau's West Coast Chief.

"What do you want from me?" Swan demanded.

"That depends on whether you're the right fellow." Harry leaned back and crossed his arms.

"And if I am?"

"Then I have something you might be interested in buying from me. For the right price, I might be interested in selling."

"What do *you* have to offer that might interest *me*?" Pure contempt in the tone, but Harry was accustomed to that. What mattered was that the fish was nearly landed.

"Can't say. Not until I know you're who I'm looking for. If I spill the beans to the wrong people, I could end up in prison. And mister, I don't want to go to prison." He paused, allowing the hint of a smile to play at the corners of his mouth. "So tell me. You the right guy?"

"That's impossible to say since you've told me nothing about the specifics."

"Tell me what kind of science you're doing."

"I cannot divulge that information. I too wish to avoid legal entanglements. Which leaves us at an impasse."

Smoke and mirrors worked fine in the movies, but Harry was tiring of this—and he feared that fatigue would lead to mistakes. Never sharp even at his best, his wits grew duller when he was frustrated or weary. And he'd also had those drinks. He shook his head. "All I'm gonna tell you is one thing: Mr. Lord's research was going real well. That thing he left me? It's a successful experiment." *Sorry, John.* Harry hoped his chagrin was well hidden.

Swan's eyes widened and hectic blotches of color bloomed on his cheeks. He swallowed a full glass of bourbon in one go. "Do you mean to tell me you possess—" He stopped himself, but his jaw kept working.

"I'm not telling you anything until you prove you have the same hobby as Mr. Lord. Otherwise how do I know you're not a cop or running some kind of con?"

"I am neither."

Harry shrugged. "Look, if you don't want to play, fine. There's another fellow too, you know. In New Jersey. I came to you first because Portland's closer to LA, but if you're not interested, I'll head East."

Although Swan looked very much as if he wanted to hit someone —or at least down a lot more booze—his voice stayed even. "I believe I *am* the man you seek, and I'm willing to pay a great deal if you truly have... this object." He rubbed his forehead in thought. "All right. Tomorrow I have an unavoidable meeting in Seattle. I'll return home the following day. You come to my house that evening at eight and bring your inheritance. At the same time, I will show you my laboratory. We'll provide proof to each other concurrently. Acceptable?"

The fish was in the net. But Harry didn't exult over it, and his sensation of being dirty and corrupt had only increased. Harry had gotten himself into this mess and deserved whatever happened to him; but not John. As far as Harry could tell, John was innocent.

"Yeah. Okay."

Swan wrote his address on the back of a business card and slid it across the table. Harry took the card, stood up, and removed his coat and hat from the hook. "See you soon, Arthur."

Swan nodded and took another sip of his drink.

HARRY WALKED a few blocks and found a pay phone. This time when he called, Townsend himself picked up. "Yeah, kid?"

"He's real interested, but he doesn't want to tell me anything until he sees Jo—the proof. I'm going to his house the night after next. He says he'll show me his lab."

"Two nights from now? I thought he'd be more eager."

"He has to go to Seattle for something tomorrow."

Townsend made a *hmm* sound.

"Hey, Chief? He didn't come right out and confess, but he sure hinted at being up to something. Isn't that enough? Can't your guys crash his house and see the lab for themselves?"

"Has he confirmed that he's attempting to make creatures like the one we lent you? Because if he's simply digging up bodies with no intent to resurrect them, there's no federal jurisdiction. And I *don't* want to get into a pissing contest with the local authorities."

Harry sighed. "He hasn't confirmed anything."

"Then report back after you see his lab."

"Okay. Hey, Chief?"

"Yes?"

Harry wanted to tell him about John. The way his eyes lit up over small gifts. The look of wonder he'd had during a simple walk in the park. How he caught on to things really fast—reading a thick volume as if it was a comic book—but didn't make Harry feel stupid. How his smile was so sweet that the scars no longer mattered and he became beautiful.

Townsend wouldn't want to hear any of that.

"Nothing. Night, Chief."

CHAPTER 11

$\mathcal{G}$AZING PATIENTLY through the lace curtains on the front window, John saw Harry park in front of the house and get out of the car. But instead of coming inside, Harry spent a moment staring at the house before shuffling up the sidewalk in the direction of the park. John was sorely tempted to follow, but Harry had ordered him to stay put, and so he did.

It was over an hour before Harry returned, his trouser cuffs wet from the rain and his eyes troubled. He appeared to be sober, however, as he nodded at John and went into the bedroom, returning a few minutes later in jeans and a white T-shirt. John thought that a better look for him, more natural than a suit. The shadow of a beard had sprouted on Harry's chin and cheeks, and John found himself longing to stroke it.

With a sigh too heavy for such a young man, Harry collapsed onto an armchair. "You've been listening to the radio."

"I can turn it off if—"

"No, I'm glad you like it. That's why I bought it." He leaned his head back and closed his eyes.

"Harry? Can I help you with something? I'm much stronger than I was." John could stand for a long time now, and when he looked down at his arms, they were no longer skeletal. Although he was grateful for the vigor, it also made him restless and a bit uneasy.

Harry peeled his eyes open. "Yeah. You look...." He pressed his mouth closed and looked away.

"Do you have work for me to do? I can clean, I think. I'm not sure whether I can cook, but I suppose I can try."

"No. Just...." Harry's jaw worked and then he raised his chin. "I don't know how long you have here. Maybe just a couple of days. And after that... I don't know. So relax while you can. Read your books and listen to Nat King Cole." He gestured toward the radio.

It was good advice. If John was sent back to that cell—or worse—he'd need all the good memories he could collect. Treasures he could cherish when despair dug its talons into him. But maybe it would be worse than ever to lie naked, weak, and filthy in the darkness, knowing how much he had lost.

John gathered his courage. "Do you want me to go back to the cell?"

"No! Jesus, no."

"Then why send me there? Why can't we stay here? I'll be no trouble, I promise. Or we could go somewhere. Anywhere you like." He crossed the room and fell to his knees in front of Harry. "Please. I'll do anything you tell me to. I'll be your faithful servant—your slave. Don't send me away. Please, Harry." Something tickled his cheek, and when he brushed at it with his fingertips, they came away wet.

Harry shot out of his chair and rushed to the opposite side of the small room, then backed into the corner as if trapped. "Don't. Don't do this, John." He sounded close to tears.

"I have to. What other hope do I have but you? And I *do* hope. I feel. I...." He pressed his hands to his chest. "My heart doesn't beat, but it aches."

Harry fled past him and out the front door, not even pausing to grab his coat and hat.

John sank to the floor and hugged his knees against his chest.

. . .

HARRY RETURNED SOAKED AND SHIVERING, his T-shirt transparent and hair dripping. But he stood in the doorway to the living room for a long time, silent except for water droplets pattering on the floor.

John spoke first, his voice barely more than a whisper. "I'm sorry. You've given me so much already. I shouldn't have—"

"Don't." Harry rubbed his face. "I need to tell you things. Everything, I guess."

"Dry off first. I can wait."

"Yeah. Okay."

Harry returned quickly, wrapped in a blanket and with hair in disarray from a towel-rub. He sat in the armchair, tucking his bare feet and legs under his body. His face still looked cold-tinged, and he hadn't stopped shivering.

"Do you want something hot to drink?" John asked. "Or soup?"

"Stop being so fucking considerate!"

Still sitting on the floor, John shrank back against the couch and ducked his head.

When Harry spoke again, his tone was soft. "Sorry. But you need to stop being nice to me. I don't deserve it."

"I don't understand."

"Yeah. Look, there's things I have to tell you. About me, and about... what's going to happen. They're not nice things."

John raised his head to look at Harry. "I'm a monster. That's not nice at all."

"I don't even know what that word means anymore. People have called me a monster, or close to it. My own daddy used to say I was a worthless piece of garbage, and Mama said I was the Devil's work."

Although Harry's tone was matter-of-fact, the words wounded John. He'd thought parents were supposed to love their child. Yes, he'd learned that Harry's father was troubled, but to go so far with his own flesh and blood? "Why would they say that about you?"

"Lots of reasons. I ain't smart. I'm not good at much of anything. I never fit in with anyone, not even my own family." Harry let out a deep breath. "And I'm a queer. That's one of the things I had to tell you."

"Queer?"

"I fuck men. Or let them fuck me."

John had to process this. He understood the concepts but not the disgusted way Harry had said them. "Do you.... When you have sex, you don't force anyone? And they don't force you?"

"It's voluntary."

"Then why does it make you... those things your parents called you? Sex feels nice, doesn't it? It doesn't hurt anyone."

"Yeah, it feels good. But two men together ain't natural."

John surprised himself with a bitter laugh. "Bringing the dead back to life—that's unnatural. A perversion. If two people make each other feel good, I think that's a beautiful thing." He looked down at his feet. "But I guess I'm no judge of morality."

After a long pause, Harry rose from the chair. Still wrapped in his blanket, he sat next to John. "It doesn't bother you."

"No. Of course not."

"It bothers most folks."

John smiled at him. "I'm not most folks, am I?"

Harry's answering smile nearly broke John's heart. "I guess not. But that's not necessarily a bad thing." He scooted slightly closer until they were almost touching. John felt the warmth of him. "Everyone always called me brainless and clumsy. Daddy said I was a waste of good food. But they let me stick around at least. Until I was sixteen and Mama found a letter I wrote to Cary Grant."

"Who's that?"

"An actor." Harry snorted softly. "Real handsome. I saw him in a movie and wrote this stupid letter. I wasn't gonna mail it, of course, but I guess I had to get those feelings out somehow, even if nobody was supposed to read them. I hid the letter in this little box where I kept a few things. That box was the only thing that was really mine. But Mama found it a couple of months later and she showed Daddy."

"What happened?"

Harry hunched in on himself. "He... he was sick then, but still pretty strong."

Although Harry didn't elaborate, John could imagine the rest: a man's hands hard against a boy's young body. A child damaged by the man who was supposed to protect him.

"I'm sorry." John knew that sympathy from a monster was inadequate comfort, but it was all he had to offer.

Harry nodded twice. "I had to quit school, find whatever jobs I could get, sleep wherever I could afford a bed. The rest of them—Mama, my brothers and sisters—they wouldn't even talk to me at Daddy's funeral. Like I was a stranger to them. It took me a long time to save enough money to go to California, but I did, eventually."

"You're very strong."

Harry blinked at him. "No I ain't."

"Of course you are. You were left on your own at an age when you should have been nurtured. You were called foul things. But you survived and found a dream and pursued it."

"It was a stupid dream."

A heavy realization hit John: Harry, in his own way, was as alone in the world as John, and perhaps nearly as vulnerable. John had always thought that being human meant having love and connections to others. How heartrending that it wasn't so.

"I don't know if anyone has ever treated you with kindness, Harry. But you've been nothing but kind to me, a monster. You didn't have to. I suspect you weren't expected to do so. But you did. That proves how strong you are."

Judging from Harry's astonishment, he'd rarely been praised. "You're easy to be nice to," he whispered.

John traced fingertips over one of his scars, a thick raised one that circled his neck like a collar. It wasn't painful, but it felt ugly. He wished he were beautiful, or even just plain. For Harry's sake and for his own. An ache had spread from his heart throughout his body, filling him with a type of want he'd never experienced. Desire. Oh God, this was desire.

Would Harry be disgusted to know that John yearned to touch him? Perhaps. But John owed him an honesty in return for the one Harry had given him.

"If I were a man, I would very much want to... to make love with you."

Harry swallowed audibly. "Shit."

"I know what I am. I know I'm not—"

"Stop." Harry put a hand on John's knee. "You're going to say you're a monster again, and I wish you wouldn't. You need to hear the rest of what I have to tell you."

"All right."

"You say that like it's so easy. It ain't."

"Then take your time with it. I'm not going anywhere."

Harry nodded, his hand still heavy and warm on John's knee. John almost wished he were still terribly weak, unable to even sit unaided, because then Harry might hold him again. Might once more clean him with a soft wet cloth. Might even touch John's skin with his own.

After a long time—four different songs played on the radio, interspersed with advertisements for a car dealership and an appliance store—Harry shifted position. "The Bureau sent me here. You know what the Bureau is?"

"The cell."

"Yeah. They're the ones who killed the man who made you, and then they took you away, and.... Fuck, John. They *tortured* you."

John couldn't suppress a shudder. "I suppose they wanted to see what I am. How I'm made. You took me away from that place."

"But I can't keep you. Told you that from the start."

"You did."

After a quick squeeze of John's knee, Harry pulled his hand back under the blanket. "Here's the whole story. It's ugly."

"Like me," John said, attempting a joke.

But Harry didn't smile. "You're not ugly."

An odd thrill swirled through John, making his skin tingle. But he warned himself to concentrate—Harry was about to reveal John's purpose and his future.

"The Bureau thinks a guy here in Portland, named Swan, is trying to make... more like you."

"Why would he want that?"

"I don't know, John. Why do people want to do stupid things? Because we're fools. Anyway, it's illegal, and the Bureau wants to catch him. But they don't have enough of the goods on him yet, so they sent me here to see if I can get him to spill the beans." Harry went silent, perhaps giving John a chance to process that.

"You work for the Bureau?"

"No," Harry said bitterly. "I applied—that was my dream—and they turned me down. But then Townsend said he'd give me another chance. If I help them nail Swan, I get to be an agent."

"That's wonderful! You can fulfill your ambition."

Harry scowled. "Right. It's all peachy keen. Townsend gave you to me to use as bait, so I can convince Swan to admit what he's up to. I'm supposed to offer you to him. Some kinda goddamn prize for Swan so I get the evidence the Bureau needs." His hand reappeared, and he rubbed his palm down his mouth and chin. "Two days from now."

John's existence in the cell had been simple. Not better—definitely not that—but uncomplicated. He had his patch of sunlight, his fragments of knowledge unmoored from memory, the name he'd given himself. He had almost no choices to make, and his emotions were largely limited to misery and anguish. Now, though, his swirling feelings made him so dizzy that he was grateful to be sitting. How was it possible to feel so many things at once, many of them in direct conflict with others? Is this what it was like for real people, and if so, were they able to endure it more gracefully?

"Two days," was all John could say, although the timeframe was hardly the point.

Suddenly Harry twisted around and grasped John's shoulders, allowing the blanket to fall to his waist. "Go. Put your shoes on and just get the hell out of town. You can take the car."

"But... your plans."

"Townsend's plans, not mine, and he can fuck himself. I'll find a way to get what he wants out of Swan. I don't need to drag you into this."

John allowed himself a moment to seriously consider Harry's offer, but he found no promise in it. "Where would I go?"

"Anywhere. I'll…. They gave me some cash. It's yours. You're really smart. You'll manage."

"I don't know anything about the world, not really. I doubt there's a place in it for something like me. And what about you? The Bureau won't be happy you let their property get away. They won't give you a job."

Still holding John's shoulders, Harry made a frustrated growl. "I don't care! Townsend was probably lying anyway. Once this thing's over, I bet he planned to cut me loose. He doesn't really want me. Anyway…." Harry let go of John and moved back slightly. "I don't want the goddamn job if it means sending you back to those bastards."

Oh.

Something enormous inside John shifted. It *hurt*, yet he felt immeasurably more whole. More real.

"You care about me," John said softly.

Harry let out a long breath. "Yeah. Guess I do."

"That's…. I never hoped for anything so precious. Thank you. I wish I could express what a gift you've given me. Will you believe me when I tell you—even though I'm a monster—that I care for you as well? Does that offend you?"

"I believe you," said Harry, eyes shining.

Moving slowly so as not to spook him, John raised his arms and settled his hands on Harry's shoulders, a mirror of Harry's recent touch. The shoulders were bare, the lightly tanned skin warm, unscarred, and perfect. Harry didn't pull away from the contact, although his breathing grew a trifle rougher and a rosy flush spread from his cheeks down to his chest.

"If I run," John said, "the Bureau will hunt me down and find me, won't they?"

"I don't—"

"Please be honest."

"Y-yes. I think they will."

John nodded. "I won't spend my limited freedom as a fugitive. I'd prefer to spend it with you."

"Even if it's only two days?"

"Yes."

"I... I can ask Townsend.... Explain things. Tell him how you really are. Maybe he'll listen and let you go."

John had seen the way Townsend looked at him. No possibility of sympathy there. He lifted one hand and very gently stroked Harry's cheek. Rough bristles and soft skin. Harry leaned into the caress. "Perhaps when you are an agent, you can come visit me in my cell sometimes. I'd like that."

"John—"

"No. We can't change who we are or the circumstances under which we find ourselves. But perhaps we can find some happiness in what we do have. Happiness is such a valuable thing, John. We shouldn't waste it."

"Happiness," Harry echoed dreamily.

Then he leaned forward and touched his lips to John's.

John knew about kisses in the abstract, just as he'd once known about grass and the sky. But the reality was infinitely grander, a bouquet of sensory information that made John want to swoon. Harry smelled like rain and soap. His lips were a little dry, and he tasted of something rich, bitter, and sweet. Oh, and his mouth was wet and *hot*, tongue slick against John's, hands solid and strong as they cradled John's face.

When the kiss ended, they remained nose to nose. Harry was panting. "You like men too?" he asked with a grin.

John had no idea what his preferences might have been before he died, but those didn't matter anymore. He knew how he felt now. "I like you."

"Even though—"

"Yes. Just as you care for me, even though." In fact, John thought, their respective shortcomings made their feelings exquisite. It was probably easy to fall for someone who was flawless, but to ache for someone who was not... didn't that mean the emotion was more genuine?

"It's really hard for me to think clearly when you're so close,"

Harry said, "and I'm not all that good at thinking under the best of circumstances. I'm going for a walk."

Harry made as if to stand, but John stopped him with a hand on his shoulder. "You've already been soaked once tonight. Stay here. I'll…. If it's all right with you, I'd like a bath."

"Yeah, sure."

John rose to his feet, no longer experiencing any weakness. Whereas two days earlier he could barely walk, now he felt as if he could run for miles. He smiled down at Harry and then made his way to the bathroom.

It took a few moments for John to work out how to run the water. He wasn't dirty, but he thought this might give Harry the space he needed. Besides, John would not likely be afforded this luxury again.

As the tub filled, he shed his clothing, stroking each item fondly before hanging it on a hook. And then he did something he'd been avoiding—he faced his reflection in the mirror.

He saw a young man, thin but not remarkably so, with skin as pale as the moon. Long scars mapped him, jagged ridges on limbs, abdomen and chest, smaller puckers scattered everywhere. His body was nearly hairless except for tawny sprigs at his crotch and in his armpits. His cock and balls—not noticeably marred—were a bit pinker than the rest of him. He had long, slender fingers, like a pianist, and rosy nipples. His narrow face with high cheekbones bore an almost aristocratic mien, with full lips, a Roman nose, and pale brows arching over bright blue eyes. Butter-colored hair grew on his scalp, quite short but no longer sparse.

The man in the mirror was handsome if you overlooked the scars.

But to John he was a complete stranger.

CHAPTER 12

*E*VEN THOUGH John had left the room, Harry still felt John's hands on his bare shoulders, John's mouth against his. And he was certain that years from now—decades from now—he'd *still* feel those things. As if John were a ghost instead of... whatever he was.

How could anyone look at John for even a moment and not see his soul? Even when he'd been hardly more than a skin-sheathed skeleton, his essence had shone in his eyes. He embodied more humanity than anyone Harry had met. When John looked at Harry, he didn't seem to see a moron, a weakling, a pervert. John's gaze could almost make Harry believe in himself.

But in two nights, Harry would be complicit in returning John to hell, and Harry was too dim to find any way around that. Sure, he could again tell John to leave, but he doubted John would listen. And besides, John had been right; the Bureau would track him down soon enough. Hunting monsters was what they did.

John had said that two days of joy were better than a lifetime of loneliness and sorrow. And maybe two days was all that a guy like Harry was due, so he ought to be grateful for even that much. If only he could do more for John.

Well, at least he could make the most of what they had.

He stood, letting the blanket drop to the floor. Wearing nothing but boxer shorts, he padded to the bathroom and tapped on the door, which was slightly ajar. When no answer came, he thought maybe John hadn't heard him over the sound of running water. He knocked again, harder, and the door swung open.

John knelt naked on the floor, face buried in his hands.

"John!" Harry rushed in and crouched in front of him. "What's wrong? Are you hurt?"

When John raised his head and looked at Harry, his eyes were dry but his expression bleak. "I'm nobody."

Regret rocked Harry. "I shouldn't have kissed you. I'm sorry. It doesn't mean you're corrupt like me, okay? You're just—"

John's laugh sounded almost like a sob. "The kiss was wonderful."

"Then why did you just say you're nobody? You're not. You're John. My friend, I think. And you're really smart and—"

"Nobody." John tapped Harry's shoulder lightly before standing and turning off the faucet. Nearly full, the tub steamed.

"I don't understand."

"I don't have any memories from before I was created. You knew that. But I assumed I'd just lost them at death, like losing my pulse. I was wrong."

"You didn't lose them?"

John shook his head slowly. "I never had them."

"I don't—"

"I'm not a man who died and was brought back to some semblance of life. I'm...." He sighed. "A man died. Maybe several—I'm not sure whether all of this body comes from a single source. But whoever those people were, their souls, their *selves*, those are gone. Perhaps they're enjoying an afterlife somewhere. I hope so, for their sakes." His head drooped.

Slow as ever, Harry struggled to comprehend. Despite his confusion, he turned his attention to John and gently took his forearm. "Get in the tub, John. You can explain more in there."

Although John still appeared miserable, he nodded once and

189

slowly climbed into the roomy tub. He leaned his head against the edge, eyes closed, and let out a long breath.

Harry sat on the closed toilet. "Feels good, huh? I haven't had much access to bathtubs since my parents threw me out. I'm lucky when I get a shower."

"It's lovely."

John was lovely, although Harry didn't say it aloud. He looked like an angel, maybe. Like a dream who'd stepped right off a movie screen. The scars didn't detract at all from that.

After a few minutes, John opened his eyes. "I don't know how to explain. I can't find the right words. But I'll try." He lifted his arms out of the water, and he and Harry watched them drip. "This body was never mine. As I said, whatever people it belonged to are dead and gone. I was thrust into an empty patchwork shell. I'm a monster squatting in a stolen home." He let his arms drop with a splash.

Harry scratched his head. "If that's true, it's not so bad. I mean, whoever used to have that body, he doesn't need it anymore. You didn't have any choice in the matter, but even if you did, you're no thief. It's like when I was staying at the March. People lived in that room before, but they moved out. As long as I paid rent, that place was just as much mine as it had been theirs." He nodded as he warmed to his topic. "Or when I buy secondhand clothes. They're mine once I hand over my money, and that's not hurting anyone."

John surprised him with a small smile. "My body as secondhand clothes. I like that. It explains the wear and tear." He briefly traced the scar on his chest.

"That body might not be brand new, but you wear it mighty well."

This time, John's smile was big enough to crinkle the corners of his eyes. "You truly see me as... desirable?"

"Yeah." That came out hoarser than Harry intended. He wasn't used to admitting his feelings to anyone—not even when he was fucking them.

But then John looked serious again. "You shouldn't. This body may not disgust you, but what's inside should. I thought I'd once been human, Harry. I worried about what kind of man I'd been, but at least

I believed I *was* a man. But now I realize I never was. I have never been anything but a monster."

Harry was tempted to remind him of their earlier discussion, in which Harry had questioned the very concept of *monster*. He still believed it was just a word people threw at someone they feared or misunderstood. Being a monster didn't depend on how someone was made—or who he wanted to go to bed with—but rather how he acted. For instance, a guy could be born the usual way but grow up to love booze more than his family, to abuse his child in every way imaginable. He deserved the label much more than a fellow created in a lab, who'd never harmed anyone.

But with rare insight, Harry understood that it wasn't just the categorization that was disturbing John so deeply. It was the loss of a past he'd hoped he'd once possessed. And the loss of a future too—a future already made tenuous by the Bureau.

Harry couldn't do anything about how John was created, and he was in a true bind over the Bureau as well. But he could offer some solace, at least.

He got off the toilet and knelt beside the tub, thankful for the rug cushioning his knees. Then he sank a hand into the water, grasped one of John's, and fished it out. *"Look* at you, John."

"What?"

"You called me strong for... for surviving so far, I guess. But look at you. Until you left that cell, you never had one minute of anything good. Nobody gave you anything but pain. But here you are, only a few days away from that place, and look what you've become. Nobody could blame you if you went wild like Frankenstein's monster. If you killed as many of us as you could get your hands on. But that isn't what you want, is it?"

"No," John replied softly.

"You could have become anything, probably *should* have become an angry beast out for revenge. Instead, you're... nice. Even after I told you how I'm going to use you. You've been kinder to me than anyone." Harry had to swallow before continuing. "You've made yourself from scratch. And if those bastards give you half a chance, you'll be a better person than any of them."

Still holding Harry's hand, John regarded him solemnly. Then the corners of his mouth rose just a bit. "You're very wise."

Harry barked a laugh. "No, I'm—"

"Wise." John brought their joined hands to his mouth and gently kissed Harry's knuckles. "And generous and kind. Thank you."

Some of the weight lifted from Harry's heart. He couldn't fix much of anything, but he'd eased some of John's sorrow, and that was an accomplishment he could be proud of.

"John? Let's just forget about everything else for a little while, okay? Never mind the before or the after—let's have now."

"Also wise."

"Good. So what do you want to do with the now? What do you truly want?"

John didn't hesitate. "I want you."

CHAPTER 13

*I*N AN odd way, the realization brought a sense of joy. That walk in the park hadn't been just a sad little meander. It was, rather, the very first time John had gone for a stroll, the first time he looked up at trees and touched grass. How many people were lucky enough to remember their firsts so vividly?

And that kiss Harry had given him. That was John's first too, just as Harry was his first friend and now might become his first lover. How wonderful! John wasn't an amnesiac desperate to resurrect old recollections. He was quite literally a new man accumulating a wealth of fresh experiences.

And Harry had made him understand this.

John wanted to show his gratitude, but Harry wouldn't even let him out of the tub right away. He insisted, in fact, on rubbing a soapy cloth over John's body, treating him with utmost tenderness. This wasn't the first bath Harry had given him, but John had been too weak to appreciate the first time. Now heat pooled low in his belly, his skin tingled deliciously... and his cock hardened. He looked down at it, surprised and pleased.

Harry was grinning. "We're off to a good start, I guess."

"I wasn't sure I could…. I've never been aroused before. I didn't know if I was physically capable."

"Never?" Harry's eyes were wide.

John shook his head.

"Jesus. Okay. We'll just… take this slow. Make it good."

He was true to his word. He took his time with the bathing, lavishing caresses on every inch of John, not even hesitating over the scars. His attentions made John feel desirable. And when Harry ran out of skin to clean, he shampooed John's scalp instead. His fingers massaged the suds in, eliciting a low groan of pleasure from John.

Harry laughed. "If you think that feels good, just wait."

John didn't want to wait. He felt suddenly voracious for contact. It took all his will to be patient while Harry rinsed him, helped him out of the tub, and dried him with a large towel. It didn't help that Harry's excitement was evident through the thin fabric of his underwear—it was heady for John to have his effect on Harry confirmed.

He thought Harry might lead him into the bedroom right away, so he was surprised when he was maneuvered instead to face the mirror. After wiping the steamy glass clear with the towel, Harry stood slightly behind John and peered over him, hands on John's shoulders. "Look at yourself," he ordered.

"I did. That's how I realized—"

"No. Look."

While John gazed at his reflection, Harry licked his neck—a long streak of damp heat—and then sucked lightly at the juncture of neck and shoulder. Before John could fully process that sensation, Harry pressed the front of his body against John's back and slid his hands from John's shoulders slowly down his arms, over his hips, and then to his belly and groin. One hand caressed his abdomen, scar and all, while the other gently cradled his balls. So many things to feel at once. Harry's hands were calloused, his lips smooth and slick, his body hard. His darker skin contrasted nicely with John's paleness.

Moaning, John allowed Harry to bear some of his weight. His legs might have given out otherwise.

"Look at yourself," Harry whispered in his ear. "This is you now. You're a marvel, a miracle. I've never wanted anyone so much."

"Not even... Cary Grant?" John asked between gasps.

Harry's laughter echoed in the bathroom. "Not even. He was just a movie star—dime a dozen. There's nobody else like you."

John's arms, pinned lightly in place by Harry's embrace, hung useless at his sides. He wanted to touch too, but he couldn't make his mouth work properly to ask for that. When Harry released his balls and began a slow stroke of John's shaft instead, everything else ceased to matter.

It was strange. He had hated his prior constant weakness, but right now he was as weak and defenseless as he'd ever been, yet it felt delicious. His thin store of knowledge hadn't informed him how magnificent it could be to willingly give yourself over to someone else's power.

"H-Harry...."

"Getting close?"

"I don't... I d-don't...." Maybe. *Something* was building within him, and he didn't want it to stop.

But Harry kissed his nape and let him go. "Bed," he said hoarsely. His flush had deepened and spread, his breathing sounded rough, and good *Lord* he was beautiful. He took John's hand, led him into the bedroom, and switched on the light. As John stood, stupefied, Harry shed his underwear.

John had never seen anyone else naked, so he had nobody to compare Harry to. But he was quite sure that no one could look as magnificent: muscular torso with a trim waist and narrow hips, a thick red cock jutting proudly from a neat bush of dark curls.

"Do you want to touch me?" Harry asked.

"Yes. Please."

"I'm all yours."

John's fingers explored Harry's skin, so smooth and hot. And he noticed something else: small scars. Not as many as he bore, and not nearly as large. Yet there were quite a few—thin lines, tiny divots, and small discolored patches—on his back, shoulders, arms and legs. Harry didn't wince when John touched them. They might have come from childhood mishaps or from abuse by Harry's father. Some were undoubtedly souvenirs of the manual work Harry had done since he was a boy. The scarring didn't seem to discomfit Harry in the least. The blemishes were part of who he was.

Even humans were marked and shaped by the forces around them, it seemed.

Harry didn't shrink from John's explorations, not even when they extended to the most intimate parts of him. In fact, he closed his eyes and leaned his head back, allowing his mouth to fall open. Clear beads of liquid formed at the tip of his cock. He'd rarely been touched with tenderness, John guessed, and he appeared to crave it as desperately as John.

Eventually, without words, they moved to the bed. Harry arranged John on his back and, grinning wickedly, climbed over him and faced the opposite direction. That left his cock dangling inches from John's mouth. John reverently palmed the heavy muscles of his ass. "I don't know what to do," he said.

"Copy me, if you want."

And without further explanation, Harry lowered his mouth over John's cock.

John *thought* he did a passable job of mimicking Harry's motions, but it was hard to be certain when he was so overcome with sensation. He'd never imagined that it was possible to feel so good. That his body, instead of being a prison, could become a vehicle of pure pleasure.

When Harry climaxed, John swallowed eagerly—the only meal he'd ever taken. Then John's bliss hit its pinnacle as well, and he roared his delight to the heavens.

Moments later, Harry lay beside him and pulled the blankets up. He snuggled tightly against John.

"I understand why you like sex with men," John said.

Harry chuckled, his breaths tickling John's cheek. "It's not always like that. That was… special."

John felt himself smiling. "Can we do it again?"

"We have all day tomorrow."

Too short, far too short. Yet a wonderful gift nonetheless.

CHAPTER 14

*T*HEY BOTH knew their hours together were limited, but they ignored the future and reveled in the present. When they awoke in the morning, limbs entangled, they made love, took turns showering, and then made love again, leaving Harry famished and exhilarated. The weather was fine, and after dressing they decided to walk to Harry's breakfast.

John smiled up at the bright sky as they traversed the route. "The sun is generous to me."

"Yeah?"

"I think it's shining today on purpose—just to make us happy."

That was a pretty thought. Harry, who'd never been gifted with a fertile imagination, could now almost picture a dazzling goddess smiling down at them.

They went to the Hotcake House, where Harry ordered an enormous meal. Although John had nothing at all, he enjoyed the aromas of Harry's food and was fascinated by the morning bustle.

Afterward they went for a long stroll. They watched the river flow by, a few moored boats bobbing near the banks and cars crawling over the bridges. They wandered through a supermarket, where John exclaimed over the bright colors and myriad scents. They went downtown and sat in a coffee shop, watching men and women go by on their way to lunch and, later, back to the office. They found a school and observed children running and yelling on the playground. They passed through parks, John pausing to fondle leaves and admire tree bark.

Although none of this was extraordinary to Harry, John treated every experience as if it were a miracle, and Harry couldn't help but echo his joy. John had such capacity for wonder and delight—what if nobody had ever discovered that? Not even John.

Eventually they returned home. John sat at the table and read one of his books while Harry made dinner. Afterward they huddled together on the couch and listened to the radio. They discovered that John couldn't sing, but his attempts made them laugh. When it grew late, they undressed and climbed into bed and made love again.

It had been a perfect day, and Harry wished he could save it in a box to treasure forever.

Despite himself, he fell asleep. And then it was morning.

They didn't go anywhere that final day. They didn't make love, but they spent almost all their hours close together on the couch. John read, and Harry mostly watched him, memorized him.

Night fell too soon.

Harry changed from jeans into trousers. Then he looked at John. "You need to leave, and—"

"No." John's gaze was even. "Don't waste time arguing the impossible."

Although Harry clenched his jaw, he obeyed and then put on his coat.

John liked riding in the passenger seat of the car. The rain had returned, and the windshield wipers played a song as they swished back and forth. Raindrops on the windows, refracting the streetlights, looked like jewels. But it wasn't a long journey, and soon Harry pulled to a stop in front of a grand house. He turned off the engine but didn't get out right away. His hands clenched the steering wheel hard enough to make the plastic creak.

John set a hand on his knee. "Did you ever read the book you gave me? *Frankenstein?*"

"Just part. It's…. I'm not good at reading."

"But you know the monster went on a rampage."

Harry nodded. "Look, if you want to run or hurt someone or—"

"I don't. Listen to me. This is important. Do you know *why* he became violent?"

"Not really."

"The monster wanted—*needed*—friendship. Companionship. Love. But he realized he'd never have those things because even his creator viewed him with hatred and disgust. And Harry, the author was exactly right about that."

"You're not disgusting," Harry protested.

"Not now. Because you were kind to me from the very beginning. I crave the same things as Frankenstein's monster, but unlike that poor creature, I received them. From you. Don't you see? That's why I've grown so strong—because you've given me what I needed to survive. To flourish." John's voice sounded urgent, but he was smiling.

"I did that?"

"Yes. And that's why whatever happens to me next doesn't matter. You've saved me from that monster's fate and made me a real person. Thank you, Harry."

John kissed him, right there in the car. If Harry shed a few tears, neither of them mentioned it, and as they got out of the car, the rain washed away any bit of evidence.

The walk to the front door took forever and yet was too short. Harry's mind churned helplessly. If he were smarter, he'd surely find a way out of this mess, but nothing came to him. John stayed close, his thoughts opaque but his stride steady; in fact, he led the way. But when they reached the house, he stationed himself slightly behind Harry and subserviently bowed his head.

Harry swore at himself, took a deep breath, and rang the bell.

Swan answered the door, which took Harry by surprise. He expected that a place this swanky would have a servant. After a quick look at Harry, Swan turned his sharp attention to John, who didn't look up.

"Who's this?" Swan demanded.

"My inheritance."

Swan's eyes widened. "But it looks so—" He shook his head. "Come in, come in." He held the door as they entered, looking behind them as if to make sure nobody followed.

Other than in the movies, Harry had never seen such a fancy house. He'd certainly never been in one. They walked through the vestibule on marble floors, past landscape paintings in gilded frames. Despite a coatrack, Swan didn't offer to take their coats or Harry's hat. Instead he led them through a vast room with several long low couches, wall-to-wall carpeting, heavy draperies, and a crystal chandelier. All it lacked were film stars standing around with cocktails and cigarettes, chatting wittily. From there they went down a short hall into a kitchen bigger than any of the restaurants where Harry had occasionally worked. Everything gleamed and sparkled as if brand-new, and he wondered if Swan ever cooked. Maybe he ate all his meals out.

At the far end of the kitchen, they reached a door. Swan pulled a key from his pocket, unlocked and opened the door, and gestured downstairs. Harry almost balked—he didn't like the idea of descending into unknown darkness—but John was close behind him, silently urging him on. When they were all in the stairwell, Swan pulled the door closed. Only a single bare bulb lit the way, hanging from a cord overhead. It seemed to Harry that Swan could have afforded a better light fixture.

Two closed doors were at the bottom of the stairs. One had a neglected air, scuffed and somewhat battered. Swan pushed past Harry to unlock the other, which swung open smoothly.

Fluorescent lights flickered on overhead, illuminating an office that contained an enormous desk covered in books and papers. Stepping inside, they saw bookshelves and filing cabinets along the cream-painted walls, and several small tables held ashtrays and more books. Although a few Oriental rugs lay scattered over the linoleum floor, there was nothing particularly elegant or grand about the space, which was clearly well used.

Swan spoke for the first time since admitting them into the house. "All right. Let me see what you've brought."

"That wasn't the deal. You have to show me—"

"Mutual disclosure. Of course." Swan gave John another long look before striding to the desk and picking up a heavy book that looked ancient. He carried it over and showed Harry the cover. It wasn't in English. German maybe? Harry wasn't sure.

"Did your Mr. Lord possess this volume?"

"I don't know."

"He must have had an extensive library."

"I guess. I wasn't allowed into the parts of the house where he did his work. Nobody was."

Swan raised his eyebrows. "That didn't bother you?"

"Wasn't my business. Anyway, I didn't really care. It was a big house. I had my own room and I got to use the pool." The part about the pool was his own addition to the Bureau's fiction. He was proud of it.

"So after he died, you didn't have access to his materials?"

"Just the notes I told you about, because they were at his bedside. He used to read there sometimes."

Swan looked thoughtful. "I wonder what happened to those materials."

"He had a lawyer who took care of the estate. I'm sure he knows."

"This attorney's name?"

Harry attempted a calculating smile. "I'd be happy to tell you—for an extra fee."

If this annoyed Swan, he didn't show it. "Of course. We can discuss that later, when we negotiate terms." He tapped the book. "As far as I'm aware, this contains the only complete written account of a successful experiment—of the sort that interests me."

"Which is?"

"The only experiment that matters in the end."

He returned the book and remained standing behind the desk. "Do you know how many people were killed during World War Two?"

"A lot."

Swan laughed. "Yes, quite a lot. Perhaps upwards of fifty million, if you count civilians. A significant portion of the world's population, in fact. And how many American losses were there?"

Frowning, Harry felt as if he were back in school. At least nobody was making fun of his inability to answer. "Don't know."

"Over four hundred thousand. Also a lot, wouldn't you agree? Did you lose any family in the war?"

"My Uncle Jimmy." It felt like a betrayal to share that information with Swan.

"Your Uncle Jimmy. A shame. I lost my brother, which was not a shame because he and I never got along at all. But I also lost a very close friend. My lover, in fact."

"I'm sorry," Harry mumbled.

Swan strolled out from behind the desk and crossed to a large wooden cabinet. He swung down a door and, with his back to Harry and John, spent some time pouring things from bottles into glasses. When he turned back, he held a tumbler of what looked like bourbon in one hand and a tall glass of orange liquid in the other. He handed the orange one, with its yellow plastic straw, to Harry. "You'll forgive me if I've forgotten the ice."

"I don't want—"

"You'll like this one. It's quite sweet." He grinned. "It's called a Zombie."

Although Harry didn't want a drink, he did want to move things along without an argument. As Swan waited expectantly, Harry took a long sip from the straw. The beverage was sweet and tasted of pineapple and other fruit, but the alcohol was so strong that he coughed.

"Just a little rum," Swan said with a chuckle. "It'll put hair on your chest."

Scowling, Harry took another swig. "Look, we—"

"I was telling you a story. I had a beloved. We went to school together, he and I. We were planning to go into business together—pharmaceuticals. When the war broke out, I urged him to get a medical deferment, as I did."

"What's wrong with you?"

"With sufficient funds given to the right physician, whatever I want." Swan drank his bourbon in one long swallow but didn't put the glass down. "My paramour refused my pleas. He wanted to be a patriot, a hero. I told him he was foolish—the country he'd be fighting for would happily put him in prison if we were open about our relationship. It wasn't *our* war. But he wouldn't listen. He became an Air Force pilot. And he was shot down over Germany. His remains were never recovered."

Harry took another burning drink. "I'm sorry."

"Yes. Very unfortunate. But those events gave me the impetus for my studies. Money means nothing, Harry—not in the end. I'm sure it doesn't feel that way to you, given your... rather impecunious status, but it's true. My love was wealthier than I, but his money won't bring him back from the dead. But what if *I* could?" He said the last part with nonchalance, but it was clearly important. He waited for Harry's response.

Harry decided not to tell him that according to John, the dead stayed dead; their bodies simply got new tenants. "That's what you're working on? Bringing the dead back to life?"

Swan smiled. "Yes."

"Have you actually done it?"

"I am quite close, but no. Small difficulties remain." For the first time since the conversation began, Swan glanced at John, who remained motionless with his head bowed. "Which is why your offer interests me—if it's genuine, of course."

"It is."

"I need to see."

Although Harry felt sick to his stomach, he didn't stop Swan from approaching John. Instead, he finished his drink and set the glass on the table. He thought he had enough information to satisfy Townsend, so he and John could just leave. Surely Swan couldn't stop them if they tried.

Swan began to unbutton John's shirt, and Harry blinked at them blearily. The Zombie had been stronger than he expected, and fog had crept into his skull. "Look, Swan—"

"Follow me," Swan said sharply. Abandoning John's buttons, unfastened enough to reveal the scars on his chest, Swan hurried to a small door Harry had barely noticed. He assumed it led to a closet.

But as he shambled inside with John at his heels, Harry entered a space considerably larger and more sinister than a closet. It was a laboratory, just like he'd seen in the movies, with steel tables and metal cabinets and glass bottles and jars full of... things. Some of the things looked like body parts. The room smelled of decay and formaldehyde.

Harry turned to leave, but Swan had already shut the door, locked it, and pocketed the key. "Excuse the smell. Unavoidable, I'm afraid."

Stomach roiling, Harry shook his head in a vain attempt to clear it. "I need to.... We need to...." The words fled his tongue.

"Harry?" It was the first word John had uttered since leaving the car.

Swan looked startled but then moved quickly, pushing John against a wall. Harry cried out but couldn't seem to get his legs to work, and as he stumbled into a table, he saw Swan shove John's neck into a metal collar attached to the wall, then lock the collar in place.

"Harry! Run!" John shouted.

But Harry couldn't even stand; his knees wobbled and he fell heavily onto his ass. John kept shouting his name as Swan struggled to jam John's wrists into manacles beside his head. Harry tried to crawl to them, but the floor heaved under him like a stormy ocean beneath a ship, and no matter how hard he tried to focus his eyes, everything doubled and tripled.

He tried to call out to John, but he wasn't sure if he made any noise at all.

His arms gave out and the floor came rushing at his face.

Failed at this too.

Then blackness.

CHAPTER 15

ONSCIOUSNESS CAME slowly to Harry, and at first he fought it. Oblivion was so much better than the pounding agony in his head, the penetrating cold, and his queasy stomach. When he finally became aware that he was pinned on his back, he fought blindly against whatever held him.

It took several moments to gain a better understanding of his situation.

He was naked and bound by thick leather straps to one of the metal tables in Swan's lab. A thick rubber gag filled his mouth so he could only grunt, and a bright light hung directly overhead, bringing tears to his eyes.

John was fastened to a nearby wall, held in place by metal bands at his throat and wrists. Perhaps around his legs as well, but Harry couldn't see from his angle. Not only was John naked and gagged. The worst thing was a bloodless gaping wound in his chest, which looked to be a long and deep slice from a blade.

John, his face a mask of sorrow, watched Harry.

Harry knew it was hopeless, but he fought his bonds until his breath came in desperate snorts and sweat sheened his chest. The effort served no purpose other than to bruise and tear the flesh near the straps. He stopped moving and stared at John, wishing he could somehow communicate his regrets and apologies. Townsend should have known better than to send an idiot on a mission, and Harry should have known better than to accept. He never should have brought John here; they should have stayed in the car and just kept driving. Sure, the Bureau would have tracked them eventually, but it was a big country with so many places to lose oneself. They could have had more days together before they were found. John could have been free a little longer.

Time passed. Harry's sweat dried, leaving him shivering. He took a closer look around the lab, as much as his position allowed, and he didn't like what he saw. Trays of glittering blades. Bottles full of murky liquid. Pieces of bone that might have been human. The cloying stink of the room seemed to grow worse, insinuating its way into his nose and throat and lungs. Fearing he would otherwise choke, he fought to not vomit.

Sometimes John emitted low noises through the gag or made a small movement that caused his chains to rattle softly. He never stopped looking at Harry.

If only Harry could touch him—just a brush of fingertips against skin. It would mean so much.

Then John shifted his gaze beyond Harry, and a door opened and closed. The odor of cigarette smoke reached Harry even before Swan stood beside him, glass and cigarette in hand. He'd changed out of his expensive sweater and now wore a white lab coat with a white shirt and black tie visible beneath. He watched with amusement as Harry renewed his struggles and grunted frantically.

"You have a choice." Harry stilled at once. Seemingly satisfied that he had Harry's attention, Swan continued. "I'm going to kill you. That part is non-negotiable."

Maybe Swan thought Harry would make a fuss over that, but Harry waited for more. His own death didn't frighten him—he wanted to know Swan's plans for John.

Swan apparently enjoyed an audience. He took a drag on his cigarette, followed by a sip of bourbon. "Still, you have an important decision. I can kill you now. Not quickly, I don't think, because I rarely have the opportunity to play. Or you can remain alive a short time longer—until I've finalized my research. Then I will kill you quickly and resurrect you. You'll be my first success." He stroked Harry's bare hip. "You're pretty enough to keep around in that capacity."

Someone else walking around in Harry's body—that was an odd idea. And actually, it didn't disturb him. Perhaps the new creation would be smarter than him, like John was. Perhaps he'd find a way to escape Swan's clutches and maybe even take John with him.

John rattled his chains, but Swan ignored him.

"So what do you think, Harry? Would you prefer the second option?"

Harry nodded vigorously.

"Excellent." Swan petted Harry's hip again and then, smiling, moved his hand to Harry's groin and fondled his soft cock. Harry growled and John rattled more loudly.

"I'm glad you wish to cooperate, because if you didn't, I might start by removing this." Swan squeezed firmly. "That would be a shame, wouldn't it? But you're well enough endowed that I might preserve the organ for potential future use."

If Swan thought he was intimidating Harry, he was wrong. Not that Harry wanted to be chopped to pieces. But he couldn't bring himself to care much about his own fate when John hung there with his chest slit open.

Swan withdrew his hand. "All right. If you wish to avoid that destiny, you must simply do one thing. Tell me the name of Mr. Lord's attorney."

Harry almost laughed. In fact, when Swan set down his drink, stubbed out the cigarette, and unbuckled the gag, Harry *did* laugh. This son of a bitch thought he was so fucking clever, but he still hadn't figured out that Harry's story was bullshit.

"You're amused? Do you believe I'm joking?" Swan looked slightly rattled, which Harry figured was a good thing.

But what to do next? Harry could confess that he'd fabricated everything, but then he'd end up tortured to death and John would remain captive. Harry suspected that if Swan learned the truth, he'd be enraged, which would lead to bad things for John.

Harry could make something up. Create a name. That would buy him a little time but not much, because Swan would rather quickly find out that no lawyer existed. In fact, he'd probably realize that Lord was a fiction too.

Then Harry remembered something: Townsend knew Harry was meeting with Swan tonight. When Harry didn't check in within a reasonable amount of time, wouldn't Townsend investigate? It might take him a while to act, especially if none of his agents were in Portland, but surely he *would* act eventually. Harry didn't want John back in the Bureau's hands but figured he was better off there than with Swan.

Okay then. Continued lies were the way to go.

"I'll tell you his name," Harry said. "But can't you let John go? You don't need him if—"

Swan cast a quick look at John. "You named it?"

"He named himself. He's a good man, he really is. Set him free. You'll still have me."

Swan laughed. "I don't think so."

Harry hadn't expected him to listen, but no harm in trying. "I get that you lost someone you loved and you want to do something about it. But there's no reason to harm an innocent person in the process, and John is innocent."

"That creature is irrelevant to you. What is the attorney's name?"

"Robert Dunn." That had been a farmer who, when Harry was sixteen or so, gave him a job for one season. Funny how that was the name that came to him now. "He has an office in downtown LA."

"Robert Dunn. Very well."

Harry expected him to run off right away. Instead, smiling, Swan walked behind Harry. Metal clattered against metal, and John became agitated again, making desperate sounds and pulling against the manacles. Harry understood when Swan returned.

He held a scalpel.

"You said—"

"I know what I said, Harry. And I will keep my promise—I won't kill you tonight. But it's too late to make inquiries about this Dunn fellow, and I'm feeling restless. It won't hurt your value as an experiment if I make some modifications now."

"You sick motherfucker! You piece of shit, you—" He went silent as Swan grabbed Harry's balls and poised the blade inches away. *Maybe I'll bleed to death. Or die of shock.* Either would be a mercy.

Harry turned his head to look at John. "I'm sorry, John. So, so sorry. Don't forget the man you truly are."

Unable to face either John or the scalpel, Harry closed his eyes.

Swan squeezed Harry's scrotum more tightly—

And then a mighty roar shook the room.

Harry's eyelids flew open just in time to see John rip the manacles out of the wall and tear the metal collar from his throat. He charged toward Harry and Swan.

Screaming, Swan let go of Harry and backed away, holding the blade in front of him. Harry screamed too, shouting John's name. But John flew around Harry's table and, heedless of the scalpel, launched himself at Swan. They fell onto the floor, where Harry could see only flashes of arms and legs.

Swan's shrieking grew loud enough to hurt Harry's ears. And then it abruptly stopped.

A moment later, John stood and staggered over. Several fresh wounds marred his torso, but the blood on his skin wasn't his own. He bent over Harry and, after unfastening the straps with some difficulty, helped him to sit up.

The first thing Harry did was take the damned gag out of John's mouth. "Jesus, he hurt you! What can I do—"

"I killed him." John's voice was heavy with anguish.

"You saved me. You were— Fuck."

"I murdered someone. Just like Frankenstein's monster. Just like—"

Harry caught John's shoulders. "No. He killed out of hate and revenge. You did this because you...."

"Because I love you," John whispered.

"I love—"

And the door to the lab crashed open.

CHAPTER 16

$\mathcal{J}$OHN LEAPT in front of Harry, ready to protect him from this new danger. The wounds inflicted by Swan now hurt, and despite Harry's reassurances, John's mind reeled from having committed murder. But he knew with every fiber of his existence that he'd do anything to save the man he loved.

Several men burst into the room. An explosion resounded. Something hit John's belly with such force that he fell, instinctively howling at the new pain.

Harry scrambled off the table and screamed "Stop!"

Miraculously the four men listened, freezing in their tracks, guns raised. One of them was Townsend.

Harry dropped to his knees beside John, his arm raised toward the agents. "Don't hurt him!" Then he turned to John. "I don't know— What can I— How do I help?"

After a moment of assessing the damage to his body, John managed a smile. "It's all right. I've been hurt worse than this." It was true. The Bureau had done worse when they first acquired him—and he'd always healed eventually, with new scars as souvenirs.

But Harry didn't seem comforted. He peered worriedly at John's injuries and tenderly swept the hair from John's eyes.

"What's happening here, boy?" Townsend had holstered his gun and marched over. He glared down at them like an avenging angel.

With another quick touch to John's forehead, Harry stood, placing himself between Townsend and John. If he remembered his nudity, he seemed unbothered by it. "Don't touch him. Don't you dare hurt him."

Townsend narrowed his eyes but didn't argue. Instead he gestured impatiently at the other agents, who put their guns away. Two of them knelt over Swan's corpse, while the third began a walking survey of the lab.

"What are you doing here?" Harry demanded.

"We followed you, of course. Do you think we'd let an untrained kid do an important mission unsupervised? We've been waiting outside for hours, wondering what the hell was going on. We broke in when we heard screams." He crossed his arms. "Now you tell *me* what happened here."

Harry lifted his chin. "Swan drugged me, I think. Tied me up on that table. He was going to...." He shuddered. "Torture me. Murder me. Use me for his experiments. John broke loose from his chains and stopped him. He saved my life."

"John." Townsend looked thoughtful and then seemed to reach a decision. He turned toward the agents still examining Swan's body. "Clark! Call in the crew. Have them bag up everything and take it away. Call the Portland Police Bureau and let them know they have one fewer problem on their hands." He swiveled back. "You come with me, Lowe."

"Not without John."

"Fine."

Harry had to help John stand, and then John slung an arm over his shoulders so Harry could help him walk out of the lab, through the office, and up the stairs. A harried-looking agent met them there. He handed Harry a coat, but Harry refused to budge unless John got clothing too. He also demanded a first-aid kit. Townsend waited impatiently while Harry clumsily bandaged John's wounds and helped him into a pair of trousers that had likely belonged to Swan.

"You see?" John whispered to him. "They were watching us. We couldn't have run."

Harry answered loudly, clearly wanting Townsend to hear. "I don't care. The only way they're getting their claws into you is over my dead body."

"I don't want you to die."

"Me either. But dammit, you're worth whatever I have to do."

Despite the wounds, despite the uncertainty as to their fates, John felt warm and happy. Harry found him valuable. In all his most imaginative fantasies while locked in the cell, John had never hoped for anything so wonderful.

THEY RODE in the back of a big car while Townsend drove. Harry kept an arm wrapped around John as if to insulate him from bumps in the road. They went only about two miles before Townsend stopped in front of what appeared to be an empty storefront. Although the windows were papered over, new furniture filled the inside.

Harry and John were allowed to wash up in the bathroom, and John was relieved to clean Swan's blood away. A doctor came to examine Harry and declared him fine, apart from some minor cuts and contusions where he'd struggled against his bonds.

Someone had evidently visited Harry's rented house, since an agent handed them familiar clothing. Another brought Harry a thick sandwich and a bottle of Coke.

John and Harry sat side by side in uncomfortable office chairs while Townsend faced them across a desk and asked Harry question after question, often repeating himself or posing the same query in different ways, as if trying to catch Harry in a lie. But Harry did not lie, not even when he slumped from exhaustion and slurred his words.

Townsend, apparently indefatigable, finally took pity on him. "Unless you have something else to add, we're done for now."

"I don't have anything else."

"All right. Look, kid, I need to tell you something. About that job we talked about with the Bureau—"

"I'm not Bureau material. I know."

Townsend cut his eyes toward John. "It's like I said before. You're too soft. A Bureau man has to make everything secondary to the mission—and you can't do that, can you?"

"Some things are more important than any mission." Harry took John's hand.

In the past, when John had simply glanced at Townsend, he assumed him to be an ordinary man—middle-aged, overweight, prone to too much smoking and drinking. But now as he truly focused, he saw that Townsend was something else entirely. Dangerous. Cunning. And perhaps not entirely human.

Townsend had ignored John up to this point, but now he shifted his attention. "Who came up with your name?"

"I did."

"Why?"

"A person needs a name."

"I suppose so," Townsend said with a chuckle. Still smiling, he asked, "Why did you kill Swan?"

"He was going to mutilate Harry. And then he was going to murder him."

"Why do you care what happens to Harry?"

"Because I love him."

Harry squeezed his hand.

"I see. And will you kill again?"

"If I have to, in order to protect Harry." John leaned forward. "Have you read Mary Shelley's book?"

"Ah, the modern Prometheus. That monster never had a name. Its creator didn't give it one, and it never took one for itself."

"I am not that monster."

"How do I know that? How could I let you loose on the world?"

"He's no monster," said Harry. "No more than any human is."

John remembered the closing lines of the book. "Some years ago, I nearly wept to live. Now it is my consolation." His paraphrase turned the monster's words inside out, a reflection of John's very different situation. But the next part he quoted exactly. "Fear not that I shall be the instrument of future mischief."

Townsend laughed again, and this time he looked more human as well. Then he poured himself what must have been his sixth or seventh drink and lit another cigarette. "You're not Bureau material, Lowe, but you followed through on your duties and you rid the world of a very bad man. Keep the money I gave you. Hell, keep the car. I'll have the boys drive it back to your place."

"I only care about John."

"Keep him too. If he wants to be kept by you, that is."

John's eyes stung with tears. "I do. More than anything."

Townsend removed a pen and small black notebook from his inner coat pocket, scrawled something down, and tore the page out. He scooted the paper across the desk toward Harry. "Wrote down a name for you. Charles Grimes. The agent who fell for a demon. You remember I told you about him?"

"Yes," said Harry, wide-eyed.

"He's in Santa Monica. Look him up."

"Why?"

"He's good at finding things. Maybe he'll help you find your way." Townsend stood. "Want a ride home?"

Harry looked at John. "How do you feel?"

How to put so much into mere words? "Buoyant. Jubilant."

"We'll walk," Harry said.

Townsend walked them to the front door and unlocked it for them. He stood there a moment, his bulk blocking the way. "The Bureau will be keeping track of you, boys. Don't get into trouble." Then he stepped aside.

Dawn had broken, the light drawing moisture from the pavement and giving the city a soft, dreamlike quality. Harry and John walked slowly side by side, hands not quite touching.

"What are you thinking?" John asked after a couple of blocks.

"I've never been good at anything. Never had any real reason to be on the planet. But I think I do now."

"What's that?"

Harry stopped in his tracks and smiled brightly, creating in John a warmth that far surpassed those patches of sunlight in his former cell. "I want to show you the world," Harry said. "Maybe I'll make a decent tour guide."

John wanted to experience it all—the sights and sounds and smells and feelings—with Harry at his side. He wanted to see what was around every corner. Snow and oceans and mountains and sand; bazaars and concerts and parties and cafés. Books. Snuggling on the couch with the radio playing romantic tunes. Making love. John was greedy and he wanted it all.

"Show me, Harry." John raised his hands high. "Show me *everything.*"

THE BUREAU OF TRANS-SPECIES AFFAIRS

For many years the United States government has been aware
that *Homo sapiens* is not the only sentient species inhabiting the country. Some other species were native to the continent, while others
immigrated along with humans. Early on, these nonhuman species
(NHS) were largely ignored when they lived peacefully within human
communities. At other times they were deemed a threat and local
efforts were made to eradicate them. The federal government was not
involved in these early efforts.

During the Civil War, both the Union and Confederate armies recruited members of the NHS, with varying degrees of success.

By the early 20th century, some local law enforcement agencies expressed frustration with their inability to deal effectively with the special needs of NHS. Localized incidents of mass violence occurred in several locations, most notably the Omaha Zombie Epidemic of 1908, the Manchester (New Hampshire) Melusine Drownings of 1911, and the Eugene (Oregon) Sasquatch Riots of 1915.

In response to these incidents, as well as a heightened desire for increased federal control, President Wilson created a new federal agency in 1919 called the Bureau of Trans-Species Affairs. The mission of this agency was to communicate with NHS, to control them, to investigate reported dangerous actions committed by them, and to bring them to justice or eliminate them when necessary. Since then, the Bureau has been quietly active throughout the United States. Its jurisdiction has expanded to include humans who engage in magical or paranormal activities.

Over the decades, a great many dramas have unfolded among the people who work for the Bureau. The **Bureau stories** are a collection of these tales. Each involves different protagonists and is set in a different era, yet all focus on the adventures and struggles of the Bureau's agents. These novellas can be read in any order.

The Bureau of Trans-Species Affairs: Strength, Intelligence, Honor

More about the books in this series.

- **Book One: Corruption**
- **Book Two: Clay White**
- **Book Three: Creature**
- **Volume One (Compilation of Books One through Three)**

- Book Four: Chained
- Book Five: Conviction
- Volume Two (Compilation of Books Four and Five)
- Book Six: Conned
- Book Seven: Caroled
- Book Eight: Camouflaged
- Volume Three (Compilation of Books Seven and Eight)
- Book Nine: Caught
- Book Ten: Chambered
- Volume Four (Compilation of Books Nine and Ten)
- Book Eleven: Consumed
- Book Twelve: Connected

ABOUT THE AUTHOR

Kim Fielding is very pleased every time someone calls her eclectic. Winner of the BookLife Prize for Fiction, a Lambda Award finalist and a Foreword INDIE finalist, she has migrated back and forth across the western two-thirds of the United States and, after a long exile, has recently returned to Portland, Oregon. She's a university professor who dreams of being able to travel and write full time. She also dreams of having two daughters who fully appreciate her, a husband who isn't obsessed with football, and a house that cleans itself. Some dreams are more easily obtained than others.

Kim can be found on her blog: http://kfieldingwrites.com/
Facebook: https://www.facebook.com/KFieldingWrites
and Twitter: @KFieldingWrites
Her e-mail is kim@kfieldingwrites.com

ALSO BY KIM FIELDING

Series

The Bureau

Greynox to the Sea

Love Can't

Ennek

Bones

Stars from Peril

Novels

Rook's Time

Crow's Fate

The Taste of Desert Green

Potential Energy

The Muffin Man

Teddy Spenser Isn't Looking for Love

Hallelujah (with F.E. Feeley Jr.)

Blyd and Pearce

A Full Plate

The Little Library

Ante Up

Running Blind (with Venona Keyes)

Staged

Rattlesnake

Astounding!

Motel. Pool.

The Tin Box

Venetian Masks

Brute

Novellas

Shelf Made Man

Man of His Dreams

Bread Crumbs

Regifted

Bite Me: An Elucidation in Three Acts

Farkas

Ash Believes the Impossible

A Very Genre Christmas

Gravemound

The Solstice Kings

Dei Ex Machina

The Golem of Mala Lubovnya

Refugees

The Dance

Transformation

Summerfield's Angel

The Tale of August Hayling

Phoenix

Grown-Up

The Pillar

The Border

Housekeeping

Night Shift

Speechless

Guarded

The Downs

Short Stories and Collections

Dog Days of December

Firestones

Dreidels and Do-Overs

Get Lit

Christmas Present

Act One and Other Stories

Exit through the Gift Shop

Dear Ruth

Grateful

The Sacrifice and Other Stories

Saint Martin's Day

The Festivus Miracle

Joys R Us

Alaska

A Great Miracle Happened There

Violet's Present

Standby

Anyplace Else

Milton Keynes UK
Ingram Content Group UK Ltd.
UKHW020754191124
2941UKWH00018B/71

9 781952 724114